NAMELESS

JENNIFER JENKINS

Month9Books

Month9Books

For Clint, I'd fight for you…

NAMELESS

Jennifer Jenkins

Chapter 1

Zo couldn't remember a time when she didn't fear the Ram. Even after the raid, when so much of her fear had turned to hate, the fear still existed beneath. It was a foundation that she came to rely upon. A constant.

Sleeping under a fir tree so close to Ram's Gate went against her very nature. While her body revolted, she couldn't think of a more appropriate place to be. Zo choked down the beastly fear clawing its way up her throat and smiled like this was just another assignment. "It's time, Gabe."

Her guard, Gabe, rested on soggy pine needles beside her. His hands were tucked behind his shaggy blond head, eyes closed in feigned sleep. He used to lay like that, with his arms arrogantly thrown back and his chest puffed out like he owned the world, when they were kids. The river would rush by carrying rumors of starving clans and battles lost—heartache

- 1 -

that pulled tight strings of tension throughout Zo's body—
while Gabe just laid back and chewed on a grass root.

Today, Gabe's pretend-sleep didn't fool Zo any more than
it ever had. They both knew he hadn't slept soundly since
they'd left the Allied Camp a week ago. With eyes still closed,
Gabe frowned as Zo left the protection of his side to bundle her
bedroll. She crawled out from under the skirt of the enormous
fir tree. Its sweeping limbs that kissed the uneven ground had
kept them as safe as one could be in this godforsaken region.
Behind her, Gabe growled impatiently as he gathered his
things to follow.

"There's no need to rush this." He pushed the branch aside
and threw out his pack with more force than necessary. Zo
flinched, not used to seeing her childhood friend angry.

"You didn't wake me for my watch again," said Zo,
unsurprised. Ever since they'd left the Allies, Gabe had been
insanely overprotective.

"You need your sleep."

"And you don't?"

Gabe sighed and scooped a blob of mud from the newly
thawed earth. He frowned and smeared it along the curved
planes of Zo's face and neck. The cool mud felt surprisingly
comforting, but it could have just been Gabe's touch. His
capable hands shook while lines of worry deepened across his
brow.

"This won't work." He stopped and cupped his muddy
hand at the base of her neck, his blue eyes pleading. "You're
too pretty. A little mud can't change that."

Zo yanked on the sleeve of her shirt until the seam split then
ripped and frayed the cuff of her pant legs. Young, unarmed

women just didn't go on casual strolls through the perilous hills of the Ram. Commander Laden said she needed to look desperate if she wanted them to believe her story. Her lie.

As if looking desperate is hard, Zo thought.

Gabe stood a full head taller than Zo. Despite his large frame, he could outrun a jackrabbit and his mind was just as quick. A valuable weapon for the Allies. But with all of his abilities, he was not the one walking into the lion's den this morning.

He untwisted the strap of Zo's medical satchel and let out a long breath before dropping his hands to his sides.

"I'll miss you," said Zo. Her voice carried the mechanical cadence she'd adopted several years ago. A small part of her— the part that wasn't dead—hated disappointing Gabe. He'd done so much for her and her little sister, Tess, since they'd journeyed from the Valley of Wolves to live with Commander Laden and the Allies.

Thinking of her wild, eight-year-old sister brought a temporary smile to Zo's muddied face. She couldn't think of Tess and not imagine her tromping through the forest trying to catch squirrels and sneak up on rabbits. It was her second favorite thing to do, next to following Zo around the Allied Camp. The little tick wouldn't take her absence well. Zo had left a note and arranged for her care, but that didn't mean the kid wouldn't be furious.

Gabe pressed his cold hands to Zo's face and forced her to look at him. "Come back with me, Zo. Let Commander Laden send someone else. Someone with less to lose."

"We're not doing this again." Zo pulled away. She had begged for this mission, and she would see it through. No matter what the cost. The Allies desperately needed information that only she could provide, if they hoped to defeat the most powerful military force in the region.

Gabe's hands curled into fists. His voice rose to carry over the wind that whipped his unruly hair. "Entering Ram's Gate is suicide! We don't even know if you can get the information Laden's after."

The truth was far worse than Gabe could possibly know. He hadn't heard what life would be like inside the Gate. They would eventually discover her, and once they did, they'd kill her. Plain and simple.

There were worse things a person could endure.

She'd do anything for the Cause.

"Goodbye, Gabe." She kissed his frozen, whiskered cheek.

His hand clamped down on Zo's wrist and he yanked her into a fierce embrace. "I'll be close, waiting to help you escape the minute you send word." He smoothed down her wild, dark hair. "I'll find a way to keep you safe, Zo. I swear it."

Zo forced a hollow smile, for Gabe's sake. "Look after Tess. Tell her I'm doing this for her. Tell her I'm doing it for our parents."

She left Gabe standing frozen in the low light of morning.

[•]

After a hard climb, Zo reached the towering wall of Ram's Gate. The wall was comprised of redwood logs at least four feet in diameter and fifty feet tall, bound together with heavy rope and shaved to a point at the top. Black tar and broken glass glimmered along the high rim of the wall to discourage clans foolish enough to attack, and souls brave enough to dare escape.

Zo looked right and left and saw no end to the wall through the thick maze of aspen and evergreens. From her training with Commander Laden, she knew the giant wall ran for miles in each direction until it reached the cliffs that dropped off to the freezing ocean below. Inside the wall were hundreds of acres of farmlands, mountainous forests, and enough homes to house thousands of Ram and the slaves they called "Nameless."

Calmer than a sane person should be, Zo dropped to her knees in the shadow of the ominous wall. Knowing these might be the last free moments of her life, she allowed herself to think about things that were normally buried deep within her. The memory of her mother's soft skin. The safety of her father's smile. Tess' dimples and her eagerness to please, despite her stubborn ways.

The moment was as sweet as it was brief. But it was hers.

Deep-voiced drums boomed and the enormous gate rose inch by inch. Men shouted orders and whips cracked. Through the gap of the slow-rising gate she saw at least forty men in tattered animal hides with harnesses on their backs. They slipped through mud while struggling to turn a giant wheel connected to a thick chain to raise the gate.

The Nameless. The Ram had kept slaves for hundreds of years, some were captured, others came willingly, while most were born into the lowly title.

Instinct told her to run, but fear and determination kept her frozen in place. She locked the people she loved back into the cage that was her heart and prepared to face her enemy.

Zo pressed her nose into the icy mud in a show of

submission. The drums ceased and the silence echoed in her chest like a painful heartbeat.

The metal of short swords clinked against armor as men approached. She peeked up to sight of a bald leader walking ahead of a wall of six soldiers. His cold eyes seemed too big for his head, protuberant like those of a frog.

"Get up," the leader commanded.

Zo climbed to her feet but kept her gaze focused on the man's fur-lined boots.

"State your name and clan," he ordered.

"I am from the family Shaw of the Kodiak Clan," Zo said, hoping her accent would pass. The Ram had raided one of the Kodiak settlements a few weeks earlier. Many of the women and children whose husbands had died in the raid would come to the Gate, choosing to offer themselves as slaves over watching their children starve to death.

The leader circled her. "Age?"

"Seventeen."

A few of the guards in the line exchanged words. One laughed under his breath.

"You're too thin to claim the Kodiak as your clan. Your jaw is more square than round."

The sound of a young girl's scream saved Zo from having to answer.

"Let me go! You're hurting me!" the girl cried.

Zo froze. *It couldn't be ...*

A guard dressed in full armor carried the kicking child up the muddy hill and dropped her at the bald leader's feet.

Zo's whole body went rigid as her eight-year-old sister, Tess, scrambled up to hug her. "I'm so sorry," Tess cried. She must have secretly followed them from the Allies, though how she survived the dangerous journey unnoticed was beyond Zo.

"Tess, I thought I'd lost you," Zo stammered. She hoped her shock registered as relief instead of panic. "Don't say a word," Zo whispered in her ear as they embraced.

"Who is this child?" the frog-eyed leader asked.

"She is my sister, sir. We were separated. She found me."

"Clearly." He circled the girls once more then reached out and grabbed Zo by the throat, forcing her to the ground on her back. His lips brushed her cheek as he spoke. "How do I know you're not a stinking Wolf? That you're not feeding me some story?" His breath reeked of stale cabbage and rotten sausage.

Zo's heels dug small trenches in the mud as she struggled against the hand tightening around her throat. Black dots invaded her vision.

The leader smiled and licked his lips as if she were his next meal. "We don't allow Wolves through the Gate." A string of spittle escaped his lips and landed on her cheek. "Ever." He released his grip and Zo gasped for air.

Tess rushed to Zo's side, her eyes wet with tears.

"With all of the clans mixing, it's getting harder and harder to sort the wheat from the tares. I can't take any chances … " He shrugged and nodded to his guard. The men moved in, pulling the sisters apart. Tess let out a shrill cry. A guard struck her tiny cheek.

"Please!" Zo fought against firm hands digging into her arms. "I come from three generations of healers. My sister is learning too. We beg the mercy of the Ram, and pledge our lives to your service!"

The Gate Master held up a hand, and his men threw Zo to

the ground. His round, glassy eyes stayed fixed on her as he grunted a soft command to one of his men. The soldier nodded, bowed, and ran back through the Gate.

"A healer, you say?" The corner of his lip pulled up to reveal rotting teeth as he smiled. "We'll see about that."

Chapter 2

The cold air traveling over Zo's skin smelled strangely mineral. She walked blindfolded with Tess in her arms, and the tip of a spear at her back. She memorized the turns as they prodded her forward, knowing it would do little to help if she couldn't pass whatever trial the Ram leader had in store. The path sloped down and the moist air grew colder. Her foot caught on a rock and Zo fell to her knees, sending Tess flying into the darkness. Hands grabbed Zo's collar and hoisted her back to her feet.

"Carry the small one," the leader ordered.

"Zo?" Tess' voice cracked, weak and distant.

"I'm here," said Zo, straining to see through the blindfold. She didn't want her sister to say more. Her accent might betray them both.

The ground leveled beneath them, and a guard yanked off

the blindfold, taking a chunk of Zo's dark hair with it. She didn't cry out.

They couldn't hurt her.

She looked at the limp form of her sister in the arms of a bare-chested Ram guard and crumbled at the contradiction. It wasn't supposed to be this way. If only Tess hadn't followed. If only …

Guards lined the opposite wall. Shadows from the torchlight made the scowls on their faces all the more sinister. Each carried a round shield at his back, a spear in hand, and a short sword at his hip.

A redheaded boy lay on a narrow bed in the center of the room silently weeping. His body was long, but judging from his young face, he couldn't have been much older than twelve or thirteen. The deep wound just above his hip swam in dark red blood. He whimpered while biting down on a stick.

Zo didn't ask questions. "I need blankets!" she yelled, as she washed her hands in a basin of scalding water. With pulsing, red hands, she took a stack of linens from a supply table and pressed it to the wound. The boy kicked and jostled.

"Hold him down or he'll bleed out!" shouted Zo.

No one moved.

Two women in white robes came in through a different tunnel entrance carrying woolen blankets. When they saw Zo, they froze.

"Help me!" Zo snatched the blankets from their hands and rolled the boy onto his side. Lifting his legs, she wedged blanket rolls under his good hip. The redheaded boy cried out in pain but Zo needed to keep the wound above his heart. She wrapped a bandage around his trunk, keeping as much pressure on the open wound as possible.

The boy's skin turned alabaster from blood loss. Zo yanked more blankets from the hands of the women, covered him up, and rubbed warmth into his arms and legs while muttering the words of one of her mother's blessings. "Hold as still as you can," she whispered into his ear. "You're going to be fine. I promise."

Zo approached the intimidating line of Ram soldiers. Each wore animal hide trimmed with fur. Thick leather straps crisscrossed their chests housing a variety of evil-looking weapons. "Where is my pack? It has the medicines I need." The men barely moved, barely blinked, with hands clasped behind their backs like dangerous statues of unfeeling.

The bald leader shook his head. A taunting, wicked, grin stretched across his face. Tess whimpered from one of the dark corners of the cave. Water dripped from the jagged, rock ceiling. The quiet symphony of sounds and silence contrasted with Zo's rapidly beating heart.

She swore and darted to the opposite wall where the healers stood just as still and lifeless. "Do you have any pseudo ginseng root?"

The aging healer looked over to the Gate Master, shook his head, and looked down at his hands.

So they would put this boy's life in danger just to see if she would fail?

I shouldn't be surprised.

Zo ran back to the steaming water and plunged four inches of her long braid into the basin. Sweat dripped from her forehead. She scrubbed the crusted mud from her hair and went to the closest soldier, holding out the dark braid. "Cut it," she said.

His gaze swept over her body before fixing on her face. His lips curled into a crooked grin.

She hated when men looked at her that way.

"Cut it!" she yelled, eyeing the knife at his hip, wondering if she had any chance of taking it from him without meeting a quick death.

A young soldier to his left stepped out of rank. His long dark hair was tucked behind his ears, his brows knit together and a muscle in his neck leapt as he frowned. The unexpected flash of his dagger made Zo scream. A small segment of her braid dropped to the ground and the young soldier took his place back in line, ignoring the disapproving scorn of the Ram leader.

Zo gasped as she snatched up the braid. She stumbled over to the sink again to rinse the hair one final time to prevent infection. Convinced the hair was clean, she darted back to the boy and removed the crimson-soaked dressing from the wound. The blood had slowed, but not enough. He'd die if this didn't work.

She shoved the hair into the wound and piled the excess on top.

The boy screamed then passed out.

Zo placed her hands over the mound of hair and uttered words of healing. The flame of her energy flickered as she willed the blessing to take effect. Her head swayed without permission as she reapplied a bandage.

When Zo finished, she slumped to the floor before they carried her and Tess away.

[•]

Joshua's dried blood tugged on Gryphon's arm. A deathly plaster, equal parts unforgiving and taunting. He scratched away at the memory of the ambush, the way young Joshua's eyes doubled in size when the arrow entered his side. It was Gryphon's fault. He'd let the kid come with his mess unit against his better judgment.

It was his fault.

Gryphon took the mountain trail home from the caves. He attacked the climb like he would any enemy. After the first mile his legs warmed. After the second they burned. He welcomed the dull pain creeping through his fatigued muscles. Pain equaled progress. With enough pain he might outpace his grief.

Joshua.

Gryphon sprinted the last hundred yards of the climb. The wind picked up as he reached the summit overlooking the ocean below. High waves crashed into the cliff wall. An arctic spray carried on the breeze, stinging Gryphon's eyes.

He turned and showed the ocean his back, casting his gaze over the valley of the Ram. Wind whipped his dark brown hair and made the metal of his weapons *clink* together. From this view he could see far beyond the training grounds and housing complexes, past the fields where hundreds of Nameless bent over acres of dying soil. Even beyond the fabled wall of Ram's Gate that corralled the vast lands of his people.

He felt powerful. In control.

Not like this morning when he couldn't slow Joshua's bleeding.

[●]

The twenty members of Gryphon's mess unit were encouraged to sleep in the barracks, even though many of them were married men. Unity meant everything to a Ram mess unit. Gryphon abided this and every other command issued by his leaders with exactness. But tonight, the thought of facing his brothers of war with all their questions and condolences seemed too much.

No. Tonight he would hide behind the walls of his inheritance like a child hides behind his mother's skirt.

The brick-and-plaster house sat back on a five-acre plot. It was one of the furthest family plots from the main gate and the center of town. A red sun dipped behind the towering wall of Ram's Gate, casting an ominous glow around the house as Gryphon climbed the dirt path. The solid oak door whined with complaint as he nudged it open.

"Who's there?" Gryphon's mother reached the entry with her arms and hands covered in white flour and her graying bun sitting at an angle on her head. She studied Gryphon and the corners of her mouth sank into the frown he'd come to associate with his childhood.

"Wash the blood off your hands." She retreated back to the kitchen without another word.

Gryphon leaned his long spear and shield against the wall and sloughed off his pack. He turned and noticed the rusted metal shield mounted above the hearth. His cheeks colored in shame. He looked away, but it didn't stop the boiling wave of anger that always came when he looked at his father's shield. The symbol of his family's disgrace.

Despite Gryphon's countless protests, his mother refused to take it down. "It's good to remember," she would say.

Then she'd go out into the forest where she thought no one could hear her and cry, rocking back and forth with her hands wrapped firmly about her stomach. As if she'd fall apart if she didn't hold herself together.

No matter how hard he worked in the training field, that shield would always hang over his head. Always.

In the kitchen, Gryphon plunged his hands into a basin of water. As he scrubbed, the water turned the color of salmon flesh.

His mother kneaded her palm into a batch of dough with more force than necessary. She used her forearm to push aside a clump of silver hair that fell into her face. "How many?" she asked with her back to him.

Gryphon couldn't scrub his hands hard enough. "One. We were ambushed." His excursions used to be so boring. They used to go weeks without running into another clan, but lately …

"Who?" His mother stood up straight, prepared to take the news like a strong Ram woman was meant to.

"Joshua." Gryphon felt his control slip. He chewed on his tongue until he could steel his emotions. "Spear," was all he trusted himself to say.

Joshua wasn't a member of a mess unit yet. The System didn't allow thirteen-year-olds to join. He had still been in training, but he'd begged to go, and Gryphon—his mentor—didn't have the heart to turn him down.

"Will he live?" she asked, kneading the dough again.

"I … " Gryphon cleared his constricting throat, thinking of the dirty Nameless girl they'd let work on Joshua in the cave. "I don't think he will."

Chapter 3

Darkness. The room was quiet except for the dissonant sound of dripping water. Zo sat up from the stone floor and put a hand to her throbbing head. Her eyes burned. Her tongue stuck to the roof of her mouth, giving a papery quality to the rotting smell of the cave.

Tess!

Zo crawled around, seeing mostly with her shaking hands. When she found another body beside her she choked on a sob of relief.

"Tess, are you all right?"

Zo moved her hand up to Tess' face only to have it batted away.

"My name is not Tess," a boy said, his voice weak, yet strangely hard.

"There was a girl with me. Do you know where she is?" Zo

could hear the hysteria in her own words. The thought of Tess alone in this monstrous place was too much to bear.

"Please!" she persisted.

The boy might have fallen back asleep. Zo couldn't tell. She crawled until she felt another blanket and tried to wake a sleeping man. He wouldn't stir. She moved to another. Then another. Tess wasn't here. The words of the Gate Master rang in Zo's ears.

"We don't allow Wolves ... Ever."

No clan could afford to refuse a healer, not even the Ram. But a healer's little sister? Would they kill her? She forced the thought away and kept searching until every inch of the cavernous room was accounted for.

It didn't take long to realize that Tess wasn't among the sour-smelling men asleep on the floor. Zo crawled back to her blanket and hugged her legs to her chest. Resting her head on her knees, she tried to imagine her mother's arms wrapped around her. Squeezing the despair away and leaving behind a blanket of gray unfeeling. A safe place where the demons of doubt couldn't find her.

"Your voice. It's familiar." The boy's words sliced through the darkness.

Zo startled at the sound. "Who are you?" she asked, choking on the heavy stench of the room.

"I know who I am," said the boy. "Who are you?" He spoke with an edge of arrogance uncommon for one so young.

"My name is Zo." She inched to his side. Her eyes had adjusted enough for her to make out the outline of the boy.

"That is a strange name. You're a ... a Nameless, aren't you?" he whispered.

Zo reached out to him, gently feeling for the bandage around his waist to confirm her suspicions that he was redheaded boy she'd healed. "How are you feeling?" She pressed her hand to his brow. The boy didn't flinch beneath her touch, but Zo could sense his unease. Commander Laden told her the Ram didn't usually trust Nameless slaves as healers.

"But you're a—"

"Yes, boy. A Nameless saved you." She did her best to keep the contempt from her voice. The clan wars weren't his fault.

She split the thin cotton cloth that was her blanket into long strips for new dressing. The boy didn't make a sound as she rolled him over to change the bandage, though he trembled from pain.

His bravery triggered a memory from Zo's childhood.

A foreign soldier beaten beyond human recognition. Her clan took him in. His defiant, black eyes followed her as she helped her mother clean, sew, and essentially piece him back together. He never screamed. Never cried to an unseen god for mercy. He had just stared at Zo without ever truly seeing past the thick haze of pain. Suffering in silence.

The boy's voice brought her back to present. "I might know how to find the girl, but first we need to get out of here."

"Do you know where we are?" she asked.

A violent shudder ran through his body. Zo tried to cover him with the scraps of her blanket but he pushed them away. "I think we're in the Waiting Room," he said.

Zo sat back. "Waiting room?"

The boy rolled onto his knees, fighting back a sob as he struggled to his feet. "A place to wait for death."

Zo looked around and suddenly understood the stench of

decay. Everyone in the Waiting Room was close enough to death that they couldn't leave on their own. Left to rot and die alone. Zo fought the bile rising up her throat. "Why would they do this to you? You need a clean bed and time to heal."

"This is a test. I must earn the right to rejoin my people." He grunted as he gathered his feet to stand. "Prove my strength."

"You can't just walk out of here," she said, "not with that wound in your side." She grabbed his arm, but he shook her off. "At least let me help you."

"I have to walk away from my own death." He took a pained step into the darkness. "No one can do that for me. Not even you, healer."

[♦]

Gryphon and his mess had been scouting the rocky terrain outside the Gate for over a week. It was rumored the Raven, a rival clan, had stockpiles of grain hidden somewhere in the mountain range. Food the Ram needed if their crops didn't produce higher yields than last year.

Food hadn't always been a problem for the Ram. Several hundred years ago the Ram had fought a major war, forcing other clans out of the most fertile areas in the region. A mighty tiger clearing the vast forest so she could stretch her legs. The wall of Ram's Gate was built by thousands of captured slaves. Ram military forces defended their lands with absolute aggression. Its people enjoyed full stomachs while lesser clans struggled on the crusts of Ram society.

Over the years, as the greedy fingers of winter stretched longer and the growing season shortened, many of the lesser clans migrated south. Over time, the Ram region, with its exhausted, frozen soils, needed food more than protection. But the traditions of war died hard, and the proud Ram refused to leave the legendary fortifications of Ram's Gate.

And so the raids began.

The Ram would do whatever it took to get food, even if it meant sentencing lesser clans like the Raven and Kodiak to starvation. Fate favored the assertive. It was just the natural order of things.

Zander held up a fist to call a halt and staked his long spear into the ground. With only twenty years behind him, Gryphon was one of the youngest in the mess company huddled around their leader. Zander stood with quiet confidence, eyeing every man who entered his circle. His gaze penetrated deeper than most. Hands flexing in fists at his sides accentuated the thick bands of muscle along his arms "We'll cross the gorge in alpha formation. Rotate on my call. Watch for Birds this time."

Gryphon distractedly adjusted the shield on his back. He buried his mourning for Joshua long enough to raise his head and meet Zander's stare.

"You have a favor to return, Gryph. The Birds need a message to carry home." Zander drove a finger into his chest. "*You*, Striker, will make sure they get it."

Everyone in the circle exchanged looks of surprise. Gryphon's best friend, Ajax, smiled and rocked onto the tips of his toes. Gryphon tightened his grip around his long spear. "Yes, sir." He hadn't expected the honor of making Striker. Usually the position went to someone with more experience. Second-in-command. It was a dangerous gift.

Zander gave a nod and the mess readied their shields for

a deadly stroll through the rocky gorge without the cover of trees for protection.

Gryphon tightened the fastenings of his shield before taking his place as Striker in the back-center of alpha formation. The mess marched out in two staggered lines. The men in front held shields at their chests while the men in the rear carried shields at their sides, ready to defend the rear if they were attacked from behind.

"How's the boy?" whispered Ajax. His dark-skinned mess brother was the only one who understood Gryphon's affection for Joshua. As young as Gryphon was, his interest in Joshua had grown into something paternal. The boy's father had died before Joshua was even born. Gryphon understood what it was like not to have a man around growing up.

He cleared his constricting throat. "Zander wouldn't let me check on him before we left. But ... " For a moment, Gryphon took his eyes off of the dangerous boulders and surrounding hills. "He's gone, Jax. I know he is."

Ajax had the decency not to hammer false hope. He resumed his watch before saying, "He died on his shield."

In truth, the kid hadn't earned his shield yet, but Ajax was right. The boy was a brave little pip, wounded in combat defending Gryphon's own sorry back. If only he hadn't let him come on the scouting trip. If only ...

Gryphon's sensitive ears heard hundreds of bowstrings stretch. "Link!" It wasn't his order to give, but Gryphon didn't care. The lives of his brothers were more valuable than Zander's pride. The arrows came like a wave of water. The phalanx tightened into a wall of shields, every angle protected. Arrows *thumped* like a deadly hailstorm. The earth beneath

Gryphon vibrated as arrows sunk into the ground around their feet.

The attack came from two sides, and was over as quickly as it began. Zander didn't have to yell his orders. "Hold till the next wave. Full advance to the left. Guard our backs, Gryph."

Another volley of arrows embedded like porcupine quills into their shields.

The mess charged left until Zander called, "Halt!" and the formation linked back into a defensive huddle. More arrows beat down upon them. The timing of Zander's orders was the difference between life and an arrow through the chest.

After another volley, the mess charged left again until they reached the side of the gorge. Gryphon and the rest of the secondary covered from behind. The enemy line weakened as Raven abandoned their bows in retreat. Cowards.

"Striker!" Zander called over the chaos. It was Gryphon's cue to back away from the pack. The mess shifted into a diamond attack pattern in front of a grouping of giant boulders with Gryphon at the scorpion's tail.

They didn't need to kill all of the Raven. Just capture one to interrogate and kill a few more to remind them whom they were dealing with. Above, inhuman hoots and cries from the Raven sounded retreat.

Gryphon only had one chance to get this right.

"Strike!" Zander called.

Gryphon sprinted to his brothers. With spear ready, he jumped onto a knot of their interlocked arms. Their combined strength catapulted him up the boulder. Time slowed to a halt. Gryphon zeroed in on a target. A boy with a single feather strung around his neck clumsily tried to restring his bow. He couldn't be much older than Joshua.

Fitting.

The boy looked up. In that split-second the image of Joshua burned Gryphon's vision. He shouldn't care. War doesn't discriminate between the old and the young. But he couldn't bring himself to kill the boy. He adjusted his aim just as the spear exploded from his hand.

Gryphon landed on the boulder and watched the boy scramble away with the rest of the retreating Raven Clan. Gryphon's spear stood erect in the mud, still teetering from the impact.

When Zander pulled himself up next to Gryphon he looked down on the empty spear and swore. His whole body trembled in rage.

Together they watched the Raven retreat up the mountain, their traditional black feathers mocking as they passed outside the reach of Ram spears.

Just before crossing over the ridge, a man stopped and stared down at Gryphon with fearless eyes. He stood taller than the Raven around him. His hair and skin were lighter than theirs. A black crescent moon was tattooed on his muscled shoulder. He raised his hands to his mouth and let out a long, low howl.

Chills assaulted Gryphon's skin. "Was that … ?"

Zander swore again and stalked away.

Until that day, Gryphon had never witnessed the call of a Wolf.

Chapter 4

The boy led Zo upward through a seemingly endless tunnel of rock. He stumbled and she grabbed the back of his shirt to help him.

"Get off me." He swatted her away without success.

His pride would kill him eventually. If not today, then ten years from now on some lonely battlefield.

Pride always killed the Ram.

"Let me help you or I swear I'll slit your sorry, little throat." Zo regretted her words immediately. A true Nameless would never speak to a Ram like that, even if he was just a boy.

Her vision had adjusted enough to make out his shock. "You just threatened me." A slow smile spread across his face, reaching his eyes and lifting his ears. He chuckled, but grabbed his side from the pain. "I like you, healer." He rested his arm on her shoulder and let her carry most of his weight. "You've got nerve."

It wasn't until that moment that she noticed his size. Only thirteen but still as tall as she was, maybe even taller. His wiry muscles would undoubtedly expand with the years of training ahead of him. According to Commander Laden, boys his age had already been through a barbaric amount of training. Beatings. Systematic starvation. All to ensure their dominance on the battlefield as adults.

"We're almost to the entrance. Then you need to let me walk out alone."

Zo began to protest, but he cut her off.

"I already told you. I have to walk away from my own death or else they'll send me back. The Ram have no place for weaklings." He looked Zo right in the eyes, clearly defending his people's action to let him suffer and die in this dark, underground hell.

I will never, ever, understand these animals.

They reached a large wooden door glowing with gold light around the hinges. There was no handle. Zo ducked out from under the boy's arm to let him support his own weight. She took a step behind him and tugged at her shirt, sticky with his fresh blood.

"Don't speak unless spoken to. Keep your head down. I'll do the rest," he said.

Zo studied the boy, trying to weigh his intentions. No one was nice for nothing.

The boy pounded three times on the door. The booming sound chased past them, likely taunting the dying men at the bottom of the cave. The latch lifted free followed by a draft of fresh air and the slow creak of rusted hinges.

A single lantern swung on a knotted walking stick. An

elderly man with hollow eyes studied them with a vacant expression. His back had rounded from too many years of heavy labor, leathery skin hung from jutting bones. The poor Nameless man stood alone, left to guard the dying. His arm shook as he lifted the ram horn from his neck and offered it to the boy. "You must call them." His corroded voice cracked and wheezed from lack of use.

The boy pressed the horn to his lips and blew. The sound of the Ram ricocheted throughout the cave, pulsing deep into Zo's very bones. She hated that sound. Back home it was known as the Call of Death. It meant another raid. Another scramble to get those she loved to safety behind the inner walls of the city. It meant hunger. Women crying through the night over the loss of a son or husband. Fear.

Always fear.

Minutes passed before the small group of healers in white robes came to gurney the boy away. He might live if he didn't have to endure anymore of these ridiculous customs. The boy would grow up and become the enemy he was meant to be.

"The Nameless girl stays with me," he ordered.

"She's been summoned by the Gate Master," said one of the Ram healers.

Zo shook her head. "I want to find my—"

The boy used the little energy he had left to strike her with the back of his hand. The force of the blow sent Zo to her knees. "Quiet, Nameless," he said, though his reluctant tone didn't quite match the words.

Zo looked down and swallowed the blood pooling in her mouth. The aftertaste served as a useful distraction, buying her much needed time to temper her emotions. Her hands shook with the need to strike back. An urge to kill those who'd done so much to her and her family gnawed at her chest. It was a monster begging for release. But lashing out now wouldn't save her sister or her cause. Sweet revenge would surely come, just not today.

As they walked the rest of the way out of the cave the boy mouthed the word, "sorry." She fingered her swelling cheek and walked into the blinding light of day, into a place different from anything she'd ever known.

[◆]

The thick scent of cherry and cedar smoke filled the room. The smell might have been relaxing were Gryphon not kneeling before the Horn—a ten-foot table shaped like the curve of a giant ram horn.

It took a lot to secure an audience with Chief Barnabas. Gryphon always hoped his first encounter with the clan chief would be due to some heroic act of valor. Instead, he found himself shrinking under the weight of the chief's stare as Zander explained the Wolf sighting.

"Yes, sir. We're sure it was a Wolf." Zander stood proud, with chin raised.

"Just one?" Barnabas had deep vertical wrinkles protecting his small mouth from encroaching round cheeks. His patronizing smile sat uncomfortably on his face.

Wolves never traveled alone. Everyone knew that.

Zander shuffled his feet. "We only saw one, sir. The Wolf stopped and howled at us mid-retreat. Taunting us, in a way."

"Shameful," muttered a female advisor seated at Barnabas'

right. The men in Gryphon's mess called her the Seer. She was said to have a supernatural gift that allowed her to see everything that happened within the Gate with her black, beady eyes. Gryphon thought it more likely that she simply had an army of informants working for her.

She leaned over to Barnabas and whispered, "Didn't you say the Wolves sent troops to help defend the Kodiak too? Maybe the rumors are—"

"Enough," said Barnabas. He leaned forward, resting his clasped hands on the table and looked down the end of his crooked nose at Zander. "Your mess suffered no casualties, yet also took no lives. Explain."

Zander stumbled over his words before saying, "The enemy had high ground. We launched our Striker but the Raven retreat was well-timed."

Barnabas sat back in his chair and gestured for Gryphon to stand. "I'm not surprised to see you make Striker, Gryphon, son of Troy."

Gryphon's eyes nearly doubled in size. "Thank you, sir." He kept his head down but a zing of pride filled his chest. His hard work had not gone unnoticed.

The clan chief said, "Your father was my Striker for a number of years. Did you know that, boy?"

Gryphon's brow wrinkled. "I didn't know you shared a mess unit." No one had ever told him. Not even his mother.

Gryphon's father had been taken in a Wolf ambush when Gryphon was still a baby. Maybe the first Ram ever taken alive. He'd left his shield and dishonor behind as Gryphon's inheritance.

"Troy never missed a mark." Barnabas' jowls shook as he

laughed at the memory. Then, as swift as a changing tide, his laughter cut off and he leaned forward. Without an ounce of humor he said, "It's a shame you didn't inherit your father's aim."

Gryphon's head sunk low again. The dishonor made it hard to breathe. What would Barnabas think if he knew the whole truth? That he intentionally spared the boy's life?

Zander rested a hand on Gryphon's shoulder. "There was no target, sir. As I said before, the Raven retreated before we could attack."

"Excuses," Barnabas grunted. "If there was one Wolf with the Raven, there will undoubtedly be more. We need to find that settlement." He drummed his fingers on the horn-shaped desk. His eyes glazed over as he stared past them at the back wall of the room.

Gryphon and Zander exchanged uncertain glances. The Seer adjusted in her seat, scowling in their direction. An insect buzzed around the room, hovering from one end of the horn to the next. Gryphon's legs complained from going so long without rest from their journey. He shifted his weight. The insect landed in front of Barnabas and without warning the chief slammed the bug with his fist, his eyes still eerily unfocused as he pondered.

Moments later, he got to his feet and gestured for the guards to escort Zander and Gryphon from the room. "Dismissed."

Gryphon exhaled. He could barely make out the low hiss of the Seer's voice as he left. "I don't like it, Barnabas. The Wolves are organizing … " The door closed. Gryphon's suspicions leapt as he considered the implications. The lesser clans had never banded together in the past. Why now? And why would the Wolves—their strongest enemy—help the others when their main settlement sat well outside the reach of the Ram?

They stepped out of the stone building and Gryphon raised a hand to cover his eyes from the bright sun. As Zander started walking toward the training fields, Gryphon called after him. "Thank you for speaking for me."

Zander twisted to look over his shoulder. "I said nothing that wasn't true." He paused. "Right?"

Gryphon nodded, but the action was delayed by a fraction of a second. "Yes, sir."

Zander's lips formed a thin line. "If you look bad, the whole mess looks bad. Especially me." He walked away without a backward glance.

Gryphon thought of the Raven boy trying to string an arrow. How many Ram would that boy grow up to kill before he died? His body shook with rage. He needed to hit something. Someone. He walked by one of the training fields and yanked a spear staked to the ground. A wild roar escaped his chest as he launched the spear over the training field, deep into a thick copse of trees.

The young boys and girls in training lowered their weighted weapons to stare. One girl actually clapped. The instructor shook his head in disgust and ordered her to fetch the spear.

Gryphon's shoulders slumped.

He'd only taken two steps toward the mess barracks when a breathless runner caught up to him. "I have a message, sir. It's from the Medica."

Gryphon froze.

"Joshua lives!"

Chapter 5

Rough fingers dug into Zo's arms as Ram soldiers dragged her through the damp, cobbled streets to meet the Gate Master.

From where she walked, the tall wall enclosing Ram's Gate lay in the distance, barely visible over the massive structures surrounding her. Ram buildings made of stone and plaster conveyed a sense of arrogant permanence contrary to every other clan's way of life in these desperate times. They were buildings built to last, instead of the adobe and hide preferred by her people. It was no wonder the Ram stood undefeated for two centuries.

They reached an open square large enough to accommodate several thousand people. In the middle of the vast square stood a raised platform sectioned off by fraying rope.

The Ram dragged Zo across the open space, until they

came so close to the wooden platform, Zo might have been able to reach out and touch it. Rows of tally marks were carved into the wood. Darks stains ran like tears down the slats in some places and splattered in others. A chill rolled over Zo's skin and she turned away. It was only a simple platform, but the feelings that seemed to cry from the structure were real. This square was a place to avoid.

Zo didn't realize she'd been holding her breath until they left the square. They had to a halt as a pregnant woman with short hair and a long thin nose walked in front of them to cross the cobblestone street. Like most of the Ram who passed, her clothes were made of coarse wool with touches of fur and animal hide. The guards gave her a slight nod of respect. Zo knew from her studies that all pregnant women inside the Gate were revered because of the declining Ram population.

The Ram woman gazed at Zo from the corner of her eye and quickly averted her focus, as if pretending Zo didn't exist. She raised a hand to her ripe stomach and moved to the other side of the street.

The guards yanked Zo into one of the stone buildings. "In here," one said, pulling her through a doorway and forcing her into a chair. A clean desk sat vacant across from her. The only light came from a humble fire in the corner of the room.

The guards stood at Zo's back as the frog-eyed man she assumed was the Gate Master entered, followed by a woman wearing a boiled leather vest and a task whip at her hip. Her hair was pulled back into a bun at the nape of her neck making her tiny black eyes all the more severe. "Leave us," the woman said to the guards.

Commander Laden had prepared Zo for seeing women

of power inside the Gate. She never believed a female could inspire such fear until now. The woman settled into her chair and smiled at Zo. "Welcome, child. Our Gate Master tells me you've proven yourself as a healer," she said with nasal sweetness.

Zo was careful to avoid direct eye contact as she nodded. Submission was everything. Laden had been quite clear on that point as well.

"You might guess that we need healers inside the Gate. It is a job left for those too old or unskilled to fight. There is little honor in the occupation, but still, there is a need." She shuffled through a stack of parchment on her desk. Her spindly fingers moved inhumanly fast, like spider legs working over the body of a recent kill.

"We provide refuge for the women and children of other clans as long as they can contribute to our society. Even young girls like your tiny sister can serve a purpose."

Zo's head whipped up. Her fingers curled into claws against the wood of the chair.

The frog-faced Gate Master smiled down from his position next to the woman, showing his rotting teeth.

"You see," the woman continued, "usually Nameless aren't allowed near the Medica or surrounding buildings. Even if they have had proper training in the healing arts and blessings, how can we trust them to do everything in their power to keep our warriors healthy?"

Zo's stomach soured.

"With you, it might be different." The woman found the paper she'd obviously been looking for and dipped the tip of a black-feathered quill into a jar of ink. The tip scratched along the surface of the paper with wild precision. "I've decided to let you work in the Medica and be given food rations, water, a blanket, and a bed."

Zo sat up in her chair, relieved to finally hear some good news.

"In the mornings your sister will be taken with other Nameless in your assigned barracks to work the fields while you tend to the sick and injured." The woman looked up and smiled. "She will have to earn her stay too. Every day you prove yourself in the Medica, your sister will live to come back to you that night."

Despite the heat of the fire, a tremor of chills rolled up Zo's spine. "P-prove myself?"

The woman set down her quill and rested her clasped hands on the desk, a pleased expression never leaving her face. "As long as no one dies in your care, your sister lives."

Zo clutched her stomach and scratched away some of the flesh around her thumbnails—a habit she often used to cope with bouts of anxiety.

It offered little relief.

The woman dusted the parchment with fine sand to clear the excess ink and handed them to the Gate Master. She stood up to leave and patted Zo on her head like she was a dog. "Welcome to Ram's Gate."

[◆]

The following days dragged like a grindstone through the mud. After training, Gryphon walked to the Medica to sit with Joshua. The boy usually slept the whole time, giving

Gryphon ample time to consider his meeting with Barnabas and the consequences of his mistakes with the Raven boy. He didn't dare tell anyone—not even Ajax—about the mercy he'd shown. No man wants the world to see his weaknesses.

Gryphon tried to hide a bulge under his shirt as he smuggled his contraband past the Medica workers. He found Joshua staring blankly at a bare wall in a room with six empty beds.

The redheaded boy jumped when Gryphon entered.

"Slow down, kid. You're going to hurt yourself."

Wincing, Joshua settled back into his pillow. "I smell food. Please, *please* tell me you have food." They both looked at the door, making sure no one heard him.

Gryphon eased onto the bed next to Joshua like an old man. After the last excursion, Zander had put the mess through a grueling series of workouts. "Is that healer still not letting you eat?" Gryphon half groaned as he tried to relax his tight muscles.

"She's a monster. I'd rather take another arrow than force down more salty beet and barley soup." Joshua's shoulders sank with the burden of feeling sorry for himself. "Look at me." He flexed his biceps. "How am I going to get big like you without any protein. A man needs his meat."

Gryphon pretended to cough into his fist before unrolling the chicken leg from its wrapping. He offered it to Joshua just as the healer strolled into the room.

"I hope you plan to eat that, soldier." The girl was young and slight, but had a stern quality to her voice.

Gryphon sat back and took a modest bite before setting the chicken back in its wrappings. "Of course."

She eyed him as she walked over to Joshua's side carrying

a tray of medicines and bandages. Her white Medica uniform was clearly meant for a man. It hung off her small frame in an almost comical way. A red headscarf covered her hair and most of her face; the exposed portion of her skin was hidden behind a cracked layer of mud or plaster. Like she herself might carry some disease. But beneath it all were unique eyes framed by thick black lashes. Very different from the old men and women who usually attended the sick in the Medica.

Joshua grumbled something about systematic starvation as he rolled onto his good side. The healer's practiced hands undressed the bandage. She unstopped a bottle from her tray. "Try to relax this time," she whispered.

Three drops into the wound made Joshua's whole body flex into a ball. He breathed hard through his teeth.

Gryphon didn't remember gaining his feet. "What was that?"

The girl ignored him. She rested her hands just outside the raw hole in Joshua's side and said, "Take. Clean. Heal." She repeated the words over and over again. They flowed like a calm wind.

Gryphon's arms dotted with goose bumps.

The healer's hands swept along Joshua's skin, starting at the wound then moving outward, as if willing the medicine into his bloodstream. Joshua's legs and arms turned limp. His eyelids sagged. His jaw slackened. The healer continued her words as she dressed the wound and rolled him onto his back. She pulled the blanket up over his shoulders and cleared the wild red hair from Joshua's eyes with a sympathetic grin before moving toward the door.

"Wait," said Gryphon.

The girl stopped but didn't turn around.

"Show me your hair." Gryphon didn't have the right to demand anything of this healer, but something about her voice sounded familiar.

She grimaced, but pulled the linen wrap from her head to reveal a tangle of thick black hair that fell in an uneven line below her shoulders.

"You're the Nameless who saved Joshua."

She stared back at him, daring for a small moment to look into his eyes. Willful, if a tad frightened.

"I've never met a Nameless healer," said Gryphon.

She flinched, but then seemed to remember herself with a tight curtsy before escaping the room.

Gryphon stared at the door until he felt sure of his privacy. Only then did he bring out a stout brick of wood and a carving knife. He hummed random notes as he worked the wood. The beginnings of a new song danced on the tip of his tongue. Lyrics formed in his mind about a faceless girl who spouted magic from her fingertips. The melody begged to be sung, but Gryphon resisted. No one would ever sing his songs. Not even him.

Ram did not sing.

Chapter 6

Though Zo didn't get to see Tess until the evenings, her every action and thought revolved around keeping her little sister safe. Was she hungry? Were the Ram field bosses kind to her? Were they working her too hard?

Zo left Tess when she reported to the Medica every morning, and every morning she wondered if it would be the last time she saw her sister's face. No matter how much skill and knowledge Zo possessed as a healer, it was only a matter of time before someone died under her care.

Healing wasn't just cleaning infection and wrapping bandages. To really *heal* someone you had to care about him enough to open your heart and let compassion travel through your hands. But how could she feel an ounce of compassion for the people who'd taken everything from her?

Zo picked up a smooth stone on her way to the Medica. She

weighed it in her hand then threw it into the forest lining the path. She wanted to scream, to release the fire in her stomach and rid herself of all the hate gathered there. But it would take more than stones and screams to relinquish her dark emotions.

She needed to find some way to care for these people. For Tess' sake. But how?

Just as she did every day, Zo held her breath as she hurried through the vast square and past the sinister platform. She reached the pale stone Medica building just as the sun crested the eastern wall of Ram's Gate. There were few Nameless here in the center of the town. Mostly Ram women walked the street. Many of them carried a long dagger or sword at their hip. Every now and then, Zoe saw a girl around her age with her head completely shaved, bringing emphasis to the Ram's trademark long, narrow nose and dark features.

Zo pulled her headscarf lower and kept her head down. She did her best to blend into the heavy stone buildings until she slipped unobserved through the back door of the Medica.

Joshua, with his flaming red hair and excess of dimples, was still asleep when she entered his small room. But he wasn't alone. The Ram soldier called Gryphon sat hunched in a chair next to him. His dark hair fell forward, framing a defined jaw and downturned lips. His knife and wooden carving were held loosely in large hands as he dozed.

Zo pressed her back to the wall and worked her way around the room, careful to keep as much space between her and the Ram soldier as possible. She set her tray of medicines on the edge of the bed. Gingerly lifting Joshua's wrist, she timed the rhythm of his heart.

Stronger today. Good.

Joshua woke with a loud yawn. "Good morning."

Then everything happened fast. Joshua, forgetting his injury, reached his arms above his head to stretch. He yelped in pain and yanked his arm back down, sending Zo's tray clattering to the floor. Gryphon jumped awake and in a split second, had Zo's back pinned against him, a blade pressed against her throat. His jagged breath blew past her ear.

"Stop! Gryphon, it's all right. I just knocked over the tray." Joshua had rolled onto his knees in bed.

And just as fast as it happened, the soldier lowered his arms and stepped away, looking around the room while blinking away sleep. "Sorry," he mumbled, sheathing his dagger. He looked out the window and swore. "I'm late for training." He grabbed a piece of bread from the ground—a portion of Joshua's breakfast—gathered his pack, and sprinted out of the room.

Zo stared after him with her hand clutching her throat.

[•]

That evening, birds squawked in the rafters of the Nameless' barracks. Women and children pulled off worn boots and layers of dirty clothes. They ate rations of day-old bread and bone broth as bland as tepid water and stone. The ragged Nameless moved in a sort of trance in the dim candlelight as they prepared for bed.

As tired as they were, everyone in the Nameless' barracks had a smile for Tess. How could they not? She carried a certain joy with her even while she worked. In a few short days she knew almost everyone's name and was a special favorite with the children. In contrast, no one said a word to Zo. She was not worked to exhaustion in the fields like they were. Some called her an "in between."

It took Zo a while to learn that Nameless concubines who lived in the main part of the city were called the same thing. They were "in betweens" because even though they didn't endure the rough manual labor that came with the life of a Nameless, they were still not members of Ram society. More to the point, they worked mostly "in between" the sheets of their master's beds.

Zo had stopped caring about other people's opinions long before passing through the Gate. She ignored sour looks from the other Nameless slaves as she massaged ointment into Tess' blistered hands. The familiar motion reminded her of their mother tending to the afflicted back home.

Her mother.

She had poured a piece of her soul into every person who came through her door. All of Zo's lessons had ended with the same speech.

"Remember, Zo. You must love them to heal them. Medicine can only take you so far."

Even though she'd saved the redheaded boy from death, his healing wasn't complete—the wound was not closing as it should.

Zo didn't have her mother's heart. She could never love a Ram, and yet how could she heal one if she didn't?

You can't love someone you hate.

Sooner or later, a Ram soldier would lie on her table and her disinterest would kill him. Then they'd come for Tess—

"It's not so bad, Zo," said Tess through a yawn. She always seemed to sense Zo's mood.

Zo bit the inside of her cheek as she massaged her sister's foot.

"Really, it's not. They give us water and meal breaks. Some of the girls even get to rest up at the house."

Zo's head whipped up. "Never go into a Ram's house, Tess. No matter what they offer you."

"Why?" she asked through a yawn.

Zo tasted blood from inside her cheek. "Just promise me you won't."

Tess swayed with exhaustion. "I promise," she mumbled just before dropping her head to the straw-stuffed mattress of her bunk. Her eyes drooped into instant sleep. Exhaustion.

Zo blinked hard to clear away the unwelcome tears. She worked into the night to erase the signs of labor from her sister's hands and feet.

By the time she finished, her candle was the only one glowing among the stacked beds of the barracks, though an old woman the others called Ann still mumbled a string of nonsense to herself in the corner.

Zo used the dirt floor for a desk as she scribbled three copies of a message using parchment and ink stolen from the Medica. The candle sent ripples of ominous light over her words.

Laden,

My sister followed me. I've secured my post, but she is not safe. I can't wait. Send your sign.

Peace

Zo studied the hurried writing, examining all the Kodiak characters for accuracy. Commander Laden wanted only to know that she'd survived. To test communication. But with Tess inside the Gate there wasn't time to wait weeks before gathering intelligence.

Her hands shook as she rolled the brittle parchment into tiny glass cylinders stolen from the Medica.

When Zo was young, and life wasn't a nightmare, she and Gabe used to sit and listen to the stories chanted by an old storyteller. One night, the old chanter told a tale about the old wars. About people who sacrificed their lives by carrying explosives on their chests to kill the enemy. Zo remembered moving as close to the fire as possible so not to miss a word. The concept of a person purposely giving their life for a war seemed too high a price to pay.

That was when the candle of hope still burned inside her chest. Things were different now. After the raid, she found herself envying those souls who'd found freedom in death. This mission was supposed to be her perfect ending. Taking her own life had always seemed selfish. Dying for the Cause … that was noble.

She'd never allowed herself to think about surviving this mission, but with Tess inside the Gate, the explosive was not strapped to Zo's chest alone. She had to find a way to execute her assignment while keeping Tess alive.

Zo packed up the bottles and snuffed out the low-burning candle. She passed Ann—still muttering gibberish—as she fumbled for the only door in the barracks.

The cold wind cut through Zo's thin, layered clothing as she crossed the main road and hiked into the thick shadows of the forest. At night it was easy to forget she was still within the fabled wall that separated Ram's Gate from the rest of the region. The sickle moon provided little light as she approached the river. She hesitated for only a moment before tossing in the bottles. They were instantly absorbed in the black river that ran south under the great wall of the Ram. If these little bottles didn't make it to Laden's men at the dam, then she'd put Tess in danger for nothing.

"Please let no one see them." She spoke aloud, but only to herself. God died five years ago, the night her parents were murdered.

Chapter 7

The sun streaming through the small window of the Medica
was too bright. Gryphon pulled the pillow over his head
and showed the window his back.

"Wake up. Can't you hear the bells?" said Joshua.

For a sweet moment, Gryphon imagined sleeping until his
body woke him, not some bell or horn. But the sound coming
from the square wasn't the usual wake-up call.

Gryphon got to his feet and rubbed the sleep from his dark
eyes. These nights with the kid were starting to wear on him.
"It's a little early for a prizefight, isn't it?"

Joshua stretched to look out the window from his bed. "It's
never too early for a prizefight!"

Gryphon laughed without mirth. He'd never understood his
clan's fascination with sport killings. Where was the victory in
defeating an untrained slave?

"Aren't you going to watch?" Joshua said.

The bells beckoned everyone to witness the fight. It was Gryphon's duty to watch the young Ram challenger take on the offending Nameless. It was said that the greatness of the crowd reflected the potential of the soldier. Still, Gryphon hesitated.

Joshua got to his feet and with uneven steps walked to the door.

"What do you think you're doing?" said Gryphon.

Before Joshua could take a step past the doorway, the young healer had him by the arm and was hauling him back to the bed. Gryphon found himself smiling in approval. She was tougher than her thin frame suggested.

"You don't understand, Zo."

Gryphon cringed at Joshua's use of the girl's name.

"It's a prizefight. It could be weeks before the next one." Joshua struggled to escape her determined grasp.

"I don't care if you don't see another fight in your life. You're not leaving your bed until that wound is closed and the infection is purged."

Joshua's lips jutted out in an exaggerated pout. "Talk to her, Gryph. Tell her I have to go."

A scratchy baritone voice filled the room. "What is the problem here?" Gate Master Leon stepped through the door.

Gryphon moved in front of his open pack to hide the wooden eagle he'd spent the night carving. Ram didn't typically waste time with such impractical things. Luckily, the Gate Master's eyes were only for the healer. Gryphon cleared his throat to address his ranking superior. "The boy wants to see the prizefight, sir. His healer recommends he stay in bed."

The Gate Master stepped up to the girl and used the back

of his hand to caress her mud-caked face. Then, like the snap of a whip, he struck her. The impact sent her across the room. The girl fell to the floor and huddled in a ball. She clutched her cheek as blood wept from the corner of her mouth.

An impulse to snap Leon's neck surged through Gryphon's fingers. He squeezed Joshua's bed frame until his knuckles turned white. Then he took a deep breath to calm his rage. Master Leon and every other Ram were entitled by law to treat this woman as they pleased. She was payment for the lives lost expanding and defending the clan. Livestock gained.

Gryphon knew what it felt like to take a hit from the iron-built Gate Master. Leon had been assigned to give Gryphon his annual beating the year he turned twelve. He hadn't been able to walk without help for a week. The Ram had long believed the only way to produce brave warriors was to teach them about manhood from a young age.

Gryphon hated the system but couldn't argue with the results.

Master Leon turned to Gryphon and smiled like nothing happened. "It's unfortunate your boy got the Nameless healer."

The Gate Master crossed the room and rested a heavy hand on Joshua's shoulder. "He looks healthy enough to me. Let him watch the game. His own prizefight is only a few years away. He needs the exposure."

Red splotches sprouted on Joshua's face as he watched the healer cower in the corner of the room. "I'm suddenly not feeling well, *sir*. I think I'll stay." Gryphon hoped Master Leon didn't hear the edge to Joshua's voice. The boy didn't want to find himself on the wrong end of Master Leon's temper.

The Gate Master followed Joshua's stare.

"Come, Nameless." His boots *boomed* against the floorboards. "You don't get the option." He yanked her off the floor and launched her out of the room.

"I'll be back." Gryphon patted Joshua's leg and left to follow the healer. Master Leon might be entitled to treat the girl as he wished, but Gryphon couldn't ignore the need to make sure he didn't take things too far. She had, after all, saved Joshua's life.

The bells summoned Nameless and Ram alike. Nameless, because these fights were mandatory, Ram, because of the entertainment value. Gryphon arrived at the raised, square platform in the city center just behind Master Leon and the girl. Through the heavy layer of grit on her face, the healer's features betrayed unique beauty. She had a small nose and a set of full lips that, at the moment, turned down as she leaned away from the Gate Master. Her ebony lashes matched the wisps of hair that often escaped her head wrap.

A new wave of lyrics came to mind as Gryphon studied her soft features. He yearned to hum the dark song as he walked through the thick crowd. Of course, he fought the urge. It wasn't long before the rush of spectators carried the girl and Gate Master from Gryphon's view. He had pushed up on his toes to spot the healer over the crowd when Ajax, his favorite brother of the mess, smiled and slapped him on the back. "Gryph! You look like hell."

Gryphon laughed and half-heartedly slugged Ajax in the stomach. "Thanks."

"The rest of the guys are near the front. Come on."

Gryphon looked back to find the healer through the throng but gave up.

"Still baby-sitting the boy?" Ajax said as they walked.

Gryphon nodded. "It's a place to sleep."

Ajax shook his head, then his smile melted into a tight line. "I have a reason not to sleep with the mess unit. Sara's going to deliver her baby any day now. You," he stabbed Gryphon in the chest with a finger, "have no excuse."

"I'm all Joshua has," said Gryphon.

Ajax gestured toward Zander who stood with arms crossed at the front of the pack. Serious as always. "Tell that to him."

Drums pounded an echoing rhythm that vibrated deep within Gryphon's bones. The crowd parted as a Nameless man was ushered to the platform. The shadows beneath his eyes made him look more tired than heated for battle. His black hair hung carelessly past his shoulders. His skin was like tanned leather, coarse enough to sharpen a dull blade.

As he stepped onto the platform a buzz of excitement ignited the crowd. Normally, a prizefight accomplished two objectives: first, it offered a young Ram trainee the chance to get his first real kill, second, it was a way to publically discipline the Nameless. But on rare occasions, a Nameless volunteered to enter the square. If he won he earned his freedom. If he didn't, well …

"The Nameless isn't bound!" said Ajax. "How long's it been since a Nameless walked onto the platform without a spear to his back?"

Gryphon frowned. "Years." He studied the man with new eyes. The Nameless was lean but not without muscle. He might have been tall without the hunched curve in his back. "I can't decide if he's suicidal or just a fool."

"Flip a coin. I don't know. Though I hope to hell he's a fool.

I'd love to see a good fight." Ajax rushed over to another mess brother to hash out betting odds. Gryphon hadn't seen him so excited since the day he discovered his wife was with child. He smiled at the memory: Ajax dancing around, pounding his chest like an animal for two solid days. The idiot was easy to love.

The young Ram challenger took the stairs of the platform two at a time. The seventeen-year-old called Sam, whose training was all but complete, accepted his training shield with a serious nod. He wore fur bands around his thick arms and forehead. His brown dreadlocks fell to the middle of his back; charms, beads, and animal teeth were woven into each knotted cord.

The crowd shoved closer to the raised square platform as the Nameless was armed with a sword and wooden shield. He would be young Sam's first kill. The kill that would earn him his shield and entry into a mess.

Gryphon kept his attention trained on the hollow eyes of the Nameless challenger until a sobbing woman near the back of the crowd sobbed, "No! Don't leave me, Jacob!" The older Nameless woman sank to her knees and wept for the man who must have been her son on the platform. Her screams echoed off the cobbles of the square as guards dragged her away.

Men all around Gryphon chuckled to each other and carried on with their bets.

[•]

Zo followed the Gate Master to the square in the center of town though she wanted nothing more than to run in the opposite direction. They cut through a thick crowd of Nameless who seemed to make up the back perimeter of the square. There was an obvious gap dividing the Nameless and the Ram who'd come to witness the fight. The closer they came to the platform, the more excited the crowd became.

The Gate Master stopped near a group of Ram boys and girls around Joshua's age. Some play-wrestled while others stood on eager tiptoes to see the people on the platform. Zo's stomach twisted as she followed their gazes. She'd always seen the platform as a place to avoid. Now she knew why.

The Gate Master grabbed Zo by the arm and yanked her in front of him. When he'd struck her at the Medica it was easy to play the victim, to stay down on the floor and even throw in a few whimpers. They liked it when you stayed down. But it wasn't the hard touches that affected her.

The Gate Master's hand moved up and down her waist, pulling her closer to him as he watched the two men prepare to fight. A bald Ram stood to address the anxious crowd. He was dressed like most men of his clan: fur-lined clothes and boots with a sword strapped to his side, as if carrying it proved his manhood. Fools.

"Today Samson Longshanks fights a Nameless to earn his shield. Let all who hear my voice bear witness."

The Ram weren't people of many words. They preferred to communicate with their weapons, or in the Gate Master's case, their hands. The young Ram stood at one side of the roped-off platform while the Nameless challenger studied him from another. Judging from the subtle slant of his eyes and his straight, black hair, the Nameless looked more Raven than Kodiak.

Zo stood tall, but dropped her head as swords were drawn. The Gate Master placed a finger under her chin and gently lifted her gaze. His hot breath burned against her frozen cheek. "You will watch this."

The men on the platform circled each other with arms extended. The Nameless did his best to maintain a careful distance from the young Ram. Zo's heart beat faster, her stomach churned as she fought a rising panic. She'd rather be in the ring than watch it happen.

The Ram's dreadlocks flew with life as he charged. Zo tried to look past the fight, beyond the high mountains in the distance. She tried not to hear the wail of pain as the Ram took his first slice at the Nameless man's stomach. Or see the spray of blood as the Ram dragged his blade along his opponent's throat. Most of all, she tried not to see the Nameless man's final moments. The moments that separated him from life and death, when his eyes softened and his face relaxed into peaceful acceptance. When steam began to rise off his weeping entrails.

The crowd cheered. Zo vomited.

"You stupid girl!" said the Gate Master, wiping his hand on his shirt.

Zo hunched over and hugged her stomach. She couldn't breathe.

"You disgust me." The Gate Master shoved her from behind. She didn't catch herself before crashing to the ground. "Get back to work!"

Zo rolled away before his boot met her side. She scrambled to her shaking feet and ran. The cobblestone road swayed. Her headscarf hung crooked. Half of her dark hair escaped and whipped her face. She stumbled down a narrow gap between two stone buildings and vomited again. With her arms wrapped around her shoulders, she melted down the side of the building and fought back sobs. She pressed her cheek to the cold stone.

Light flakes of spring snow fell through the ever-present haze.

Zo hadn't cared enough to cry about anything for a long, long time, but seeing that man killed before her eyes brought back too many hard memories. Memories too close to a life she had known. A life she used to care about.

Footsteps crunched on the gravel behind her. "Are you okay?" The voice sounded vaguely familiar. Zo wiped the bile from her chin and carefully turned around to see Joshua's mentor, Gryphon.

He looked the same as he had that morning. Tired from too many nights sleeping in a chair in the Medica. His long nose was slightly too wide, but his fierce jaw seemed to have been chiseled by a master stonecutter. Under the dark hood of his brows, the depth of his golden brown eyes drew her in. He stood with his arms hanging loosely.

"Are you hurt?" he asked. He took two steps closer.

Zo inched backward.

He stopped with hands extended, showing his palms as if she were an injured lamb he didn't want to scare. "I'm not going to hurt you." His head tilted like a curious child, but the sword on his belt was nothing close to a child's play toy. She kept her distance.

"I'm sorry for—" His mouth hung open like there was more he wanted to say. He ruffled the dark hair on the back of his head. "Thank you for helping Joshua. You saved his life."

Zo didn't trust her voice. A "you're welcome" should have

come easily, but for some reason she could not tell this man, this killer, "you're welcome." The idea of being "welcome" was the last thing she wanted any Ram man to feel around her.

When she didn't speak, he slowly turned and jogged away, likely off to lull some other Nameless into a false sense of security.

Chapter 8

Zo and Tess sat together twenty yards off the road on the bank of a stream. Tess used her small hands to help Zo apply mud to her face. She took her time, making swirls and shapes that she said reminded her of cloud formations.

Even with her nose scrunched up in concentration, and her tongue poking out the corner of her mouth, Tess looked like a little angel. Innocent and untainted by the evils of life. Unless Zo could help her escape the Gate, Tess would one day have to wear this mud costume. If she lived that long.

She bore the "pretty" curse too.

Unlike Zo, some of the Nameless women didn't mind the hungry eyes of the guards. Some even welcomed them. Life for slaves inside the Gate could be easy if you were pretty. Better food. Better clothes. Better beds, once they left you there. That's exactly why mud had become Zo's best friend.

As a Wolf, Zo had to be especially careful to go unnoticed. The resentment between her clan and the Ram went deeper than blood or even food. It was an age-old feud between two powerful brothers that had fermented over hundreds of years. Though Zo couldn't remember the details of the dispute—something to do with inheritance and land—she did understand the raids. The nights when Ram soldiers burned fields and killed Wolves who were outside the protection of the Valley of Wolves.

Every Wolf grew up on stories of Ram violence and evil raiding. Even before they could talk, they understood that the chilling sound of a Ram horn meant death and devastation. Boys became men at a young age, forced to join their fathers in defending the pack, then to take on the impossible role of protecting the family when their own fathers fell to the spear. Girls learned to hold their heads high with dry eyes, knowing that one day the mighty Ram would fall, just like a great moose falls to a pack of dogs.

When Tess finished her muddy masterpiece, Zo pulled her to her feet so they could head out for another day of work.

Tess kicked the same rock all the way from the Nameless' barracks. Her light-blond ponytail bounced extra high with every stab. "Why are you staring at me?"

"Who's staring?" said Zo.

The mud on Zo's face stiffened with the dry heat of the morning sun. Baking ugly. They enjoyed a peaceful walk until Tess had to take the fork in the road that led to the farmlands. Her assignment.

Zo pulled her sister to her chest and squeezed. "Remember—"

"I know," said Tess, counting off the details on her thin fingers. "Don't talk to anyone about home. Drink lots of water. Don't go into houses. Anything else?" she said, tapping her foot on the sticky road.

"I think that covers it. I'll see you tonight." Zo kissed her round cheek.

Tess' ponytail bounced as she ran to catch up with the rest of the children. Zo picked at the raw nail bed surrounding her thumb and forced herself to walk in the other direction. Tess' survival depended on Zo's healing ability in the Medica and so far, things weren't going so well.

[•]

The blunted sword grazed Gryphon's calf, but he didn't feel it. He swung his shield to deflect Ajax's next blow. One by one, the men of his mess abandoned their training to watch the sparring.

Gryphon pushed through the attack. His sword vibrated with the power of swift lightning every time it connected with Ajax's blade. Ajax took a step backward. Then another. His ever-present smile faltered. Sweat rolled into Gryphon's eyes, stinging and burning until he blinked it away.

Gryphon purposefully let Ajax turn him to expose his weak side. Ajax lunged for the back of Gryphon's legs. A favorite attack that Gryphon anticipated. Gryphon smacked the other man's backside with the flat of his sword. Ajax fell forward. Gryphon jumped on his back, grabbed a fistful of hair, and held his blade to his friend's neck.

"Damn it, Gryphon!" he growled. Gryphon laughed and hopped off his friend's back. Ajax didn't technically call "yield" but he never did. He just got really, really angry.

Zander was the one to keep protocol. "Gryphon takes Ajax ... again." Even Zander had the good humor to smile. Ajax had rarely lost a spar until Gryphon came along.

"What's the tally up to now, twenty-three to nothing?" Ajax spat blood from his mouth.

"Does it matter?" It was twenty-four.

"Of course it matters. I think I dropped my manhood back there."

Gryphon cleaned the grit off his sword. "It's your pride you should worry about."

"You little goat tit!" Ajax took Gryphon in a headlock and whirled him around until they both collapsed on the ground laughing.

"How is your wife?" Gryphon asked once they'd caught their breath.

"Big." Ajax laughed again. "She's a strong woman. I'm sure she'll do fine. The healer said it could be any day now."

The sound of deep horns silenced them both. The low-sounding horn was not the typical summons, but instead a call to war. Gryphon scrambled for his gear and sprinted toward Zander with the other members of the mess. Every man huffed with adrenaline.

The horns sounded again before Zander could speak. "To the front gate." He pulled his shield to his chest and assumed his role at the head of the mess.

The training fields inside the great wall were less than a mile from the front gate. Gryphon's mess filled the town square with almost fifty others. Metal clinked against metal as the small army looked to their leader. Barnabas, the clan chief, stood on a platform next to a bloody animal carcass. Shouts of outrage rang out. Every man looked wild, like they wanted to kill something.

"Soldiers of the Ram!"

"Hah!" the men all cried.

"Today we've been threatened inside our own territory!" With his massive arms, Barnabas held the dead ram above his head. The animal's horns had been sawed off, leaving only bloody holes in their place. The great-horned ram were considered sacred, their horns a symbol of the clan's power.

Ajax gasped next to Gryphon.

Barnabas launched the carcass into the crowd of soldiers. Blood sprayed armor. "Find who did this! Bring me back his head!"

Runners shot like daggers out to a few different mess leaders, bringing orders and ration satchels.

"I'm afraid we're in for a long night, men," said Zander, shouldering one of the packs. "Let's go hunting."

[◦]

Zo stared at the intimidating crowd of Ram soldiers from the steps of the Medica. She'd asked Commander Laden for a sign, but it wasn't until she saw the dead ram with her own eyes that she dared believe it. The bottles worked. The Wolves knew she had survived. They knew about Tess. She didn't have to fight the Ram alone. Others were ready to help. Ready to act on whatever information she sent them.

For the first time since she'd entered the Gate, Zo felt powerful. Like she might actually make a difference.

Thinking to take advantage of the commotion, she decided

it was time to do something she'd lacked the nerve to do until now. She raced back into the Medica and snatched a used blanket from a laundry pile before bolting out the door again. She wove through the buildings of town until she came upon the first of many training fields. As she'd hoped, the chief's announcement left the fields empty and the practice weapons hastily dropped in the field to be gathered later.

Zo looked around to make sure no one was watching then dropped her blanket onto the ground over a discarded short sword.

It might have been a foolish risk, but one Zo felt she needed to take.

Walking back to the square to reach the Medica, she noted that Ram soldiers hurried about with preparations to leave the Gate. The silver sounds of swords sliding into sheaths and boots tromping on the cobbles sent chills up Zo's back. She hugged the blank*et and weapon* to her chest, realizing for the first time just how dangerous her little stunt had been.

She made it to the steps of the Medica and exhaled deeply. Almost there.

The door flew open before she could reach the handle and a giant Ram collided into her. Blanket and sword flew from her hands as she landed hard on her backside.

Zo crawled over to pick up the blanket and cover the sword but she saw the boot of the Ram standing right next to the blanket, the hilt of the sword peeking out underneath.

"It's not what you think."

Gryphon adjusted the strap of the pack thrown over one shoulder. His brows knit together as he bent to pick up the blanket, careful to keep the sword hidden. Disappointment dripped from the corners of his lips as he frowned. "Healer?"

"It's for Joshua. He's been talking about training since the day I took him into my care. I thought to let him practice from bed until he's able to move around without causing himself harm."

Gryphon narrowed his eyes. "You know what would happen to you if someone found you carrying this?"

Zo nodded. "He isn't improving like he should. I'm worried for him. I thought this would help raise his spirits." Zo mumbled the explanation then looked down at her feet. In truth, she knew that much of the reason for his limited improvement was because of her. She liked Joshua, but was still having trouble opening up her heart enough in the blessing to heal him.

"Gryphon, it's time."

Zo looked over her shoulder to see a stout Ram waving Gryphon over to join a small group of about twenty soldiers.

Gryphon thrust the blanket and sword back into Zo's unsuspecting arms. "Heal him, Nameless. Do whatever you must, just heal him."

Zo nodded, numb and confused when Gryphon followed the other soldier and left her gripping the forbidden sword to her chest.

Minutes later, Joshua startled when she entered the room.

"Daydreaming again, Ginger?" said Zo as she struggled with an awkward pile of blankets.

The boy was still too pale. Sweat beaded above his upper lip and forehead—his body's effort to fight the infection.

"I can't believe I let you sneak up on me again." He pressed a hand to his forehead. "I swear, the Medica's softening my brain. I'm getting weaker while the other guys my age are getting stronger." He wrung his hands into the bed cloth. "It isn't fair."

Zo knew better than to correct him. It was the illness, not the Medica, that slowed his reflexes. The herbs she gave him for pain weren't helping either.

"What's with the blankets?" Joshua asked as Zo fumbled with the pile.

She lowered the bundle onto his bed. The weapon object dropped out, landing smartly on Joshua's ankle.

"What the—where did you get this!" He held up the weighted short-sword with reverent fingers, his eyes wide with shock. His fingers settled naturally into the familiar leather grip.

"Be quiet. Are you trying to get me killed?" Zo hissed.

She covered the sword in blankets and went back to close the door. "I borrowed it from one of the training fields while the soldiers were rushing to the gate." She scratched at the mud on her cheek.

"Zo, you can't just go around carrying weapons. You're a Nameless. If someone saw you with this they'd kill you before asking questions."

She shrugged. "You've been driving me crazy with all your talk of training." Zo bit down on her bottom lip as she watched him admire the stupid sword. A warm energy entered her chest, like hot liquid passing too slowly down her throat. It was almost painful.

Joshua reluctantly pulled his eyes from the blade. "I don't know how to thank you."

She ruffled his red hair and scooped up the blankets. "Thank me by getting better."

He would. The uncomfortable, warm sensation in Zo's chest confirmed it. The boy would live.

Chapter 9

It had been two weeks since the Allies sent their sign. Two weeks and Zo hadn't come close to finding any information that would help her people. Without the responsibility of Tess, she would have done a lot more than snoop around important buildings and mentally chart the movement at the gate.

Every time Zo formulated a new plan to get the information she was after, Tess' innocent face came to the forefront of her thoughts. How could she take the risks necessary to help her people when it meant putting her little sister in danger?

After weeks of servitude, Zo still hadn't seen half of the rooms in the Medica. She passed countless doors on her daily trip to the supply room. The brown plaster on the walls didn't crack and flake so much in this wing of the building, evidence of the continuous add-ons the Medica received over the years.

The nicer rooms were usually reserved for injured Ram

soldiers and leaders. No one trusted her to heal the high-ranking. As a result, Zo was assigned to work in the older wing of the building, where she attended mostly women and children.

"What are these?" The Ram supply clerk came around the table and snatched up the blankets Zo deposited.

"They're blankets," said Zo, her voice flat and hollow.

The clerk's pockmarked face reddened. "I know what they are. What are they doing on my table?"

"They need to be washed," she said.

The clerk hissed a string of curses as he added the load to a pile in the back of the supply room, grumbling about taking orders from an ugly Nameless.

Zo hurried away. After rounding the first bend in the corridor, she heard a muffled man's voice drifting through the door of one of the newest rooms. Zo made sure the hall was empty before pressing her ear to the door.

"Zander and his men are a part of First Company, sir. Their search quadrant is the farthest away," said a shaky voice.

"I want them here, now! It's been five days!"

"Yes, sir."

"I can't lead our people south until I quell these little rebellions. I want whoever killed that ram! I want his head staked to my wall!" The voice held an air of command, like a man who wouldn't be questioned. Zo pushed closer to the door, hoping to hear something, anything, that might help the cause.

"Have we found the Wolf pup who taunted Zander's company a few weeks ago?" said the leader.

"No, sir."

There was a loud crashing sound, like a chair thrown against a wall. "I can't have Wolves roving these hills, Captain!"

Zo forgot how to move. Her thoughts turned immediately to Gabe. His promise to stay close. To help when she needed him. Was he really foolish enough to linger at the Ram's doorstep?

Yes. Yes, he was. He'd enjoy the challenge, not to mention the bragging rights. The fool.

"We gave Zander the coordinates of the last spotting. His mess will find them. They are the best."

"Yes, as long as that Striker doesn't botch the job," said the leader.

"Sir." The shaky captain cleared his throat. "According to our numbers, Gryphon is the best—"

"Training figures do not impress me! I want results outside the wall."

"Yes, sir."

The sound of footsteps pulled Zo from her trance. She hurried down the hall before anyone could catch her snooping around important doors.

[◆]

Gryphon's mess puffed white clouds of morning air as they ran. Their steps fell sure, if somewhat slower than they had five days ago. Zander finally called halt when they reached the top of a steep plateau. The men could barely hear his orders over the gusting wind. "Shields ... shelter ... rest."

The group of brothers didn't need further explanation. They staked their shields into the half-frozen soil in a perfect ring then huddled along the inside wall formed to escape the wind. Zander tossed them all some dried meat and flat bread. They chewed while he spoke.

"How far to our target search point?" Zander asked Lincoln, the navigator of the group.

Lincoln pulled out the compass and chart. He scratched the peppered beard that made him look much older than he was and walked his fingers along the map. "We're practically there, sir. No more than two or three miles out."

Zander nodded. "We'll split up to cover more ground. My team will veer west. Gryphon's team will veer east. Make a full circle. Search every rock, every trail. Meet back here at sundown."

Gryphon swallowed hard on a dry crust of bread. Since when did he have command over a team? Striker was one thing, but this …

"Sir?" he said.

"Walk with me, Gryphon."

Gryphon followed his captain out of the circle of shields. His muscles were stiff from the brief rest. They stopped behind a lone tree to hide from the loud wind.

"Sir, I'm one of the youngest in the mess. I have no right—"

"You have every right if I give it to you," Zander growled. "You're the best I have, Gryphon. Don't let me down."

Gryphon nodded, gulping down the contents of his churning stomach. "Thank you, sir."

Zander walked away, his words nearly swallowed by the roaring wind. "Thank me by finding some Wolves. The chief wants them alive."

(•)

They slept for two hours before readying their packs and weapons. Gryphon, Ajax, and six others followed a trail northeast, while Zander and the rest of the mess moved northwest. Gryphon had never been this far north, even the wind blowing through the high grass sounded foreign. Spring came later here. The spongy carpet of green gave way beneath their boots as they zigzagged across the hilly terrain.

"Five square miles is too much for one group to search," said Brutus, one of Gryphon's mess brothers, between gulps of air when they stopped for water. Brutus wasn't a feather over five and a half feet tall. He had a shaved head and bloated muscles that commanded respect. "Split us up. We can cover twice the ground."

Gryphon corked his water skin and shook his head. "Too dangerous. We have no idea what's out there. We can't risk it."

Brutus showed Gryphon his back and muttered, "Too afraid to get the job done."

Gryphon yanked his brother around and stabbed his spear into the ground, an inch from the man's foot. "Are you calling me a coward? If so, have the honor to say it to my face!"

Brutus glared at him before ducking his head. "No, sir."

Gryphon released him and addressed the now silent group of men. "Let's pick up the pace."

They ran through midday and into the afternoon without seeing a footprint. Gryphon pushed on, determined not to fail Zander and his brothers in the mess.

It was Ajax who finally had the nerve to say what the rest

were likely thinking. "The sun's sinking, Gryph. We need to head back."

He was right, of course, but it didn't make the decision to quit searching any easier. Gryphon nodded. "Back to the rally point."

As they followed the slope downhill, a short burst of light caught Gryphon's eye. He blinked, searching for a source of water in the gully below, but then saw a hint of movement in the thick foliage.

Gryphon barely spoke above a whisper. "Movement below. Southwest patch of bushes."

To the group's credit, they marched on like nothing had happened until they were within twenty yards of the bushes.

Another beam of light blinded Gryphon. He heard the quick thump of a bow just before an arrow entered his shoulder.

"Link!" Gryphon ordered. They tightened into a perfect ball of shields just as another secession of arrows pelted against them.

"I count five archers!" said Ajax.

"Six," groaned Gryphon, gesturing to the foreign arrow in his shoulder.

Ajax barely spared Gryphon a glance as he leaned over and ripped it out.

"Ahhhhh!" Gryphon growled. His vision swirled as he tried to clear his head through the pain.

"They're running!" one of the men called.

"Not again!" Gryphon pushed through the phalanx of shields and took off at a dead sprint, leaving his brothers behind.

The enemy ran deep into a shallow ravine as Gryphon

charged after, running along a narrow ridge ten feet above them.

Shouts from his brothers who couldn't match Gryphon's pace sounded from behind. Going off alone, without the protection of the mess, went against Ram training, but he refused to lose this man. This Wolf.

With every jarring footfall, Gryphon thought of the shield hanging above his family hearth. The shield that kept him from becoming what his father never had. He pushed himself harder. The distance between he and the Wolf narrowed, but so did the small ridge above the gorge. He'd have to jump.

The Wolf bringing up the rear of the group slid to a halt. He turned to face Gryphon, drawing a sword from his back sheath. Gryphon almost stumbled in shock as the fool charged. Gryphon leapt off the ledge. Ram and Wolf collided in the air, but Gryphon's momentum carried them swiftly to the ground. The hilt of the Wolf's sword slammed across his face. The Wolf's free hand reached for a dagger, but Gryphon grabbed his wrist to stop him.

The Wolf was strong, and judging by his surprised expression, he hadn't expected Gryphon to match him. Gryphon blocked another hit to the face, grateful he was too close to get the long end of the Wolf's sword. With both hands occupied, Gryphon arched his head back and butted the Wolf in the face. Blood poured from the enemy's nose, but his hand moved even closer to the dagger.

Ajax pulled Gryphon off to let the rest of the mess take over.

It took four of them to get the deadly sword from the Wolf's hands. They bound his arms behind his back and tied a rope around his neck.

"What were you thinking?" Ajax's dark complexion matched his mood. He made a tourniquet and wrapped it around Gryphon's shoulder.

"I got him, didn't I?"

Ajax fought a smile as he cinched the dressing with more force than necessary. "Yes, you did."

Gryphon kept his eye trained on the prisoner as he took the length of rope. The pain from his shoulder streaked through his whole body, pulsing and terrible, but he didn't show his enemy weakness.

Blood dripped from the Wolf's nose onto his lips and chin. He didn't seem to be any older than Gryphon. One eye was swollen shut. A deep gash ran from cheek to chin. He stood tall, looking Gryphon directly in the eyes.

Gryphon couldn't help but be impressed.

It was a shame the Wolf had to die.

Chapter 10

Zo carried a stack of Medica records through the torch-lit square, eyeing the raised fighting platform with contempt as she passed. She'd never been out at night before, and as ashamed as she was to admit it, the flickering lights and shadow-cast faces caused fear to weave throughout her body. She missed the colorful painted lanterns and rich laughter that had dominated the nights of her childhood with the Wolves. Here the air carried a hard, cold energy that made her want to turn back and wait out the nightmare until morning.

She tugged on the heavy wooden door of the Building of Records and slipped inside. A shadowed figure cornered Zo the moment she entered. He smelled like bad cheese, the kind with too much curd and too many days left to age.

"State your purpose here, Nameless." Of all the men inside the Gate she'd hoped to repel with the mud, the Gate Master topped the list. The trouble was he never looked at her face.

"I have records from the Medica."

The Gate Master eyed the papers with disgust. "The Seer and her mindless records," he mumbled.

Zo waited for him to move but he simply stared at her. "The more I see you, the more I know you're not a Kodiak." He lifted up her chin to examine her face. "Those blue eyes and full lips. There's Wolf in your blood. I swear there is."

If it weren't for Tess, Zo might have bitten off one of his fingers.

The Gate Master raked her cheek with his fingernail, clearing away a line of plastered mud. "You might actually be something to look at underneath that filth. Maybe we should take a walk to the steam caves and find out."

"The records ... " Zo whispered, still casting her gaze to the floor.

A young boy burst through the door. "Master Leon! Master Leon!"

The Gate Master pushed Zo aside. "What is it?"

"Zander and his men are back. They caught a Wolf! They caught a Wolf!"

The two men hurried away and left Zo unattended in the Building of Records.

Unwilling to think of the poor Wolf they had captured, she ducked into a room, clutching the stack of records to her heaving chest.

The room was instantly familiar. The bare walls. The orderly desk piled with neat stacks of parchment and scrolls. The Seer's office. She dropped the Medica records on the desk and went to leave when a page of the Seer's neat script froze her feet to the floor.

"Military Records," she whispered aloud.

She dove toward the desk and rifled through the pages. The stack of parchment was an inch thick, filled with numbers and records of troop movement, supply inventories, and more. She snatched the stack off the desk and shoved it into the front fold of her white Medica robe, looking over her shoulder all the while.

It took everything in her not to run through the hall to get out of the building and back to her bunk. The papers crinkled with every hurried step, itching her chest, reminding her of the risk she'd taken. She stepped into the evening air and a smile stretched across her face. The papers tucked close to her chest gave her purpose. Meaning. She wanted to skip. To prance around the square and make a mockery of the monster that was the Ram.

Her smile faltered when she spotted Joshua's friend, Gryphon enter through the giant gate. A blood soaked wrap covered his Ram-sized shoulder. She stopped walking. The urge to help him came from a place deep within. It was warm and completely foreign, but there all the same. She shook her head, blaming Joshua for making her soft.

She didn't see the prisoner Gryphon dragged behind him until they passed her.

"No!" she sobbed.

For one moment the earth froze mid-rotation, the heavens shattered and fell like daggers from the sky, and everyone standing within earshot turned to see the Nameless who dared speak against the Ram.

Zo's eyes locked with Gabe's, the history of their childhood together passed before her eyes, then Gabe's head slumped forward and he collapsed to the ground, drawing the attention away from Zo and back to him.

Zo didn't squander the distraction. She tugged up the front of her robe and sprinted all the way to the Nameless' barracks. Throwing herself on the bed, she sobbed until crying turned to breathless convulsing and convulsing turned to rage.

[●]

The graying healer wrapped another layer of gauze over the hole in Gryphon's shoulder. "Make sure to drink it all. It will numb the pain and help you sleep tonight."

Gryphon almost choked on the sour concoction when he saw Joshua. The boy sidestepped the old healer and tackled him on his Medica bed. "You're a hero! Everyone's talking about it!"

"When were you released from the Medica?" said Gryphon, amazed.

"Zo cleared me three days ago. I feel great!"

The image of Joshua sick and pale in his bed only ten days prior didn't match the lively kid before him. "You shouldn't use the healer's name, Joshua. She's a Nameless. You *know* that."

Joshua took a step back and frowned, his fists balled. "Her name is Zo. She saved my life."

How could Gryphon argue? The girl had worked a miracle. "Fine, just don't let anyone else hear you."

"I won't." He bounced up and down. "I want to know everything. They say you took down the Wolf yourself. That you dove like an eagle off a cliff. Is that true?"

"Nope."

"Then what happened? Give me *every* detail!"

Gryphon told him the whole story. Zander's command that Gryphon lead the second group. The blinding light that preceded the arrow. The chase. The bravery of the man at the back of the Wolf pack who turned and charged him.

"What an idiot! The Wolf was outnumbered," said Joshua.

"I don't think he actually planned to take us, kid. Just slow us down so his friends could escape."

"Wow." Joshua sat back staring off into nothing. "That might be the bravest thing I've ever heard."

Gryphon nodded. "You should have seen him. No fear at all."

Joshua blinked out of his trance. "And they call *you* the hero?"

Gryphon swatted at him but Joshua easily dodged.

"I need to tell Zo." Joshua's eyes went unfocused again.

"Is she impressed by bravery?" said Gryphon, wondering why he cared.

"She doesn't believe in it. That's why I need to tell her."

"Naturally." Gryphon snickered over his mug. "Isn't she a bit old for you, kid?"

"Stop making fun. She's sad all the time. I think something inspiring would make her happy."

Gryphon's shoulders rose and fell with a heavy sigh. Once Joshua set his mind on something there was no deterring him. "Don't get too attached to this Nameless girl. It will only bring you trouble."

Joshua jumped to his feet and bounded to the door. "I've got training tomorrow. Need to get some sleep." He went to leave but stopped and turned. "Her name is *Zo*, Gryph."

Chapter 11

Zo couldn't stop thinking of Gabe as she silently slipped out the door of the Nameless' barracks. Just knowing he was somewhere inside the Gate made it hard to concentrate on her footing as she navigated the darkness. There was a good chance that at this moment he was being tortured for information. No use hoping for a better alternative.

Gabe had plenty to hide. Beyond knowing the plans and location of the Allied Camp, Gabe was one of the few people to ever be invited into the Raven settlement as an ambassador for Commander Laden. If what Zo heard in the Medica was true, Chief Barnabas would do anything to have that kind of tactical information. Yes, the Ram needed the Raven food stores, but Zo had a feeling there was more to it than that. What if the Ram really did intend to move the entire clan south? She knew the Wolves sat on the most fertile land in the region. Would the

Ram try to take it from them? No one—not even Commander Laden—believed they'd have the nerve to strike so far from the Gate.

But what if they did?

Zo's foot caught on a low branch and she stumbled to the earth, bruising her knee on a rock. She pushed her palms into the soggy ground and let her head hang forward. She welcomed the pain of her throbbing knee. The dark emotion that had long ago hijacked her rational self actually enjoyed the pain. Told her she deserved it. Even uncomfortable feeling is still … feeling.

The thick mud on her face itched like a wicked rash and she eventually climbed back to her feet. Clumps of rock-hard clay ripped away layers of Zo's skin before they fell to the dark forest floor. Her body reeked like manure, but she couldn't complain about the results of the mud and smelly perfume. With the exception of the Gate Master, the Ram soldiers had left her alone.

The moon glowed like a thousand torches reflecting off the white stone of the mountain as she walked to the river. This far away from the barracks she could almost imagine she was outside the Gate.

At home picking peas in the garden while Gabe romped around the yard with Tess laughing uncontrollably while riding on his shoulders.

Free.

Zo forced thoughts of Gabe away and traveled with the silence of the Wolf, keeping to the balls of her bare feet, avoiding low branches and twigs by instinct as much as practice. She reached the river near the base of the mountain in record time.

Zo pulled out one of five glass bottles from her satchel and double-checked the stopper. She hugged the bottle to her chest before carefully dropping it into the river. Her hands shook and she repeated her actions until all five were lost to the fast moving current. Five chances for the Allies to learn Gabe's fate and discover the location and times of the next Ram excursion. Five promises to look deeper into the threat of a Ram move and to send more information soon.

Commander Laden had been very clear about the information he needed her to gather. His list was as precise as it was long: the number of battle-ready troops, supplies, weapons, coordinates for a possible Ram excursions. Anything that might help the Cause.

Zo watched the hope of her people float away, absorbed by the dark water. She was contributing to the alliance. Paying back a small fraction of the pain Ram soldiers had caused her.

The soft breeze died down, making Zo's odor hang heavy in the stagnant air. Her stench burned her nostrils as she looked longingly at the clean rushing water. One bath wouldn't kill her. She'd have Tess double up on her mud paint tomorrow.

Zo pulled off her woolen shirt and untied the rope holding up her too-large pants. The cold water numbed her bare skin as she stepped deeper and deeper into the mountain river. Her shivers turned violent when the water reached her shoulders. She fought against the current while she scrubbed at her skin, using her blunt nails to rake away the layers of plastered mud and grime.

Out of habit she softly hummed a washing song to calm her nerves. A song her mother had taught her before her world turned upside-down.

[•]

It was well past dark when Gryphon was finally released from the Medica. He walked the mountain trail home with Joshua chatting away under his good arm. Using his hands to tell his training story, the boy bounced up and down.

"Toban shouldn't have beaten me in hand-to-hand. I had him in a lock," Joshua held up his arms to demonstrate, "and was ready to demand 'yield' when he elbowed my bad side. Right in the button! Even after Master Cadmos instructed him not to."

Gryphon fought a smile. "How long were you down?"

"Half a minute. Maybe twenty seconds. It doesn't matter. He didn't follow the rules."

Gryphon stopped and took both of Joshua's shoulders in his hands. "There are no rules in war, Joshua. A good fighter expects his weaknesses to be exploited and uses that foresight to his own advantage."

A faint voice could barely be heard over the river. Gryphon put a shushing finger to his mouth. He stepped off the trail, following the sound.

"I thought you said we were going to your family home," said Joshua, trailing behind like a spring duckling. "Your mom made food."

Gryphon whipped around in a crouch and placed his fist to the ground. The signal for caution.

Joshua nodded, a look of anticipation in his eyes. He deftly pulled a dagger from his leg sheath and inched to Gryphon's side with exaggerated stealth.

Gryphon sighed inwardly. Joshua's thirst to prove himself would be the very thing that got him killed someday.

"You can put the knife away, kid."

"What if it's dangerous?" Joshua whispered.

Gryphon rolled his eyes and moved toward the water. The whispered singing of a shaky female voice grew louder. It was a sad, intoxicating sort of melody that wrapped its fingers around Gryphon's heart and squeezed. He inched to the ledge of a small cliff, looking down on the river no more than fifteen feet below.

The moon turned her skin to milk, casting hard shadows along her curves as she stepped from the river onto the bank. Her hair hung like a midnight veil in an uneven line at the middle of her back.

Gryphon caught a small glimpse of her profile as she reached for her clothes. He leaned closer to the ledge, hypnotized by the moon's generosity. This was clearly no Nameless field hand, and Ram women didn't sing.

Joshua stumbled forward, snapping a twig in two with his awkwardly large foot. The girl stopped her washing song and glanced up to them, clutching her clothes to her chest.

"Sorry," Joshua mouthed.

Gryphon shook his head and looked back to the girl.

She studied the trees around them while she dressed. Her body was tense, ready to flee at the first sign of danger. She looked so different from any of the Ram women he knew, yet so familiar. Her face was more square than round, her body longer and leaner than a typical Ram daughter. Graceful.

Then he saw it. A black crescent moon tattooed just below her shoulder.

Gryphon turned to Joshua. "She has the same tattoo as the Wolf I just captured."

"Wolf!" Joshua whispered too loud.

The girl darted into the trees like a deer.

Gryphon turned predator as he jumped from his perch into a full sprint, dodging branches and bushes to catch his prey. He heard Joshua's frustrated efforts to keep up behind him, but Gryphon couldn't wait. This rabbit was far too quick.

The girl zigzagged through the forest. Several times Gryphon thought he'd lost her, and then he'd catch a glimpse of a ruffling white shirt in the corner of his eye and he'd correct his course. He followed her up the mountainside into a thick patch of fog. The trees blurred to white, the fog so dense he could barely see the ground as he ran. Gryphon slowed to a jog. He didn't need a broken ankle to hinder him in his next excursion. A lame shoulder was bad enough.

He heard movement and crept toward the noise with silent steps, his eyes useless in the dense white fog surrounding. Joshua's loud feet twenty yards away actually served as a good decoy. For once.

"Wolves never travel alone," Barnabas had said.

A branch snapped behind him as the girl dropped from a tree onto Gryphon's back. She held a blade to his throat. "Show me your hands!" she said. Her voice was too calm for the situation.

Gryphon froze, his hands carefully raised in surrender. She should have bled him then and there, but for some reason she hesitated. A costly mistake.

With his hands already raised, Gryphon grabbed her by the hair and flipped her forward onto her back. She let out a cry of pain as she landed on the rocky ground. He jumped on her, pinning her arms down with his knees. He wrenched the knife from her hand and forced the tip of the blade to her delicate cheek.

The fog cleared enough for him to see the whites of her almond eyes. She didn't beg or even so much as whimper, just stared at him with a penetrating glare.

"How did you get inside the Gate?" he snarled, unable to imagine her scaling the wall. He could feel her labored breath. The rhythm of her heart accelerated.

"Answer!" He forced the blade deeper, breaking the skin.

"I owe you nothing, soldier. Kill me if you must." Her smooth face was eerily calm, as if ending her life would save her the trouble.

Gryphon looked up in time to see Joshua charge him with both arms outstretched. The force was enough to push him off the girl.

"Leave her alone! She didn't do anything to you!"

Gryphon dropped his blade. His grip stayed locked around the girl's wrist as he wrestled Joshua to the ground next to her. A regular string of quail lined up for the plucking.

"Get off of me!" Joshua said, kicking and swatting. "And don't you dare hurt her!"

Gryphon looked between Joshua and the girl in disgust. "She's a bloody Wolf, kid. I can't let her live."

"It's Zo! It's Zo!"

Gryphon sat back and released his hold on Joshua. "Trust me, this is not her."

Joshua slapped at Gryphon's hand until he reluctantly let go of the girl's wrist. "Say something," Joshua said to the girl.

She didn't move.

"Say you'll slit my throat. Say it!"

The girl pushed up to rest on her palms, brushing away wet strands of hair from her face. "Your throat is safe, boy. It's your ox-for-brains friend who should watch his back."

Joshua tackled her with a warm hug. "It *is* you. I knew I recognized that voice. I've never seen you without that mud mask thing or without your hair all wrapped up on your head. You look so … different. I mean, look at you." He gestured at her whole body, blushing. "Why do you wear that stuff?"

"Because she's a Wolf. She knows we kill Wolves," said Gryphon. He used his armband to bind her wrists. He'd heard Wolf women were considered the fairest of all the clans. Now he understood why. It was a lethal beauty that made Gryphon's senses fuzzy and his rationale distorted.

Joshua seemed to lose his voice. The poor kid.

Gryphon forced the girl to stand. His fingers wrapped all the way around her biceps. Breakable. Weak. His hold loosened, until he remembered his orders. It was as though Zander's voice tumbled along the walls of his thoughts, stirring a sense of duty he felt toward his brothers and clan. "*If you value the lives of your family, you will kill every Wolf on sight. No exceptions.*"

But how could he kill her?

The girl looked up at him, as if reading his thoughts. Her lower lip trembled from the cold of the night, or perhaps it was fear. Fear of knowing she would soon die.

Chapter 12

"Go ahead and do it." Zo's legs buckled beneath her.
Gryphon let her sink to her knees on the cold earth.

"You can throw my body into the river when you're done."
The Allies watched the river. Someone would know Tess was
alone. Commander Laden would send a team to retrieve her.
The Ram would move south and the Wolves, with the help
of the Allies, would be prepared to fight. Tess would be free
before the end of this year.

She would.

Joshua joined Zo on the ground and put an arm around her.
"Don't worry, Zo. Gryphon's not going to kill you."

Joshua looked up at Gryphon for reassurance.

"The chief will want to question her." Gryphon frowned.
"But I'll speak for her, Joshua."

"You'll *speak* for her?" Joshua jumped to his feet. He had

to crane his neck to meet Gryphon's cold eyes. "You'll *speak* for her!" He shoved him in the chest with both hands. Gryphon didn't even sway from the contact. Joshua pushed him again and again until his shoving turned to full-on punching. Gryphon just stood there and took it, watching Zo with a hollow expression.

They all knew what would happen if Gryphon took her back.

Zo couldn't stand it any longer. "Joshua, stop." She used a low tree branch to help her stand. The muscles in her back throbbed from Gryphon's rough handling. "I can speak for myself."

The poor kid dropped to the ground. His head hung between his knees, he grabbed two fistfuls of his own red hair.

Zo stepped toward Gryphon. "Send the boy away. For his own sake." Zo was in no position to make demands, but the prospect of losing her life made her bold. She wouldn't be a victim any longer.

Gryphon studied her through the curtain of his dark hair. "He has a right to stay."

Zo stepped closer until their toes almost touched and the smoke of her breath reached his dimpled cheek. Her voice barely carried over the sound of the river. "Kill me here. Don't hand me over to the chief's guards." The image of the Gate Master entered her mind. "Please." Her bright blue eyes met his. The time for submission had passed.

Gryphon shook his head, his jaw set.

"What?" She shoved him. "Too much of a coward to do the job yourself? Aren't you a Ram?" She had to get him angry. No one would know to help Tess if Zo's body didn't end up in that river.

Gryphon tensed.

Joshua got up from the ground and put a hand on his mentor's chest while looking at Zo. "That wasn't a great thing to say," he forced a whisper through his teeth. "I think you should let me do the negotiating from now on."

Gryphon pushed Joshua's hand away. The wrap around his wounded shoulder was dark with fresh blood. The bandage needed replacing. "Why did you come to the Gate when you knew we kill your kind?" he asked.

Zo chose her words carefully. Tess' life depended upon them. "Why are you so convinced I'm a Wolf?"

"The Wolf I captured had that same mark on his shoulder."

Zo opened her mouth to speak but no words came. The mark of the Allies was a well-kept secret. She wouldn't be the one to divulge it. "The waxing moon is a common symbol of hope. I'm surprised you've never seen it before."

"You look like a Wolf too." Gryphon's face colored and he looked away.

Zo sighed inwardly. It always came back to her cursed face. "Either kill me or don't. Nothing I say will sway you." She folded her arms and showed him her back. It was the ultimate sign of disrespect inside the Gate. She braced herself, ready for him to strike her, but nothing happened.

A lifetime passed before she heard the crunch of his approaching footsteps.

Gryphon walked around to face her. This was it. Tonight she would join her parents on the other side of this cruel life. She closed her eyes and took a deep breath. *Please let Tess be safe. Please let her not mourn my death. Let Commander Laden find her.*

Warm hands clamped down on her tied wrists.

Zo's eyes shot open and all of her fears raced back in one swift, agonizing moment: torture, no body for Laden's men to find, Tess alone, the Gate Master. "No, no. Don't take me back there. Please!" her voice slipped and cracked. "Please! I'll do anything! Just don't take me to the Gate Master!"

Gryphon pressed the blade of his short sword to her neck. "I don't trust you, Wolf," he whispered. "If you ever do anything to harm my people, I swear I will end your life in a way that will make you regret ever surviving this night."

Joshua ran up and hugged Gryphon. "Thank you! Thank you!"

Gryphon yanked the band from her wrists and walked away, leaving Joshua and Zo to stare at his back in the moonlight.

Zo sunk to her knees. "I don't believe it." She held her unbound hands to her cheeks, her jaw hung slack.

Joshua put an arm around her. "Welcome to the family, Zo. I think he likes you."

[•]

Gryphon punched a tree. Not a good idea, but enough to take his mind off the girl, if for only a moment. He took off on a wild sprint through the mountains. He pushed himself past the point of fatigue, weaving through evergreens, jumping over rocks and streams until he reached the peak he'd visited the day Joshua should have died.

The first day he met the young Wolf healer.

He panted to catch his breath; his head hanging in shame. Zander's warning assaulted him. *If you value the lives of your family, you will kill every Wolf on sight. No exceptions.*

He should take the girl to the guards for questioning. What they did to her shouldn't be his concern. It shouldn't. But no matter how hard he tried, he couldn't bring himself to walk her to the chief's interrogators.

And they called him a hero?

How could he kill the girl who had saved Joshua's life? She'd more than earned her place inside the Gate.

Right?

Gryphon balled his fists and yelled at the mountain peaks to the south. A battle cry that brought him to his knees. No matter how hard he tried, the truth overpowered any excuse he conjured for letting her walk.

The truth was he didn't only spare her because of Joshua. He spared her for the same reason he'd spared the young Raven boy in the field.

He hated himself for it.

He was weak.

Like his father.

A melody ran unchecked through his mind. Tragic and beautiful, the lyrics moved with clouded understanding of this young woman, a girl really, whose eyes were blue wells of mystery and whose countenance was a lonely grave of sadness. It didn't make any sense, but somewhere beneath the pretty face of his enemy was a person he wanted to know. To understand.

Gryphon had never realized treason could be so complicated.

Only one man might be able to help him know if this girl was a threat to the clan. Who could explain the mark on her back, and clear his dark suspicions. Only he had the power to make Gryphon's shame bearable.

The only question: Would the Wolf prisoner talk?

Chapter 13

"He won't tell the Gate Master." Joshua rolled his eyes for the fifth time. "I'm telling you, once Gryphon makes up his mind, it's done. You don't need to worry."

Zo shook her head. The only thing worse than a Ram soldier was an unpredictable Ram soldier. "I can't take any chances. There are other things I have to worry about. Other … " she wanted to say "people" but it was better not to remind Joshua of Tess. He hadn't asked about her sister since the day they left the Waiting Room. Hopefully he'd been in so much pain at the time that he didn't remember her.

They reached the main road, barely visible in the darkness. Left would take Zo back to her barracks, right led to the city center and Joshua's training barracks housing the other adolescent boys his age.

"Just promise me you won't do anything crazy." Joshua's

forehead wrinkled, making him seem older than thirteen. "I'll talk to Gryphon."

Zo nodded and Joshua attacked her with a hug before taking off at a jog down the dark road. She watched him go with mouth gaping. Did he really just hug her? She needed to lie down. A person could only take so much surprise in one night.

"Hey, Zo."

Zo whipped around to see Tess. She had one hand on her hip and a sinister smile plastered to her face.

"What are you doing here? If someone saw you ... Tess, you're in huge trouble."

"I'm in trouble? You can't leave in the middle of the night without telling me where you're going. I know you have your little secrets," she wiggled her fingers in the air, "but you need to tell me when you're leaving, so I don't think some soldier has snuck in and carried you off." Her hand went right back to her hip, her gaze daring Zo to tell her she was wrong. She looked just like their mother when she got this way.

Zo sighed. "You're right, Tess. I'm sorry."

"Of course I'm right! Now who was that boy?"

"First, tell me what you planned to accomplish by sneaking out?" said Zo.

Tess looked at the ground and dug her toe into the dirt. "Everyone's talking about a Wolf. A man they captured. They say they're going to kill him in front of everyone. They say we all have to watch."

Zo cringed. Her hand shook violently as she tried to tuck a loose piece of hair behind Tess' ear.

"Do you know who it is, Zo?"

Zo frowned. "No, I don't," she lied.

The sound of crunching gravel made Zo grab Tess' arm and wrench her into the bushes on the side of the road. A small group of men and women walked past laughing. Luckily they were too caught up in each other to notice Zo and Tess.

Gabe was as good as a big brother to Tess. When she was only four, she used to beg Zo to kiss him so he would always be there to give her horsey rides. The memory made Zo smile despite the circumstances. Tess would discover the lie as soon as Gabe climbed the platform. At least tonight she could sleep without nightmares. If only Zo could claim the same ignorance.

"That's where I thought you went," Tess whispered once the Ram were out of sight. "Freeing the Wolf. I wanted to help. I can be very useful, if you'd only let me."

"No." Zo started walking back to the barracks with her sister in tow.

"Please, Zo. I'm so little no one will even see me."

"Absolutely not." They walked through the woods, parallel the road, to avoid detection. Tess stopped when they reached the barn-like structure that served as their barracks.

Zo turned around, impatient to lie down in her bunk. "Come inside, Tess."

The moon made Tess' face even more pale than usual. "You're not the only one who gets to be angry, Zo. They were my parents, too," her little voice trembled.

[◊]

Gryphon marched into the main part of the city to request an audience with the chief for the second time that day. The first time he came, the sun was just peeking over the distant mountain. Chief Barnabas had still been asleep and Gryphon was all but thrown out of the building. By midday, Gryphon's nightlong craze had subsided into something more practical. He approached the line of guards who blocked the entrance to Barnabas' home with wet palms. "I want to speak to the chief. Will he see me?"

A guard Gryphon knew by reputation eyed him for a moment before saying, "You can't just show up and demand a private audience with Barnabas. If he needs you, he'll send for you."

Gryphon cleared his throat. "It's regarding the Wolf prisoner. I am Gryphon, son of Troy."

This time the guard straightened. He raised an eyebrow at the men at his side, and they nodded. "I'll let him know you're here." The guard tugged on the ram horn door handle and ran into the ornate building to deliver the message.

Gryphon exhaled.

One of the remaining guards, the youngest, from what Gryphon could tell, stepped forward. "Is it true what they say about you? Did you really fly off a cliff to capture the Wolf?"

Curse Gryphon's mess and their exaggerating tongues. "No."

The guard opened his mouth to respond just as the two metal-framed doors opened. Gryphon filled his lungs to calm his hyper nerves and marched into the chief's private home.

"You can wait in here." The guard said, before turning on his heels to leave.

The candlelit waiting room smelled like stale bread. The walls were lined with shelves filled with dusty scrolls. Ancient swords and spears hung above every doorframe in the room. Shields were respectfully absent, likely buried with their owner, as they should be. Gryphon's cheeks burned as he once again thought of his father's shield hanging shamefully in his family's front room.

He'd worked too hard to fix his family's broken honor to let senseless mercy get in the way. Mercy for a Nameless, of all things. He scratched the back of his head and looked at the door. He shouldn't have come. The clan deserved to know the truth about the healer. It was his duty to disclose everything. *Right?*

Just as Gryphon turned to leave, an old woman wearing a long sage-colored dress entered the room. Deep wrinkles lined her face and thin, white hair created what seemed to be a halo around her head and neck. She rested her cane in front of her, the sound of wood striking the stone floor echoed off the room's four walls. She nodded to the scrolls stacked orderly on the shelves. "Find anything that interests you?" Her lips barely moved as she spoke.

Gryphon didn't think he'd ever seen someone so old. "Those scribblings mean nothing to me." He gestured to the weapons above the door. "Action always speaks louder than words."

One of the woman's tufty, white brows rose so high it became lost in the cloud of her hair. "You don't read?"

Gryphon shrugged. "What is the point of it?"

The old woman's deep laugh turned into a cough that rattled her frail chest. Gryphon crossed the room and helped her sit in a lone chair in the corner.

"You're laughing at me." He couldn't see what was so amusing.

It took her a moment to collect her breath. "You mock yourself, soldier. I'm just enjoying the entertainment." She lifted his chin with the tip of her cane to get a better look at him. "I see the apple doesn't fall far from the tree. Your father, Troy, was just as foolish in the beginning."

"You knew my father?"

Layers of translucent wrinkles lifted with her smile. "I knew him better than most."

The last thing Gryphon wanted was to discuss his fallen father. "Who are you? What sort of place do you have in the chief's home?"

Her eyes twinkled, and for just a moment, Gryphon thought he could see the young soul trapped in her aged body. "Before I passed on the responsibility to the woman you call the "Seer," I kept records for the Ram during the reign of the last two chiefs. Now I fill a more docile role." She sagged in her chair, clearly exhausted from the conversation. "Your father used to call me the Historian."

Again with Gryphon's father. It seemed he could never escape him.

A guard entered and looked between Gryphon and the old scroll keeper. "The chief is ready for you."

"I'd like to chat with you sometime about these scrolls and the past," the old woman said.

Gryphon nodded. He didn't know if he wanted to talk to the woman, especially if she planned to discuss his father. "Enjoy your words." He dipped his head in respect.

"Enjoy your ignorance," the Historian mumbled as she looked down at her wrinkled hands.

Gryphon followed the guard through a series of doors

and winding halls until the walls opened to a great room that smelled of lavender and fish oil.

In the chief's living quarters, Barnabas lay stomach down on a padded table. A beautiful woman massaged his naked backside while he ungracefully ate a messy plate of trout with his fingers. One of the old yellow scrolls lay open at his side. He didn't bother looking up from the page.

The guard who escorted Gryphon dropped to one knee and whispered a message into his master's ear. Barnabas grunted and dismissed the guard. "It seems you've met my grandmother."

"I didn't realize she was your family, sir."

The chief frowned and went back to his reading and trout, leaving Gryphon to stand waiting in the middle of the room.

When the chief finished his meal, he snapped his fingers and a new servant appeared to retrieve the fishy plate. "Did you know Linus the Mighty was barely five and a half feet tall? Doesn't sound all that 'mighty' to me!" He wiped his mouth on a silk cloth.

"Who are we talking about, sir?"

The chief waved him off. "I'm talking about the past, son. You and the past have a great deal in common."

"What do you mean, sir?"

"I mean we are not as original as we think we are. These scrolls will tell you as much. My father and grandfather studied them day and night. Histories of ancient empires and military structures that changed the world."

Gryphon shifted his feet, anxious for the chance to discuss his reason for coming.

"Where other great empires failed, we will prevail. Do you know why, young Striker?"

Gryphon shook his head. "Why, sir?"

The chief held up a preaching finger. "Because we have managed to pick the weeds in our society, getting rid of imperfection and making room for the healthy to thrive. There has never been a more pure race in history."

The woman massaging his back rolled her eyes. Gryphon fought a smile. How many times had this girl heard the chief's ranting? The more Gryphon watched the girl, the more he thought she looked like Zo.

Like a Wolf.

If that were true, then the chief was disobeying his own order. When Gryphon was still a boy, Barnabas had ordered the killing of all the Nameless Wolves inside the Gate. It had been a source of contention since Wolf women were highly favored among ranking officials.

Just thinking of all the Nameless killings made Gryphon nauseous.

"Sir, if I may be so bold, I'd like to visit the Wolf prisoner."

Barnabas propped up onto his elbows. "Why do you want to see him?"

"I'd like to question him."

Barnabas snorted. "And what makes you think he'll talk to you?"

Gryphon shrugged. "He might not."

Barnabas grumbled and went back to his reading. "I suggest you concentrate on your spear throwing and leave interrogations to the experts." He sank back onto the table and looked away. A clear dismissal.

Gryphon turned to leave, but ground his teeth together. "He's the bravest enemy I've ever faced, sir," he blurted. "I brought him in. I believe I've earned the right to face him."

Barnabas slowly raised his head. Painful silence filled the space between them.

Gryphon cleared his throat. "If nothing else, I'd like to look him in the eyes before his execution."

Barnabas' mood shifted like a match struck in total darkness. He pounded his fist on the table and laughed. "You sound like a woman." His deep chuckle turned his face red. When Gryphon didn't join in, the chief sobered and frowned. "You're serious, aren't you?"

"Yes, sir. I think he'll speak to me. I might be able to learn something about our enemy."

Barnabas harrumphed and sunk back into the cushions. He waved his hand. "Your heroics have earned you the right, I suppose. Only prepare yourself for disappointment. The Wolf hasn't muttered a word since he came here. Even my interrogators have failed, and we both know how persuasive they can be."

Gryphon could only imagine. "Thank you, sir."

Chapter 14

"I want you to keep this pressed firmly against the wound. Understand?"

The little girl pinched her eyes shut and nodded. Zo frowned at her effort not to cry. Even little girls had to be brave inside the Gate. Thankfully the weighted training weapons children used were blunted.

"What's your name?" Zo squatted down to meet the girl's eyes.

"Iris," she whispered.

"Iris, the next Ram Chieftain? I've heard of you."

The little girl opened her eyes and giggled. "I'm not a going to be a chief."

"Oh, no." Zo put her hand to her mouth in mock surprise. "I guess I wasn't supposed to tell."

The girl giggled again until the door flew open. It banged

against the wall, making both Zo and the child jump. On sheer reflex, Zo turned to shield the child from danger with her own body. She didn't have time to analyze her own reaction. The girl was young, but she was a Ram in blood. Zo's instinctive concern surprised her.

"I need you to come with me, healer." Gryphon looked down at the cowering girls and frowned. "I ... I didn't mean to frighten you."

Zo tried to remain calm for the child's sake. "Should I finish with Iris before we go? I'm almost done."

Gryphon moved to the corner of the room and leaned against the wall. "Of course."

Zo reached for a strip of cloth but accidentally knocked the whole basket to the floor. Her stomach rolled as she hurried to pick up the mess.

"Re-remember what I told you, Iris. Keep this bandage on for two days. Don't get it wet if you can avoid it. If it falls off before then, come back and I'll refit one for you." Zo glanced at Gryphon as she grabbed another strip of cloth. His bulky arms were folded across his broad chest, his chin down, his eye appraising under a hood of thick brows.

"Uh, if I'm not here," Zo's hands slipped as she tightened the wrap, "someone else will help you."

Iris slid off the bed and gave Zo an easy hug before running out the door. Thankfully, it wasn't too hard to care for these Ram children. Especially when they were as young as Iris. Zo couldn't blame them for the pain the Ram had caused the other clans over the years. She looked over to Gryphon's towering form and rose to her feet, hugging the basket of cloth to her chest. Gryphon and others like him were not so innocent.

"You're coming with me." He took a step toward her.

Zo looked at the ground and nodded. She carried the basket over to a table and, in a last-moment decision, tucked a thin scalpel up her sleeve before turning to face her enemy. She would end her own life before they had the chance to torture her, if it came to that.

Gryphon's hands tightened at his sides. "The man we're going to see will require medical attention. You'll need more than the knife to help him."

Zo froze, unable to hide the shock on her face. Her little stunt had likely squashed what trust he might have had for her. "I ... I'm sorry—"

"Just get a kit together. We don't have much time."

They left the Medica, Zo walking three steps behind Gryphon on the cobbled road through town. "Will you let me speak?" she asked as they turned onto a dirt trail leading into the thick forest fringing the town.

Gryphon looked back and nodded. Zo absently put one hand to her cheek, wishing she'd had time to apply another layer of mud that morning. "I didn't plan to hurt anyone with the scalpel. I thought you were handing me over to the guard."

Gryphon fought a smile. "So you planned to fight your way to freedom without hurting anyone?"

"No."

Gryphon's calm demeanor was like a giant snake holding perfectly still until its prey became complacent. She knew he would strike eventually, and when he did the bite would kill.

"Why would you carry a knife, if not to fight?"

"To control how I die." She blurted the words before she could help herself. A Nameless shouldn't speak so freely.

Especially not to the one soldier inside the Gate who had seen her for what she was. A Wolf.

Gryphon nodded. "We all want to control our lives, healer. Few of us get to."

Zo wanted to hit him. She wanted to scratch out his honest-looking eyes and spit in his face. He knew nothing about losing control in life. Nothing.

They traveled deeper into the woods. The sun filtered through the trees, lighting up patches of earth with brilliant afternoon light. Zo longed to remove the wrap covering her head and neck and let the light breeze finger through her hair. The green season was nearly here. At home she would have been sowing tubers and peas on her family's plot. Tess should have been out causing trouble with her two best friends. Her little sister's greatest worry should be winning the relay race at Spring Festival.

Zo hitched up the medical kit on her hip.

"We're almost there," said Gryphon.

They reached the entrance to a cave guarded by two heavily armored men. Each wore a fur vest and boots. Like most Ram, they stood as tall as trees, with white battle scars marking their arms and chests. Zo took a half step behind Gryphon so he stood between her and the guards. Two snakes were always worse than one.

"We've come to see the prisoner," said Gryphon.

The size of Zo's eyes doubled. Gabe. They'd come to see Gabe!

Weeks ago she had kissed Gabe's cheek and left him forever. He had been buried with the rest of her friends and family in the grave of her heart. She wasn't supposed to ever see him again.

"Are you coming?" Gryphon's voice pulled her out of her stupor. His lip pinched in on one side as he looked between Zo and the cave entrance.

"Yeah, sorry." Zo hitched up her kit again. If Gryphon connected her to Gabe, he'd have no choice but to turn her in. "I guess I'm still a little shaken from my last cave experience," she lied.

Accusation lifted from Gryphon's face. "Joshua told me about the Waiting Room." His brow wrinkled with concern. "Are you going to be all right?"

Gryphon glanced at the guards and quickly added, "Because if you can't treat the prisoner, I have no use for you."

Zo swallowed. "I'll be fine."

[◆]

Gryphon held the torch to his side so the healer could share the light. "Be careful of the ledge. It's a long way to the bottom if you fall." His voice echoed off the moist rock walls.

The girl didn't respond. Were it not for the sound of her soft footsteps, he wouldn't know she was there. Gryphon should have taken the scalpel from her, but part of him felt he deserved a knife to the back. Penance for letting her live last night.

At least today he'd get answers.

The air grew heavy. The thought of walking beneath thousands of pounds of rock always made it a little difficult for Gryphon to breathe. After several minutes, the cave flattened into a large cavern. The flickering light of the torch seemed barely able to combat the persistent darkness.

"The prisoner is this way." Gryphon took the healer by the arm and led her to the far corner of the cavern where the guards said he was chained.

Faint rustlings echoed high above them. Water dripped from the tall ceiling, landing with heavy *plunks* at their feet and on their bodies. Gryphon wiped water from his eyes more than once.

The girl shivered under his hand. Gryphon noticed she walked closer to him in the dark confines of the cave. A bat swooped down and screeched at the intruding torchlight. The healer gasped and jumped into Gryphon's side. His arm fell naturally around her. It was only a moment before she jerked away from him.

"Sorry," she mumbled.

Gryphon couldn't speak around the lump in his throat. Grateful for the darkness, he pressed on until he found the wall. "Hold this." He handed the torch to the healer and pulled out an oil soaked cloth from his pack. He wrapped it around the end of another stick to create a second torch.

"Switch with me." Their hands brushed. The light cast harsh shadows across her face, if possible, making her look even more devious, even more beautiful.

"Aren't you going to light it?" she asked. The glass jars in her medical kit knocked against each other as she shivered.

"Not yet." There would only be one chance to witness the prisoner's first reaction to the girl. He couldn't afford to miss it. He trailed a hand along the wall until he saw him. The once proud warrior lay huddled in a ball on the floor. Thick chains ran out from the wall, connecting to clamps around his wrists. His eyes flashed opened but his body didn't move beyond the even rise and fall of his chest.

Gryphon stepped closer. "Before your arrow found my shoulder, I was blinded by a small, but strong burst of light." Gryphon only assumed it was the other man's arrow that bloodied him. "What was it?"

The Wolf prisoner didn't raise his head from the cold stone floor, but his lips stretched into a bloody smile. "Old trick." He wheezed and coughed, sucking up dirt from the floor. His chains rattled with him.

"They say you don't speak."

"I do as I please." He coughed some more. The man pushed himself into a sitting position. The pinky fingers on each hand were missing. The left side of his face was twice the size of his right. The eye was pinched shut.

"Should I help him?" The healer spoke behind Gryphon's shoulder.

He held up a finger for her to wait.

"Did you bring a woman?" The man laughed. The chains rattled as he put a mangled hand to his head. "I've been lying here for heaven knows how long, waiting for my next *visitor*," his words took on a biting edge, "and you bring me a woman?" He laughed again. "I swear, nothing will ever surprise me again."

Gryphon took the torch from the healer, lit it, and threw the spare to the prisoner. The man snatched it out of the air before it hit the wet ground. He squinted against the light as he used the wall to inch up to his feet.

"What are you doing?" he asked.

Gryphon stepped aside and yanked the healer into the light of his torch.

The prisoner didn't flinch. He didn't even blink as he examined the girl. If Gryphon could trust his gut—something he never did well around the healer—the man's lack of reaction spoke volumes.

"I don't think I understand," the Wolf said. "Is she for me?"

Gryphon kept a careful eye on him as he spoke. "In a way, yes. She's a healer. I've brought her to tend to your injuries."

Zo shifted uncomfortably under Gryphon's grasp.

The prisoner exhaled. "Under normal circumstances I'd be disappointed. But today—" he lifted his deformed hand and sighed. "Today I prefer a healer."

Gryphon nodded for her to go to him. She looked up at Gryphon with wide eyes. He fought the urge to comfort her, to tell her he wouldn't let the man harm her. He didn't understand why she would be afraid of a Wolf, if she was one, too. Good acting or genuine fear, he couldn't decide.

The healer moved toward the man with careful steps. "I can treat you better if you sit." Her soft, smooth voice carried a low echo around the cave. The hairs on Gryphon's arms prickled.

The tall Wolf studied her for a moment then slid down the rock to sit on the damp floor. Gryphon took the torch from him and wedged it into a crack in the wall before finding a place to sit beside them.

"We've met more than once in battle," said Gryphon. "A few weeks ago my mess was attacked by a group of Raven. You were with them. You gave a Wolf Cry before disappearing over the mountain."

The Wolf didn't pull his gaze from the healer. Gryphon could hardly blame him. The usual layers of mud didn't taint her in this light. "Your spear missed its mark that day," said the Wolf.

Gryphon frowned at the memory of the young boy trying to string an arrow. The slight adjustment he had made to alter his aim that cost him the kill. "Yes, it did."

"You spared him. Why?"

The healer stopped cleaning the prisoner's hand. She peeked at Gryphon from the corner of her blue eyes.

"Tell me about your tattoo, Wolf. The one on your arm."

"Will you tell me why you spared the boy?"

Gryphon pounded his fists into his forehead. "Why do you think? Do *you* find pleasure in killing children?"

"I'm not a Ram."

Gryphon growled under his breath. He didn't have time for this. There was really only one way to confirm his suspicion that the Wolf and healer were working together. Gryphon had hoped it wouldn't come to this …

He yanked the healer to his chest, whipped her around, and wrapped two hands around her neck. She kicked and bucked, using both of her hands to pull apart his deadly grip. The girl was stronger than she looked.

"What are you doing?" Like a swift change in the wind, the arrogance of the Wolf evaporated into fear. More fear than he'd shown when he stood alone to face Gryphon the day he was captured. More fear than he'd likely shown the interrogators.

Gryphon's hands closed around her neck. He was careful to put pressure in key areas. The girl struggled, using her sharp nails to claw at his flesh. She gasped and whined.

The worst sound Gryphon had ever heard.

Gryphon's hands overlapped her delicate neck. She stopped fighting, her hands resting on his, her piercing eyes looking directly into his. Acceptance. She must have never really believed he'd spare her.

Gryphon wanted to comfort her. To explain that he wasn't really killing her. His stomach rolled. He tasted bile.

"I'll tell you what you want to know!" the Wolf yelled.

The girl passed out. Gryphon gently laid her on the damp floor, keeping her head in his lap. She wouldn't be unconscious for long, but the Wolf didn't know that.

"What have you done!" The Wolf jumped up and fought against his chains. A vein in his forehead bulged with fury. "I'll kill you, Ram! I swear I'll kill you!"

Gryphon raised his hands. "She's not dead."

The Wolf yanked on his chains like a rabid beast. When he finally sank to the floor in exhaustion, the blood drained from his face. His chest rose and fell with exaggerated effort. "What have I done?" He pushed his palms to his eyes, as if to block tears. "I've killed her." Leaning forward, he rocked back and forth on his elbows and knees, openly weeping.

Gryphon should have felt proud. He had the key to breaking the Wolf. Somehow, the victory soured at the sight of this man before him. Brave enough to give his life to defend his own men, but too weak to put his cause before a woman.

Holding her now, Gryphon felt he understood.

"I will not harm this girl if you answer my questions."

The Wolf snorted, biting his fist in agony. "How can I trust you? When you have what you want, you'll kill her."

Gryphon stared at him for a long while until the Wolf's wild eyes focused on his. He took out a long dagger from a hidden sheath at his calf and sliced his own hand. "On my honor, the girl will live if you help me." Gryphon stretched out his bloodied hand.

The Wolf eyed it with contempt. Then his gaze rested on the healer, and he broke. "There is no hell hot enough for me after this." He took Gryphon's hand and shook it. "What do you want to know?"

Chapter 15

Zo's head weighed too heavy for her neck to support. The gentle rocking motion made her want to sleep forever. Light brushed her eyelids in abrupt patches. The brightness teased her awake until she blinked away the sun.

"You're going to have a headache." Gryphon cradled her in his arms as he walked. His chest warmed her side, while her free side numbed from the cold.

Startling recollection rushed through Zo's mind. The cave. Gabe's horrific injuries. Gryphon wringing the air out of her lungs. She looked up at him and instinctively moved her hands to protect her throat. "Put me down."

Gryphon looked at her hands and frowned. "I'm sorry about that. It was the only way to know for sure."

"I said, put me down!"

Gryphon stopped walking and let her slide out of his arms. Zo couldn't get hold of her nerve. There was no chance that Gabe hadn't reacted to Gryphon's attack. He was a classic hothead. Especially when she was involved. She straightened her clothes and yanked her headscarf from Gryphon's shoulder. "Are you going to kill me?"

He folded his arms and leaned back onto the trunk of a tree. "Do you want me to?"

She sneered. "I don't care what you do, just don't stand there acting superior." The words rolled out of her mouth before she could harness them.

Gryphon's eyes narrowed. "I won't have to. Your tongue will get you killed soon enough."

They locked eyes for several minutes, until realization hit Zo like a brick to the face. "Wait. You're going to let me go?"

Gryphon shrugged. "I took you to the cave to make sure I could trust you. I thought the Wolf would recognize you, or at least make a move to save you when I grabbed you." He shook his head. "Even if you do have some Wolf in your veins, you must not be that important."

The words should have come as a relief, but Zo's stomach twisted.

"Besides," Gryphon went on, "a life for a life. You saved Joshua. We're even." He handed her the medical kit. "The road will take you back to the Medica."

He stepped off the trail and trudged through the overgrown forest, leaving her staring after him.

There was no way that happened. No possible way. Suspicion filled her with doubt. What was Gryphon playing at?

[◖◗]

Dusk pushed away the sun, making the sky bruised and angry. Gryphon inhaled the heavy air, confident the humidity would turn to rain by nightfall. He'd spent the whole afternoon wandering in the back wilderness of the Ram's Gate. He did his best thinking among the giant evergreens with the sound of the ocean crashing against the cliffs in the distance.

How could he use the Wolf prisoner's information without breaking his oath to keep the healer safe? He couldn't report the girl's involvement without incriminating her, and he also couldn't warn his people without explaining how he came by the information.

Gryphon still couldn't believe Wolves and their allies were camped downstream so close to the Gate, receiving messages from the girl in corked bottles. Right under the Ram's noses! The Wolf prisoner said they were gathering information. But for what purpose?

It bothered him that they'd sent a girl to infiltrate the Gate. A girl! She might be fast and decent with a knife, but the healer was no warrior. And worst of all, she was pretty. Far too pretty to go unnoticed inside the great walls of the Ram. The Wolf claimed the girl had volunteered for the position. If that were true, she must not have understood her slim chances for survival.

Had they not warned her?

Gryphon shook his head and walked the five miles down the sloping hills to join his mess unit in their barracks among the fifty mess cabins that lined the inside of the Gate. The log and mortar buildings formed a giant horseshoe around the main entrance, closest to the danger that existed outside the menacing walls of Ram's Gate. The rest of the Ram people lived on farms and in the hills that led to the cliff, each with a healthy number of Nameless slaves to help tend their fields.

Gryphon pulled open the cabin door to the barracks to see all of his brothers seated on the edge of their beds. At the front of the room, the Seer, with her black, beady eyes, stopped talking and glared at him.

"I'm sorry to interrupt." Gryphon quickly settled onto his bunk. Like every other mess cabin, the room was a perfect square with bunks lining the outer four walls. "I didn't know we had a briefing." He could almost feel Zander's eyes boring into him.

The Seer cleared her throat and continued. "Now that everyone is here." She paused and glared in Gryphon's direction once more. "I'd like to inform you of a change that will affect all of the unmarried members of this mess unit."

Gryphon caught Ajax's eye, but Ajax only shrugged.

"We have decided to lower the marrying age from thirty to twenty-two." The Seer raised her hands to silence the quiet murmuring in the cabin. "We expect every man in this mess who qualifies to choose a bride by the end of the week. If you fail to do so, one will be assigned you."

Being only twenty years old, Gryphon thought he had a whole other decade before the Ram would expect him to marry and start a family. For now, he was still a bachelor, but there were at least five or six men in the mess between the ages of twenty-two and thirty. Their reactions to the Seer's news were mixed. Some smiled and received congratulating punches while others looked like they just found out their favorite hound had died.

No one dared ask the purpose of changing the age-old

matrimonial custom. One didn't have to keep the meticulous tallies and notes of the Seer to know the Ram's population was on the decline.

There was only one way to become a full member of Ram society and a hundred ways to fail. From birth, every member of the clan was put through a series of tests. Young boys and girls endured grueling training sessions and scheduled beatings. Systematic starvation. Survival missions outside the wall without weapons or provisions. It was all part of the great weeding—the Ram way of determining who was worthy enough to be named a member of the most powerful clan in the region.

"Those of this mess who qualify for marriage will report your request before week's end. After the matches have been arranged, the Ram will celebrate your engagements with the Wolf prisoner's execution in the square. Consider it an early wedding gift from your generous chief."

[◊]

The next day, Zo numbly worked at a table in her wing of the Medica, her eyes glazed over, her mind far away from the task of rolling cotton gauze bandages while her patients rested. Most of her thoughts were of Tess. Thankfully, Gryphon didn't know anything about her little sister, and she needed to keep it that way.

Life experience had taught her that no matter how convincing Gryphon's promise to not report her to Ram authorities, chances were he'd betray her eventually. He must have had an angle—a reason for keeping her secret.

You could never trust a Ram.

From now on she would have to be extra careful with her correspondence with the Allies. Any wrong move could tip the scales and prompt Gryphon to talk.

The handle of the workroom door slowly turned and Zo's attention came back to focus. A slender figure in her trademark leather vest and boots stepped through the doorway.

The bandage Zo had been rolling spilled onto the floor, up and over the woman's fur-trimmed boots. "Madam Seer," Zo said, keeping her eyes trained on the ground.

The Seer reached down and picked up the roll of cotton. "Such a waste." Her artificial smile stretched in a flat line. "Are you always so careless with our supplies, Nameless?"

"No, Ma'am. I was just startled."

The Seer sighed and motioned Zo out of the chair. "I've come to discuss some reports." She sank into the chair and gestured for Zo to sit on the stone floor.

Zo obeyed, crossing her legs and clasping her hands in her lap to keep them from shaking. "Reports?"

This was it. The Seer knew she'd stolen the military records from her desk. Zo looked around the room for something, anything, to help her fight this woman, to kill her before she had the chance to order Tess' execution. Zo would hide them in the woods. Scale the deadly cliff to the ocean. Anything to escape before they hurt Tess. There was a pair of scissors on the table. They would do the job, if she could get to them before the Seer had time to react.

"The Medica reports I received recently indicate that your patients have been well cared for. No deaths to speak of. However, there was one bit of information that I found curious."

"Curious?" Zo managed to whisper.

"Our use of glass vials and bottles is up ten percent." The Seer crossed her arms in front of her flat chest and stared down at Zo with her crazy bird eyes. "Do you know anything about that?"

Zo cleared her throat. "I haven't been here for very long, Ma'am, and none of the other healers in the Medica speak to me. I am sorry, but I have no information for you."

The Seer stared at her for a measure of time. Zo kept her head down and counted to fifty, employing some of Commander Laden's interrogation tactics to keep calm.

Finally, the Seer rose to her feet and headed for the door. She reached for the handle and paused. "The funny thing about numbers, Nameless, is that they never lie. I can calculate down to inches the amount of medical gauze you will use this year based on a few variables that I make it my business to know. When a number stands out to me, it is because a variable is out of place." She opened the door, but turned back to add, "I hope you are not one of my bad variables. For your sister's sake."

Chapter 16

Zo thought of the Seer as she rubbed ointment into Tess' hands and feet before bandaging them up for bed. Thick calluses had formed on her sister's fingertips, and heels, where her too-small boots rubbed against them. As usual, Tess' eyes drooped and her head lolled to one side in exhaustion.

For Zo, sleep seemed as likely as a full stomach for a Nameless inside the Gate. Especially with the Seer's threats of missing bottles and "bad variables" squeezing at her thoughts. Something was wrong with that woman, and it wasn't just her manic obsession with numbers. Zo needed a backup plan. A way to keep Tess safe, in case Zo was discovered.

She pulled the blanket up to Tess' chin and kissed her forehead. "Good night, bug." Zo bent closer to Tess' ear. "I'm going to take a walk tonight."

Tess' brow bunched up.

"Just to clear my head. Everything's fine."

Tess digested Zo's explanation for a moment until her eyes fluttered with want of sleep and she rolled to her side. "You wouldn't tell me if it wasn't fine," she mumbled, on her way to the place where dreams exist. Zo hoped it was a safe place. Where her back didn't hurt and she was able to run around and play like a child should.

I have to get her out of here.

When all the other Nameless women and children in the barrack were asleep, and even Anne—who usually stayed up mumbling nonsense into the darkness—was quiet, Zo crept out into the crisp spring night. She shivered and pulled tight a thin jacket, crossing the cobbled road that divided the forest from the town. She climbed the gradual slope until she couldn't see the torches that burned outside each of the barracks in town. Here, surrounded only by trees and darkness, Zo felt herself relax for the first time since her run-in with the Seer.

As a child, Zo used to be afraid of the forest at night—all the reaching shadows and unseen dangers waiting to snatch her up. Wolves and bears and other beasts that didn't enjoy being woken. Sharp rocks and hidden animal dens that could easily twist an ankle or worse.

These fears seemed laughable now after seeing Gabe chained to a wall. The unknown is only scary until the harsh reality of life is so brutally exposed that you wish you could close your eyes and only see darkness. The Ram had taught her just how scary reality could be. By comparison, they made the forest seem like just a shadowed cluster of beautiful trees.

She followed the trail upward until her breathing was labored. The farther she hiked, the louder the sound of the waves crashing into the side of the mountain in the distance. When she broke the tree line at the mountain's summit, she nearly collapsed.

It wasn't the climb that made Zo's knees wobble, nor the breathtaking height that plunged so abruptly into the black ocean below. She sank to her knees and reached out over the edge of the cliff to touch the free air. A sob escaped her chest as she looked down the seamless wall of the mountain. No handholds. No footholds. Just sheer rock that ended in certain death if anyone was foolish enough to attempt the climb.

Commander Laden hadn't exaggerated. There was no escape from this place. Not even a dangerous "back-up plan" in case the Seer discovered her involvement or Gryphon decided to turn her in.

From now on, she'd have to be sparing with the bottles stolen from the Medica supply room. Only the most vital information could be floated downriver. If Tess hadn't followed her into the Gate, she wouldn't have bothered being so cautious. But as it was …

Zo dragged her feet as she hiked back down to the Nameless' barracks. She slowed her steps the closer she got to town. Once the dangerous road came into view, she took a moment to listen for patrolling guards.

A barn owl hooted in the distance. The wind rolled lightly through the trees, but no guards. She had just taken a step outside of the forest when a man dropped down from a tree above her head. Zo's scream was caught by a rough hand clamped over her mouth.

A large man with a long scar across his face looked in both directions on the road. He held a black executioner's hood in his hand. "If you value your life, you will not make a sound."

The hand covering her mouth fell away as the black hood came down over her head, blocking the light of the stars and moon.

[•]

If only Gryphon knew how to write! An anonymous letter was the safest way to give his superiors information about the enemies camped downstream. The old Historian had said he was a fool not to bother with reading and writing. She'd been right about that, at least.

"What's bothering you?" said Joshua. "Something bad happened. Tell me."

"It's nothing, kid. Fix your stance. A little girl could knock you over when you rest on your heels like that." Joshua had been begging Gryphon to help him with his hand-to-hand techniques. The training session had barely begun and already the kid sensed Gryphon's unease.

Joshua stood up and abandoned his stance. "Something's definitely wrong. I can tell by your eyebrows. Whenever you're worried a crease forms between them."

"Stance, Joshua! Or we're done for the day."

Joshua obediently bent his knees and rolled onto the balls of his feet, his hands out, his back curved. "Fine. Don't tell me. We can just lie to each other and pretend that everything is fine."

"Thank you." Gryphon suppressed a smile. "Now advance."

They grappled until Joshua complained his back ached

from being thrown to the ground too many times. He dusted himself off and received a friendly slap on the shoulder.

"You're getting better," said Gryphon.

"It's about Zo, isn't it?"

Gryphon rolled his eyes and gathered his pack. The kid could be a pesky fly when he wanted to.

"Tell me."

Gryphon sighed. He leaned against a tree and crossed his arms. "It actually has nothing to do with Zo."

Joshua lifted his freckled brow.

"I've obtained some information regarding an enemy camp."

Joshua's mouth fell open. "No way."

Gryphon raised his hands. "I'm not sure if my intelligence is accurate. I want to write it down and stay anonymous."

"Why? Where'd you get it from?"

Gryphon looked away. "I can't say."

Joshua shrugged. "I could write it for you."

Gryphon snapped to attention. "Where did you learn?"

"My friend, Lance, has been teaching me. His mother's a scribe for the Seer. It's not that hard—"

"No one can know about this."

Joshua smiled. "Whatever you say, only, can we do it at your mom's house? I'm starving."

(•)

Gryphon stared at Joshua's scribbling in awe. He squinted, as if by doing so he might divine the meaning of the text. "You included everything?"

Joshua jammed another piece of buttered bread into his mouth, leaving little room to speak around it. "Yep."

"You're absolutely certain they will not know this is from me?" Gryphon inwardly growled at his own inability. He scanned the page again, following each line with intense focus.

"I'm sure." Joshua swallowed hard and packed more bread in his mouth. "I can teach you to read, if you want."

"Really?" The thought made Gryphon surprisingly hopeful.

"Sure." He plucked the page from Gryphon's hand and flipped it around. "Lesson number one: don't read it upside-down."

Gryphon ruffled Joshua's red hair. "You're lucky I like you." He left the boy to his food and walked out of his family home. With Joshua's words clamped in his fist, Gryphon set off to plant his information and relieve some of the guilt of his betrayal.

Chapter 17

*Z*o struggled to breathe through the thick hood covering her face. Her bound wrists burned. Blood rushed to her head as men took turns carrying her over their shoulders. It was a bumpy ride that made her want to be sick inside the hood.

There was no point in risking her captors' anger by voicing the questions rolling around inside her head. Why would a Ram do this? She was their property! Where were they taking her? She could only hope they didn't connect her with Tess. Had Gryphon already broken his promise to keep her identity a secret?

After an incalculable amount of time, the guard carrying Zo stopped and set her on the ground. When Zo found her feet she resisted the urge to force her knee into the man's stomach and run. A cold knife slipped between her wrists, cutting the ropes with ease. "Take hold of the ladder and start climbing."

Zo grasped the rung of a rope ladder. "What do you want from me?" Her throat was a desert and she didn't trust her legs to stand without keeping a firm grip on the ladder.

"Climb." The voice sounded younger than she expected.

Obeying, she reached blindly for the next rung and began the vertical climb. The ladder swayed and jerked as someone followed her. After several minutes of climbing, Zo had to stop and rest. How high was she? Her breath came hard as she hugged the ladder. The muscles in her forearms throbbed. Someone below tapped on her boot. "It's not much farther."

Zo nodded through her hood and reached for the next rung. Her boot missed its footing and her arms couldn't support her weight. She screamed as she fell, knowing she'd already climbed too high to survive the impact.

The fall lasted both a lifetime and an instant. The person below caught her around her middle with one arm. The wind rushed from her lungs and she cried out in pain. The man growled with effort as he pulled her between himself and the ladder. "Quick, I'm going to lose you."

Zo grasped the rungs, grateful for the support at her back. She felt herself crying, but didn't have the breath to sustain the emotion, making her sound more like a barnyard animal than a girl who had just faced her own death.

"We need to get off this ladder. Climb with me."

Together they worked their way up another dozen rungs before a pair of hands wrapped around her wrists and hauled her onto a platform. She clung to the man who held her, desperate not to accidently step off the ledge. Her stomach churned as vertigo set in. She felt like she was falling to one side even though her feet were planted on the floor.

"This way," the man said.

The planks of the floor moaned beneath her clumsy feet. The sound increased as others behind her reached the platform and followed. A heavy wool curtain brushed her arm as she walked into a space where the sounds of the forest muted. A room? They pushed her to sit on a soft sort of pillow and pulled the hood from her head.

Zo squinted against the light of a single candle burning in the center of a room. The walls were a patchwork of dark wool that moved like water from the wind outside. A motley group of men and women sat in a circle surrounding her.

"Who are you? What do you want with me?" She could tell they weren't Ram by their worn clothing and the dirt that lined the wrinkles of their skin. But they also didn't carry the defeated expression of the Nameless.

A tall man with heavy arms clasped his hands together. He leaned forward. "I am called Stone." He gestured around them. "Welcome to the Nameless Nest. It was built by my late friend, a Raven, whose death you witnessed in the last prizefight. Do you remember him?"

Zo swallowed down the bile rising in her throat as the gory images of the prizefight assaulted her thoughts. She nodded, her mouth dry. "I remember him."

"We've been watching you, healer. We watch all the new Nameless when they enter the Gate. Even your little sister."

Zo's fingers curled into talons. "Don't. Talk. About. My. Sister." Adrenaline poured into every crevice of her being. She was tired of being bullied. No more! "Just tell me what you want."

The man stared. Five seconds passed. Ten. "You're

different. It's more than just your healer status. I can almost sense the fight in you. You are not really a Nameless, are you?"

The ragged men and women in the circle leaned forward to hear her answer.

"Why else would I come to the Gate?" Zo's voice barely carried over a whisper.

Stone's brow lifted, accentuating an uneven scar along one cheek. "There are rumors that the clans outside the Gate are working together." The light of the candle danced across the planes of his wide face. He inched closer and dropped his voice. "You're fresh from the outside, healer. Tell us what you know."

"I don't know anything beyond rumors."

Zo wanted to tell them everything about the Alliance of the clans, of her work as a spy inside the Gate, but how could their knowing help her cause? All it would take was one Nameless to talk, and Zo and Tess were as good as dead.

The leader reached out and grabbed her arm. "Will the clans unite against the Ram?"

Zo yanked her arm away. "I don't know." The lie was a mountain crushing her chest. All these rebels wanted was a little hope. They defied the Ram enough to meet. Didn't that qualify them for at least a portion of her confidence?

This is not my fight, she reminded herself.

The man's lip curled in disgust. "I don't believe you. And if you can't provide us any information, we can't afford to let you live." At a wave of Stone's hand, two men stepped forward and took Zo by the arms. "Throw her off."

Zo bucked and pulled against the men, but they managed to drag her out of the wool tent. Outside, the night bent to early morning, giving just enough light to see the staggering distance between the platform and the ground below. "Please, don't do this!" They brought her to the edge and Zo went wild, grasping at their arms and shirts, anything to keep her from being thrown over.

"All right!" she cried, thinking about what Tess' face would look like if she didn't return. "I'll tell you what I know." They let her melt to the wood planks. Her vision spun in circles as she crawled as fast and as far away from the ledge as possible.

Her body shook all over when she finally found her way back inside the covered tent. Curling in a ball, with head tucked between her knees, Zo re-taught her body how to breathe.

"You have one minute," the leader, Stone, ordered.

Zo covered her face in her hands and rocked back and forth on the creaky boards. "The Ram. They'll kill my sister if they find out. I can't let that happen." Her voice caught on the fierce edge that separates victims from warriors. "I *won't* let that happen."

Stone walked up to Zo and rested a warm hand on her shoulder as he crouched down beside her. "Look around you, healer. Do you think you are the only person in this room whose family is at risk? We gather because, for our children's sake, we cannot be silent any longer!"

Zo looked around the room and met the hollow, desperate eyes of the Nameless.

"We know how to keep your secrets, healer," Stone whispered.

He had a point. And even if he didn't, she'd already proven that she was a coward—more afraid of her own death than keeping Tess safe. The shame was unbearable.

Zo studied her hands as she spoke. "I officially joined the Allies after my parents were killed in a raid. My father's closest friend took me and my sister under his wing. At the time, I didn't realize the magnitude of having Wolves, Raven, Kodiak, and others in one camp, united under one banner. All I knew then was my rage." Zo used the back of her violently shaking hand to wipe a tear.

"I've spent almost half my life working with the Allies. This mission was my opportunity to finally help the Cause. My chance to vindicate the lives of my parents. I HATE the Ram. I always will."

Zo went on to explain her mission. The bottles. The Seer. Her encounter with Gryphon. Everything. She told them that she was chosen because her healing abilities would make her valuable and because the Ram wouldn't see a lone girl as a threat.

"Tess wasn't supposed to follow me," she added.

The group of Nameless sat back in amazement. One woman wiped at tears around her eyes. Zo could only imagine what their lives had been like. Always afraid. Constantly feeling like they were alone in their opposition to the Ram.

"I overheard the chief talking about a Great Move. I believe they mean to move the entire clan south—maybe to invade the Valley of Wolves."

Stone paced the creaking floors. "We expected this. The Ram are running low on options. Food supplies are depleting. If they stay for much longer, without finding the Raven grain stores, they'll starve." He held out his hands, gesturing to the group. "We all will."

Looking at him now, Zo guessed from his broad forehead

and thick build that he or his parents belonged to the Kodiak before their names were stripped from them. The Kodiak were known for being as direct in conversation as they were in battle.

"A move, wagons, resources, men before families ... " He spoke to himself like someone who had lost his mind. And maybe he had. It would take an insane person to rally against the greatest army known to man.

"Take her back. I have to think." Stone walked to the corner of the room, away from the others.

After the Nameless revolutionaries helped her down the rope ladder and walked her back to the barracks, Zo slipped into bed just minutes before Tess' large eyes flitted open and another day began. Zo didn't mention anything about the Nameless' rebellion or her meeting with Stone, but she couldn't shake the feeling that change was coming. Something big.

[•]

The following morning, when he was sure no one was looking, Gryphon staked Joshua's writing to the door of the Hall of Records. The next person to walk through the building would find it. The chief would have the information about the Allied camp on his desk by the end of the day.

Gryphon walked at an even pace as he left the center of the town. He felt lighter knowing that he'd finally done something right. Barnabas could take it from here, and once he did, the Wolf healer's little bottles wouldn't do any harm.

Gryphon thought of Zo and shook his head. Who would have thought such a little person could find space in her body to house that much nerve?

"What are you smiling about?"

Gryphon looked up in surprise. "Sara, is that really you behind that belly?"

Ajax's wife swatted Gryphon's arm. "Did you think the healthy son of Ajax would be small?" She massaged her lower back. "If he doesn't come soon, I might crawl into an early grave." She laughed, but Gryphon didn't see the humor in the situation.

"Is he late?" Gryphon put his hand on her back and guided her to a felled tree trunk. With the Ram's population on the decline, expectant mothers were treated like war heroes. But Sara meant so much more than the mother of another Ram baby to Gryphon. She was as good as an older sister.

"Stop coddling me, Gryph. I'm fine." Despite her words, she let him help her sit. "I just came from my family home. I'm afraid I have some bad news."

"What is it?"

"Eva accepted a claim today."

Eva was Sara's eighteen-year-old sister. Sara had been conspiring to match her and Gryphon ever since she learned the marrying age had lowered from thirty to twenty-two.

Gryphon hardly knew the girl, and so wasn't too disappointed. "Who made the claim?" he asked.

"Taurus." Sara sighed. "Eva says she's happy, but … "

"You can tell she isn't."

"Yes."

Gryphon sighed. He rested his hand on Sara's stomach and felt the baby move. "Why would she accept the claim if she doesn't care for him?"

Sara's brow wrinkled. "I'm not sure. It doesn't seem like her."

Gryphon's hand was still on Sara's ripe belly when he saw his friend coming around the bend in the road.

"Get away from my wife!" Ajax barked.

Gryphon grinned up at him, his hand unmoving. "I think I might steal her from you."

"Like hell." Ajax grabbed Gryphon's hand and threw it back at him. He turned and helped Sara to her feet. "I was worried when you didn't come."

Sara kissed the tip of his nose, effectively turning the overgrown bear into mush. "You worry too much."

Gryphon suddenly felt out of place. "Take care of yourself, Sara. And remember, I'm eligible in two more years if you decide to trade this oaf in."

Ajax kicked him away but lines of amusement wrinkled around his eyes. "Get out of here, you good-for-nothing vulture."

"Say hi to Joshua." Sara called over Ajax's shoulder as Gryphon walked away.

Chapter 18

O n the day of Gabe's execution, Tess huddled under Zo's arm as they walked with heads bowed low. Once the lane opened up into the main part of town, Zo instructed Tess to stand with the other Nameless children from their barracks. "I don't want to remind anyone that you and I are sisters," she explained.

Tess looked like she might cry. "I don't want to watch." Her lip jutted out. "What if I know him? What if they do something awful to him?"

Zo touched her cheek. "When you get in the crowd, be sure to stand in the back behind someone tall. No one will make you watch." Zo hoped she was right. The Ram wanted the Nameless to witness these things. They wanted them to remember what came from defying their rule.

A heavy crowd of Nameless surrounded them when

they reached the town square. Zo squeezed Tess' hands and parted ways from her. She allowed herself to be carried to the opposite side of the square until the current of bodies settled into stationary restlessness.

Guards cleared a walkway for five men and one woman with hands bound behind their backs. They each had collars around their necks where thick rope connected them. Gabe walked at the back of the line with his head low. His skin was transparent, his eyes hollow sockets.

Where was the pride he used to carry? Where was the confidence in his step? He was a mere ghost of the man she once knew. Dead already. *What have they done to him?*

From the corner of her eye, Zo noticed a tall soldier cutting through the crowd in her direction. She tugged on her headscarf and slowly dropped into a crouch to get some fresh dirt for her face. A heavy set of boots stopped in front of her.

"Are you the Nameless healer?" the man asked.

Zo thought about lying but didn't dare. She slowly rose to her feet while keeping her eyes trained on the ground. "Yes, sir."

He took her arm without saying a word and dragged her toward the platform. "Wait." Zo did her best not to struggle, but the closer they got to the center of the crowd the more she believed she was joining Gabe. "I haven't done anything wrong."

The guard yanked her forward.

"I haven't done anything wrong!"

Heads turned in her direction, but Zo didn't care. Tess was here. Tess would see them kill her. She would have to watch her die, like Zo had had to watch their parents.

The guard knocked people out of the way as he worked to get Zo to the corner of the platform. Gabe's head rose at the commotion. Life entered his eyes. Zo could see him mouthing the word "No" over and over again. The corded muscles in his arms jumped as he pulled against his ropes.

The guard brought Zo to the platform stairs, and to Zo's relief, walked right past. She could feel Gabe's bright blue eyes staring at her as she walked by him. She might have been able to touch her childhood friend if she tried. She reached the center where a group of padded chairs were sectioned off.

"Is this the girl you wanted, sir?" The soldier shoved Zo forward, stopping directly in front of the Gate Master.

He excused the soldier with the flick of his hand without taking his gaze off Zo. "Sit with me." He gestured to a cushion beside his chair.

Zo eyed the seat with contempt but thought of Tess and sunk to her knees in submission.

"Your service in the Medica is insufficient." He cupped her cheek in his rough hands. "You will move from the Nameless' barracks to live in my household."

Before entering the Gate, Zo knew this day would come. No matter how much dirt and grime she smeared onto her face, a guard would eventually want her. The idea had been less terrifying before she met the Gate Master.

The low rumble of the Ram horn made even the most important people seated with the Gate Master break conversation and rise to their feet. The crowd parted for the chief and his entourage of guards and advisors. Zo kept her head down as they passed. The Gate Master pulled away her headscarf. Her dark hair tumbled down her back. Clean and kept in an unhelpful sort of way.

Zo looked up in time to see Gryphon at the tail end of the precession. Leather straps crisscrossed his bare chest, storing two wood-hilted daggers. A short sword hung from a sheath at his side. He met Zo's gaze for a brief second before his attention traveled to the Gate Master's hand at her hip. His brow furrowed. His lips thinned into a straight line. The expression looked wrong for his face. His commanding build always made him seem older, but walking behind the chief he looked like a pup with only his big toe dipped into the pond of manhood.

The Gate Master leaned over to a man with a long white beard. "So much attention for bringing in one little Wolf." He shook his head. "Are we that starved for heroes inside the Gate?"

The horns stopped, but Gryphon didn't give his attention to the chief like the rest of the audience. His expression darkened into pure and utter loathing as he glared in Zo's direction.

"Today we celebrate the capture of a Wolf! Several of you will marry within the next few weeks. Consider today's unique entertainment an early wedding present from your chief." The crowd clapped and cheered, Nameless included, though their hands came together with almost too much vigor, desperate to show their devotion.

A soldier yanked on the rope around Gabe's neck and brought him to his knees. "Striker Gryphon, son of Troy, has brought us a little present." The chief grabbed a fistful of Gabe's thick, blond hair and pulled up his head to show the handsome face of the Wolf.

"Today, the Wolf and other enemies to the clan," he

gestured to the line of accused on the stand, "will die for their crimes."

Again, a predatory roar erupted from the massive crowd. Zo wanted nothing more than to find Tess and shield her from what was to come. The Gate Master's leathery hand inched up her arm to the back of her neck, leaving a trail of fire on her skin. The sensation triggered her gag reflex.

[•]

Gryphon looked down from the stage at Gate Master Leon as he caressed the bare skin around the healer's neck. The man whispered something in her ear. She closed her eyes, as if willing him away. Hot anger coursed under Gryphon's skin. An impulse he could only compare to the adrenaline he felt on the battlefield. Only this anger was much more complicated.

Chief Barnabas took the rope from his servant and handed it to Gryphon. "The Wolf is your prisoner. How will he die?" Gryphon could have said anything: *Let him be hanged. Let him be stoned. Let him lose his head.*

The Wolf looked up at him without fear, prepared to meet his end with dignity. No pleading. No begging for mercy. How could Gryphon kill such a worthy opponent with his arms tied behind his back? Some men deserved that shame. Not this Wolf.

Gryphon looked out at the expectant crowd, then back at the Wolf. He cursed under his breath and drew his own sword. "Let him die fighting!" he shouted. His declaration echoed throughout the entire square.

The murmurs of the people rolled like a giant wave,

crescendoing into a chorus of chaos and cheers. Gryphon looked down at the brothers in his mess. Most had smirks on their faces. Ajax looked furious while Zander kept his arms folded, composed as ever. Joshua stood a ways back with the boys in his age group, his head whipping from right to left in confusion.

"Release the prisoner and arm him." Barnabas rested a hand on Gryphon's shoulder. His voice was all but swallowed in the buzz of the crowd. "I never figured you for a politician, Striker." He smiled approvingly and walked off the platform to take his padded chair close to Gate Master Leon and the healer.

Ajax was at Gryphon's side before he had time to process the chief's words. "What. The. Hell?"

Gryphon smiled and shrugged. "He doesn't deserve to die without a weapon in his hand."

Ajax shook his head. "This is nothing but your own blood lust."

Gryphon's eyes darkened. "This is mercy, Jax. A chance for him to die with dignity. It's what I'd want if the circumstances were reversed."

Ajax looked down, still shaking his head in anger. "Do you think this maggot would show us mercy?" He yanked on one of the straps of his breastplate. "Your *mercy* will get people killed one day."

The Wolf stood statue still on the opposite side of the platform. His unkempt hair was hastily tied back by a Nameless attendant. He held a loose grip on a short sword and a Ram shield at his side.

Gryphon locked eyes with his enemy and didn't break

contact until the Master of Arms walked up to the center of the platform where they stood and placed his hand on the ground between them. The whole square went quiet. "On this day Striker Gryphon, son of Troy challenges the Wolf prisoner in a battle to the death," he roared.

The officiator lifted his hand from the ground. The two fighters prowled the perimeter, back and forth in a deadly dance until the Wolf sprang forward, fast as a gust of wind. His blade met Gryphon's shield like quick whips of lightning. The force knocked Gryphon on his heels then sent him reeling backward into a roll. Gryphon pushed up onto the balls of his feet, weapon ready. He didn't have time to regret his "mercy" before the next attack from the Wolf and his lightning arm.

Gryphon dodged and rolled again. The Wolf was abnormally fast, especially considering his current condition. Gryphon went to strike his left shoulder then swept the surprised Wolf's feet from under him. He jumped on top of the Wolf and jammed his shield into the Wolf's mangled hand. The Wolf cried out and dropped his weapon.

Heavy legs wrapped around Gryphon's chest and slammed him backward into the ground. Gryphon twisted and broke free from the trap as the Wolf struggled to reach his sword.

The two wrestled for advantage, rolling around the ring like animals until the Wolf pulled a dagger from Gryphon's own sheath. Fire burned across Gryphon's thigh before he realized what had happened.

The Wolf shouldn't be this challenging. He'd been starved and tortured in a cave until only a few hours ago. The man fought with heart unequalled by any opponent he'd ever faced. Inhuman strength.

"I said I'd kill you." The Wolf spoke through gritted teeth as the two men locked arms again.

Gryphon could feel himself weakening. Blood poured from the wound on his thigh. He grappled for a better hold as the Wolf hissed and spit in his ear. "I won't die in front of her."

Gryphon caught a glimpse of the healer from the corner of his eye. The Gate Master held her back from the platform by her hair but she didn't seem to care. Her eyes were only for the Wolf. Through all the shouts from the ruckus crowd, Gryphon singled out her lone cry.

Gryphon exploded out of the Wolf's hold and flipped him onto his back. He felt the crunch of the Wolf's jaw under his fist. Gryphon took him by the throat with both hands and squeezed.

I must be crazy.

The Wolf kicked and flopped about like a fish on dry land. Gryphon held strong. His practiced hands tightened around his neck but slipped on the blood gushing from the Wolf's nose. His arms shook as he fought to hold the man down. His fingers found their mark again, and this time he didn't let go.

The Wolf's legs slowed. His hands went limp and dropped to his sides. Several people in the crowd gasped.

Gryphon picked up the dagger with both hands, raised it high above his head, and stabbed the Wolf in the chest, just below the shoulder.

The crowd went completely quiet in anticipation. Gryphon's chest rose and fell as he wrenched the dagger from the Wolf's body. He gathered himself off the ground like an old man, one foot and then another. His whole frame trembled from the effort. A cold sheen of sweat collected on his forehead.

He held out the red-stained dagger, blade up, for the chief's inspection. Hundreds of excited Ram looked to their chief with bated breath. Barnabas lounged in his chair, propping up his head with a fist. Time dragged on like a cold winter but the chief eventually nodded his approval.

Gryphon sighed in relief while the audience exploded into cheers. He motioned for a pair of young guards to cover the body in lamb's cloth.

His relief died the moment he saw the healer. Her stoic eyes stayed fixed on the Wolf's limp form. Gate Master Leon grabbed her chin and shouted something while gesturing in the Wolf's direction before striking her with the back of his hand. She hit the ground, but no one heard. She didn't flinch when his boot met her side.

Gryphon found himself walking toward the Gate Master, his fists balled and eager. But before he could do anything, the chief took the platform stairs two at a time. He slapped Gryphon on the back and said, "The clan is indebted to you, son. Name your reward."

Gryphon knew this offer was coming. He'd planned to ask for command of a new mess. The same request any forward-thinking Ram in his position would make. Redemption for his father's disgrace was his to claim. The shield hanging on the wall of his home would be forgotten. He would be the youngest mess leader in his clan's history.

The actual words that slipped from Gryphon's mouth shocked him as much as the stunned crowd.

"I want the healer." His arm stretched out, finger pointing down at the limp form at Master Leon's feet.

Barnabas stared at him with mouth gaping until a clipped

burst of laughter erupted from his chest. Slow at first, it grew until his whole belly shook. The crowd mimicked his reaction, as usual. Between bouts of laughter the chief waved for his guard to bring the stunned girl up to the stand. Master Leon turned three degrees of red as they ripped her from his grasp. He glared at Gryphon with pure and utter loathing.

Gryphon squared his shoulders and stared back. He would not be bullied. As the healer approached him with her head cast down in shame, a chilling oversight settled in. Everyone in the clan would assume he took the girl as a personal slave. A *very* personal slave.

Gryphon walked over to the Wolf's limp form and used the rest of his energy to pull the man up over his good shoulder. He was so exhausted from the fight that his legs shook under the weight. The crowd parted for him as he struggled down the platform with the Wolf slung on his back. It was customary for the victor of an honor killing to bury the body of his opponent in the soil of his own fields.

The healer trailed him looking white.

"Go and enjoy her, Striker," the chief called over the crowd, accompanied by laughter and jeers from the Ram.

Chapter 19

Zo studied her dirty shoes as she trailed Gabe's killer. Gryphon leaned heavily on his dark friend, with one arm draped over his shoulder for support as he struggled under the weight of Gabe's body. Their conversation didn't hold her interest; neither did the waning moon or the pale stars against the almost night. No, she only bothered to look at her feet and the earth below them. Looking down, she could be anywhere. The earth here in hell wasn't so different from home. If she hadn't left, Gabe and Tess wouldn't have followed. If she'd had the courage not to chase after the pain of losing her parents, the disease that she was couldn't have spread.

"You're going to get someone killed," said Gryphon's dark friend.

I already have, Zo thought, hitching the heavy strap of her pack higher on her shoulders.

"Everyone thinks you're an arrogant fool showing off for sport, but I know you better," the dark man continued.

Gryphon dropped his arm from his friend's shoulder. His pace slowed as he limped along. "You don't know me as well as you think you do, Jax. Not by half."

"I know you're far worse than a fool!" Ajax snapped. "You think you show compassion, but all you show is weakness! Weakness our enemies will one day exploit."

Gryphon stopped. Zo kept her eyes trained to the ground standing the standard three feet behind them. She didn't dare look up to see Gabe, his hand swinging freely under the blanket that covered the rest of his body.

"What are you saying?" Gryphon's voice shook despite his quiet whisper.

"I'm saying I know you didn't miss your mark with the Raven boy the day you made Striker. You never miss in practice and you're twice as good in the field."

Zo stole a quick glance at Gryphon. It was the second time she'd heard mention of the boy he'd spared. Gryphon glared at Ajax, his jaw flexed, his fists balled menacingly at his side. His voice was calm but his words had teeth. "If you have doubts about my ability to perform in the mess, I suggest you take them up with Zander."

Ajax shook his head and walked away before looking back. "The men are talking, Gryph. The spear miss, letting the Wolf fight, and now this girl?" His dark eyes targeted Zo. She looked down. "It's like you want them not to respect you. Like you want trouble."

Gryphon grumbled something dark and incoherent then said, "What would you have me do, Jax?"

Zo stole another glance in Gryphon's direction. He rubbed the sweat from his face with a bloody palm. Even in his fatigue, his biceps leapt—a commanding reminder that this soldier was not to be taken lightly.

"Keep your head on. Remember what we're fighting for. I overheard Zander talking to Barnabas. The clan will move south before next frost. We're leaving the Gate and all the people of the clan will look to their soldiers for protection. This is the time when legends are born, my friend. We can't afford to go soft now."

Gryphon looked over at Zo and frowned. "I won't let my brothers down."

Ajax took Gryphon by the shoulder. "I hope not. We're going to need you."

Zo mentally tucked the information away for when she could find a day to escape to the river and drop a bottle or two. Though they were far away from her usual spot on the mountain, she could still hear the river over her left shoulder as they walked farther and farther away from Tess' half-empty bunk in the Nameless' barracks.

After Ajax left, Gryphon led Zo another half-mile down the wild path. He walked slowly, favoring one leg. His face paled from blood loss. Zo didn't offer help. The Ram would be less of a threat with his injuries and exhaustion. Not that she cared much anymore. Even though Gabe's death was just one more reason to fight, her body begged for rest. The simple task of putting one foot in front of the other became as arduous as walking through thigh-high mud.

Her cheek pulsed from the Gate Master's most recent attack. She held her side without even realizing it. The pain from what she assumed was a broken rib was the only thing keeping her lucid. Sapping the numb anguish that had settled into her soul.

After several miles of walking, the forest thinned into an open field. A log building sat on a modest rise in the distance. Behind it the great wall of the Ram loomed tall and jagged against the night sky. They must have walked the entire diameter of the territory with Gryphon carrying Gabe on his back. The wall and a handful of miles were all that separated Zo from Commander Laden and his men. The thought should have given her hope, but all she felt was pain. Pain for Gabe. Pain for Tess. Pain that she and her sister would both spend the night grieving alone.

[♦]

Gryphon's whole body hurt. Sticky blood pooled in his boot as he walked. He held one arm to his stomach like an injured bird protecting a bad wing. His right leg buckled when he gave it too much weight. He couldn't wait to lie down and fall asleep. Maybe in his dreams he could sort out the mess he'd made.

Gryphon told the healer to wait outside as he stumbled into his family's old barn. He laid the Wolf down in a pile of stale hay and stretched until his back popped. His skin was wet from perspiring and his feet felt weighed down by rocks. Pressing two fingers to the Wolf's throat, he frowned and left him there, shutting the door behind him.

Zo still wouldn't look at him when he exited the barn and motioned for her to follow. They neared the house and the door flung open. Joshua bounded from the porch like a jackrabbit.

The way he moved, it was no wonder he'd beaten them home. Gryphon extended his good arm to accept the kid's help, but Joshua shot past him.

"I can't believe you get to live here now!" he exclaimed. The healer's eyes grew round as Joshua wrapped her in a tight hug. The bottles in her ever-present medical satchel rattled together. A rogue smile cracked her stoic expression. Joshua had that effect on people.

"A little help," Gryphon grumbled as he tried to slough off his pack without jarring his shoulder.

"Oh, yeah. Sorry, Gryph."

"What? You're not happy to see me too?" Gryphon said.

"Not as happy as your mom. She's pretty upset, though."

Gryphon sighed. "So you told her, did you?"

"I had to when she saw you coming up the hill with the Wolf slung over your shoulder."

Gryphon felt the healer stiffen at his side. "Help me inside, Joshua." He turned back to see the pale girl. She looked like she might be sick. "Come with us," he ordered.

Gryphon leaned his spear against the wall and dropped his shield next to the mat. "Mother?" he called. The ghosts of voices that once filled the house haunted him. He refused to look up at his father's shield.

"Gryphon!" cried a woman in the next room. Her steps came quick and light. She stopped three feet before him, and like all proud Ram woman, let him close the remaining distance.

In two steps he pulled her under his good arm. "I'm sorry, Mother. I didn't plan to fight."

His mother wiped a tear from her eye and swatted the back

of his head. "Why? Why did you do it?"

Gryphon shrugged. "He didn't deserve execution, Mother."

"I didn't deserve to lose my husband," she said flatly. "War is war. We do what is required for us to survive."

"I had everything under control."

She eyed him like he was a kitchen mouse pretending to be a breadcrumb. "Look at yourself! Under control?" She closed her eyes and kneaded her forehead with her fingertips. Heavy frown lines permanently pulled down the corners of her mouth.

Gryphon tucked her deeper into his embrace and kissed the top of her head. "I'm sorry, Mother." The woman had endured more than her share of heartache. He hated to add to her pain.

Her fiery golden eyes whipped up to meet his. "If you leave me without grandchildren, I swear I'll jump up and down on your grave." She almost smiled before her eyes rested on the healer. "Who is she?"

Joshua put an arm around the girl. "This is the healer who saved my life."

"A Nameless healer?" Gryphon's mother narrowed her gaze. "Why would the Seer place a Nameless as a healer?"

"It's a long story." Gryphon sighed. "I'll tell you everything in the morning."

Gryphon's mother stepped around her son and grabbed the girl's chin to get a better look at her face. "Turn," she ordered, gesturing for her to do a slow spin. Zo obeyed.

"Give me your hands." His mother made a *tsking* sound and let them drop, shaking her head all the while. "You haven't worked a day in your life, have you, child?"

The girl kept her head cast down. "Not in the fields, madam."

"Madam, nothing. You'll call me Mrs. Drea like the rest of our Nameless."

"Yes, Mrs. Drea."

Gryphon found that he'd held his breath through the entire exchange. The girl had never submitted to him with such earnestness. Obviously his mother was more intimidating.

"Mother, we've had a long day—"

"If this pretty thing is a healer, have her patch you up tonight. I won't have you bloodying another set of linens. The girl can sleep in the barn until I find a place for her with the others."

Gryphon's mother grasped Joshua's hand. "Look after my son, Joshua. He seems to be losing his mind."

When they were alone, the healer started unloading glass jars filled with brown and green liquids onto a small table in their front room. "Wait." Gryphon scratched his head and took a step toward the door. "I—I need to check on … something. I'll only be a minute or two."

"I'll come with you," said Joshua. The boy moved to follow him.

"No!" Gryphon inwardly cringed at his own abrupt tone. The last thing he needed was to pique Joshua's curiosity. "Stay with the girl."

"*Zo,*" Joshua emphasized. "She has a name, remember?"

Gryphon couldn't help but look at the girl. She met his gaze for a moment then looked away. Gryphon cleared his throat. "Zo." His deep voice struggled around the word.

It was the first time Gryphon had ever spoken her name out loud. A minor rebellion compared to the other mistakes he'd made over the past weeks, but somehow it felt intimately worse. Like an admission of the way he truly saw her. She was *Zo* to him as well. The thought made him even more lightheaded than before.

"I'll be back soon." Gryphon snatched one of the room's two lanterns. He stumbled on the doorframe and left to greet the dark night. A light rain mixed with the sheen of sweat on his skin, as if the sky tried to clean away his sins. But even an angry storm couldn't wash away the film of guilt lining his stomach. How had a string of rational choices led to this?

"Idiot." He spoke aloud. Someone had to say it.

He took a calming breath before carefully opening the door to the barn. He held the lantern aloft as he searched the stalls. Gryphon felt naked without his shield. Exposed. After double-checking the stalls, a horrible reality settled upon him. The Wolf was gone. He pumped feeling into his fingers as his search became more frantic. Gruesome possibilities clenched at his gut like iron pinchers.

Gryphon tried not to panic, taking a long moment to think like his enemy. Where would he go? He might be able to scale the wall, but that would take a great amount of effort and he was seriously wounded. He'd need time to heal before any escape would be possible.

Suddenly Gryphon remembered the Wolf in the cave. The way he'd reacted to seeing Zo in danger. The man's promise to kill him repeated over and over again. Gryphon sat down on a stool in the middle of the dark barn. He rubbed his face with his hands.

"You're in some trouble, I imagine," called a strained voice from a dark corner of the barn.

Gryphon's head whipped up. He held up the lantern.

"Where are you?"

"That is, unless they put you up to it." The Wolf's voice bit through the blackness. "Make a show of killing me, then let me live so you can knife me for more information later."

Gryphon rose to his feet. "Come out. We need to talk."

"My shoulder has already stopped bleeding. Perfect blade placement."

Rain pelted against the roof of the barn. Gryphon couldn't even hear the crunch of hay from his boots as he crept toward the sound. "I spared your life, Wolf."

"Yes, but to what end?"

A crack of lightning struck outside. The ground shook from the impact as light exploded through the seams of the building, showing Gryphon his enemy only five feet away. The Wolf used the wall to support him. He held a pitchfork in his hands, the three deadly points fixed on Gryphon's heart. "Don't move, Ram."

Gryphon held up his hands to show he had no weapon. His mind raced for a way out of the situation. He could run, but he'd earn himself a fork to the back. Not a good idea.

"Where is she?" the Wolf demanded.

When Gryphon didn't answer right away, the Wolf stabbed at him with the fork. Gryphon jumped back but the metal grazed his arm, ripping his shirt. Gryphon dropped his hands. Furious. "You just made a big mistake."

"Where is she?" cried the Wolf. He stabbed at him again, only this time Gryphon was ready. He sidestepped the jab and took hold of the shaft of the pitchfork. The lantern dropped to the ground, the light snuffed out. The men struggled until they both stumbled to the damp barn floor. Gryphon landed hard, losing his grip on the weapon.

The door to the barn flew open. Lightning flashed behind Joshua, Zo at his heels. The sight of them stunned Gryphon. Joshua raised his sword and the Wolf charged him.

Zo pushed the boy aside in time to catch the tips of the pitchfork in her stomach. The weapon clattered to the floor. Joshua cried out as Zo's pale face dropped from the light of his lantern.

Gryphon slammed the stunned Wolf into the ground. His head connected with a stall door. Unconscious.

"I told you to wait at the house!" Gryphon yelled. The poor boy met him at Zo's side. She clutched her stomach and forced down a cry.

"Bind and gag him. I'll be back soon." Gryphon went to help her stand but noticed dark stains pooling from the holes in her shirt. He switched his hands with some hesitation, pulling her arm around his shoulder while scooping up her legs.

"Where are you taking her?" Tears collected in Joshua's eyes. He used his sleeve to wipe them away.

The girl rested her head on Gryphon's shoulder, and he no longer felt pain from the fight. "To the house. She needs her kit and a warm fire."

Zo reached a hand out to comfort Joshua. "It's not deep, Ginger." She gently ruffled his red hair. "I'll be fine."

C•]

Up at the house, Gryphon rested Zo on the floor by the hearth. He rushed to bring blankets and her kit. Her eyes didn't even register fear as he pulled out his knife to cut through the clothes around her waist, the fabric wet and sticky. Three shallow holes oozed ink dark blood. Zo's whole body trembled. "Who was that man?" she asked.

Gryphon could tell by her voice that she really didn't know. "My enemy." He hovered over her, his clumsy hands outstretched, wanting to help but not knowing how. "Tell me what to do."

Zo closed her eyes and started taking slow breaths.

Gryphon grabbed her by the shoulders. "Tell me!"

She opened her eyes and slapped him across the face. Gryphon sat back on his heels and rubbed his cheek, stunned.

"I ... I'm sorry. I don't like to be touched."

Gryphon could only watch with mouth gaping, his hands curling and uncurling at his sides, as she propped herself up against the wall and stripped a portion of her shirt into a bandage. She gasped at the effort of wrapping the cloth around her small waist, and cried out as she pulled tight the dressing.

"Let me help you." Gryphon inched closer but kept his arms by his side.

"Wash your hands," she said.

[◆]

As the soldier washed, Zo pulled out a few bottles from her kit. She felt awkward blessing the herbs and tonics for herself. The wound burned. Her concentration wavered. So much of healing rested in the love of the healer. With her enemy sitting inches away, Zo conjured the words of the blessing in her mind, and worked to bind her love to ... well, herself.

The familiar click that usually registered in her heart didn't come. Instead it rested just on the edge of where it should. Taunting like an aching knuckle in need of a good pop.

"Ready." The soldier held up his clean hands for inspection.

Zo nodded. "Good. Soak the wool in these." She pushed four jars toward him with shaking hands. A new wave of chills rocked her frame. Her head felt light from blood loss.

The soldier hesitated then gently took hold of one of Zo's shoulders. She flinched under his touch. He frowned and pressed the wool to her stomach. The sting made her eyes water, but she didn't cry out. Not with her enemy watching.

Show them no pain. Commander Laden's coaching echoed in her ears.

Chapter 20

G ryphon didn't remember falling asleep after moving Zo to his bed. His joints popped as he peeled his worn body from the hard floor. He turned to find Joshua leaning against the doorway of his room. The boy's swollen red eyes and deep frown made him seem older.

"Sorry kid. I meant to come and—"

"What's going on?" Joshua folded his arms and scowled, effectively scrunching up the freckles on his face.

Gryphon looked back to make sure Zo was asleep before grabbing Joshua by the collar and hauling him outside. Dark clouds swept over the early morning sky. The cold bit through Gryphon's damp shirt. "I've messed up, kid." Gryphon studied the horizon. "I couldn't kill the Wolf."

The boy was young, but he was still a Ram. He understood the shame in Gryphon's words and knew him well enough not to console him. Gryphon had failed the clan and deceived his brothers. For a Wolf.

"Why?" Joshua's disappointment carried over the wind.

Gryphon thought of Zo, the pain in her deep blue eyes as the Wolf walked up the platform to face execution. "I don't know what's wrong with me." He shook his head. "It doesn't matter. I made a decision and now have to face the consequences."

"You're not turning yourself in, are you?"

Gryphon hesitated long enough to send Joshua into a full-scale panic. "You can't! You're the best man we have!" Beneath his words Gryphon heard something completely different. *"You're my only family!"*

Gryphon swallowed against the rock in his throat. "Go look after Zo. Get some sleep if you can."

"Where are you going?" asked Joshua.

Gryphon took two steps toward the barn then called over his shoulder, "To fix my mistakes."

[●]

Dust particles danced in the beams of sunlight that filtered through ceiling planks of the barn. The Wolf lay face down with his wrists tied behind his back and a gag in his mouth. With his ankles bound to his wrists, his body looked like a crescent moon on the ground. Joshua had taken his time.

Gryphon cut the ropes connecting his ankles to his wrists and removed the gag.

"How is she?" said the Wolf with his first free breath. He tried to stand but fell. "Is she badly injured? I need to see her. I need to make sure she's all right."

"I'll smuggle you out of the Gate once we've attacked Zo's contacts at your command post down river. Once you leave the Gate you are my enemy. If we meet on the battlefield, I'll tear every limb from your body and have no problem sleeping that night. Do you understand?"

The Wolf barely seemed to hear Gryphon's words. "Why is she here? What are you doing with her? I need to see her!"

Gryphon picked up a piece of straw from the ground and split it in two. "The girl will heal. It was too dark for her to recognize you. Everyone inside the Gate believes I killed you on that platform."

"So she thinks I'm … "

"Dead."

The Wolf nodded his head. "But you're going to tell her the truth, right? That I'm alive."

Gryphon bit the inside of his cheek. "The boy will bring food and water."

"I'm not leaving her behind. Not again."

Gryphon replaced the gag and tied the Wolf's hands to a post. "I don't know how things work where you come from, but inside the Gate a pact is a pact. You told me what I needed to know inside the cave. Now trust me to keep my end of the deal. I didn't have to spare you. I've sworn with my own blood to protect the girl. That means something to a Ram."

[●]

Zo breathed in the musk of her pillow. The smell of pine and lemon grass tickled her nose. She inhaled deeper. A body lying on the other side of the bed shifted, and Zo's eyes flew open. She relaxed when she noticed the red hair sticking out from under the covers. The planes of Joshua's adolescent face seemed softer in the morning light. She reached out and touched his fiery hair, wondering if there was some way to keep Joshua from becoming a monster. Maybe she could find a safe place for him and Tess. Somewhere far away from spears and bloodshed where they could live in peace.

Joshua turned over and wrapped an unconscious arm around her middle. Pain exploded from the wounds in her stomach, but she didn't move him. Instead, she held him under the wing of her arm and thought of Tess waking up alone in the Nameless' barracks without her warmth to keep the morning chill away. No one would walk her to the fields. No one would love her and tell her to be brave and keep her head down.

The pain in Zo's stomach became more internal. The sorrow of her situation was too overwhelming to endure. The image of Gabe suffocating under Gryphon's strong hands sent her over the edge of an emotional cliff. Tears burned hot on her cheeks. Tears she hadn't allowed herself to cry in a long, long time.

"Does it hurt?" said a deep voice by the door.

Zo looked away, hurriedly wiping the tears from her face. She knew Gryphon had had no choice but to kill Gabe, but it didn't make looking at him any easier. To her he would always be the man who killed her childhood friend.

The soldier stepped closer and lifted Joshua's arm from her waist. "Do we need to replace the bandages?"

Zo sniffled and nodded, gesturing for her kit.

Gryphon washed his hands in a basin of water in the corner of the room then sat on the edge of the bed. He lifted the hem of her shirt to expose her stomach. His movements were gentle. Fluid. The caked blood tugged at Zo skin as he slowly pulled the bandages away.

"We need to flush out the wound." Zo gestured to a tall bottle of alcohol and a tiny brush. "You might need to scrub, soldier."

Gryphon frowned. "Won't that be painful?"

Zo laughed. The tone of her voice scared her—it was the sound of a woman who'd lost her mind. Why did he care if it was painful? In his eyes she was no better than a goat in a pen.

The soldier lowered himself to his knees and set his shoulders. He uncorked the lid and poured the clear liquid into each hole, looking up at her for guidance between each pour. Zo wanted to cry out, but gritted her teeth and focused on breathing through the explosions of pain.

"Are you all right? Should I give you a minute before … " He gestured toward the brush.

"Just do it." She waited for him to start before dabbing at the tears forming around her eyes. In truth, she couldn't have imagined a better hand. He seemed to read the wound, and by touch, determine the perfect amount of pressure and strokes to remove the dried blood and dirt.

When he finished, Zo sighed with relief and looked him in the eyes. She couldn't bring herself to compliment his work. This was Gabe's killer.

With most of the macabre debris cleaned away the wound looked much less dire. She winced as she tried to sit up to get a better view of it. He took her by the shoulders and lifted her into place. Her body felt cold where his hands had been.

"Looks good. We just need to close the wound."

"You don't mean stitching, do you?" Gryphon's brow furrowed.

"You don't have to, soldier." If Tess were here, she could do it, though her stitches weren't always straight.

"Call me Gryphon." He looked through Zo's kit and found a fishbone needle and thread. He placed one hand on her stomach while the other held the needle ready. "Tell me what to do."

Zo couldn't decipher his motives for helping her—for being so kind.

Gryphon worked quietly. His fingers moved with stealth and precision. When he tied the final knot, Zo couldn't help staring. "You've never done that before?"

"I'm no healer."

There it was. The pride of the Ram jumping up to greet her. Of course he hadn't healed a person before. It wasn't considered a proud profession. Certainly needed, but not desired above bashing in heads on raids.

"I need to find you a better place to lie down. If my mother wakes up to find you asleep with Joshua in my bed she'll ask more questions than I want to answer."

Zo nodded in agreement. The last thing she wanted was to be questioned by the Ram woman again.

Gryphon helped Zo stand and kept hold of her arm as they walked outside to the servant quarters. The small building had a chicken coop connected to the back and an oak front door that sat crooked on its hinges. As they entered, four men jumped out of bed and stood at attention.

"This girl will take Nan's old bed. She's been wounded and needs rest. Tend to her and your business today."

Gryphon looked back at her with a hint of a smile. "I'll check back in a few hours." He closed the door behind him.

Zo stared at the door wondering why, with all of his injuries, he hadn't asked to be healed.

[●]

Back in his room, Gryphon's head sank into his pillow as he labored to steady his nerves. Just as he closed his eyes to rest, three solid knocks sounded at the front door. The tease of sleep made it painful to pull himself away from the bed. Joshua stirred but didn't wake from his new spot on the floor.

Gryphon leaned heavily with one hand on the doorframe as he pulled the door open. He jumped to attention when he discovered Zander on his porch standing with hands clasped behind his back. "Injuries?"

Gryphon cleared the frog from his throat. "Deep gash on right thigh. Shoulder healing well from the arrow I took on our last mission. A few deep bruises. Nothing major."

Zander nodded. "The chief received an anonymous tip that we have spies waiting down river. Scouts returned last night to confirm the location. A group of Wolf, Kodiak, and Raven no more than five miles away."

Gryphon inwardly sighed relief. At least the Wolf hadn't lied back in the cave.

Zander continued, "We head out in three days, following the engagement festivities. You are excused from training until then. I expect you to be rested and ready."

"Yes, sir."

Zander turned to leave, but paused. "Gryphon?"

"Yes, sir?"

"I've been thinking about yesterday." He unconsciously

massaged his biceps. "There are only two reasons I can imagine you choosing to fight that Wolf. Either you saw it as a chance to perform for the clan or you really wanted to let the Wolf die with dignity." He dropped his hands to his sides and looked Gryphon in the eye. "Truth is, I don't really care what your motives were. It was foolish to put yourself at risk when so many people are counting on you."

"Sir, I'll be fine."

His commander raised a hand to silence him. "Your actions prove you don't always consider the needs of the mess before your own."

The words stung.

"You're selfish, Striker. You might be the best at what you do, but I can't fully trust you." Zander frowned and walked away. "Three days," he called over his shoulder.

All Gryphon could do was watch his captain leave, knowing he'd deserved those harsh words. What would Zander think of him if he knew the extent of his betrayal? Had Gryphon forgotten his brothers? Did his mercy make him weak?

Joshua's voice startled him. "Where's Zo?"

Gryphon slammed his palm into the doorframe. "Don't you have training?" he yelled. "Stop thinking about that girl and go help your clan." He pushed Joshua out the door with a little more force than necessary. Joshua didn't look back as he sprinted down the road.

Gryphon slammed the door to his room and fell into bed with a groan. A hollow ache gripped his insides. Relentless churning that wouldn't subside. How had he allowed this to happen? In only a few short weeks he'd gone from making Striker to betraying his entire clan. How could he make this right?

Chapter 21

Zo awoke to find Joshua's extra large smile hovering over her.

"Who's Tess?" the boy asked. Zo found herself holding Joshua's hand. She didn't remember grabbing it.

"She's my little sister." Zo rubbed the sleep from her eyes.

Joshua frowned. "You have a sister?"

Zo had mentioned Tess in the Waiting Room. Joshua must have been too delirious at the time to remember.

"Do you miss her? Is she with your parents?"

I hope not. Zo cringed, thinking of the subtle mounds of dirt that marked her parents graves. Images replayed in her mind: dark clouds blocking the cold sun, faces twisted in mourning, wind blowing the few flowers away, the sound of the half-frozen dirt covering their bodies. All buried and left with the rest who couldn't follow the pack to a new home.

"She's alone. I'm worried for her. Wait—how do you know about Tess?"

"You talk when you sleep."

"Oh." Zo hoped she hadn't said too much. She still wasn't sure what to do about her little sister. The worry was constant and gut-wrenching. Her sister. Alone. "Maybe you shouldn't mention her to Gryphon."

"Why not?" Joshua yawned the words. "Wait. She's not *here*, is she?"

The door of the Nameless quarters squeaked open, and Joshua ducked behind the bed. An old man carrying a bucket and shovel limped into the large room. Joshua straightened with a sheepish grin playing about his lips.

"What was that about?" said Zo, while nodding to a Nameless slave in Gryphon's household.

"Ah, nothing. I should go." Joshua bent down, kissed Zo's cheek, and ran out the door. Zo touched her hand to her cheek. She'd seen countless Ram exchange a similar kiss at parting, but never with a Nameless.

"That was interesting." The old Nameless man shook Zo's hand and smiled through a mouth only half full of teeth. "I've heard a lot about you, healer. Which for a Nameless, is not a good thing."

"What do you mean?"

"I mean Nameless talk when taskmasters aren't watching. You, child, need to learn to keep your head down." The old man gave her a look that said far more than words could. She hadn't considered the possibility that the Nameless rebels weren't limited to the brave circle in the Nameless Nest. How many were there? Trusting a handful of people to keep her secret was one thing, but the vast Nameless population?

Zo's empty stomach soured. *I need to get Tess out of here!*

[•]

Gryphon came with a plate of food and Zo's kit around dusk. He noticed her wince as she sat up.

"Are you hungry?" Gryphon set the food next to her bed on the floor and pulled up a three-legged stool. He kept his injured leg stretched out to the side. Zo held a thin blanket to her chest. She brushed a clump of dark hair from her face, revealing piercing blue eyes.

"Eat." He nudged the plate toward her.

When she didn't take the food he shrugged and reached in his pack for a knife and block of wood. The girl was on her feet and across the room before he realized the problem.

He raised an eyebrow then looked down at the knife in his hand. "You still don't trust me?" He smiled sadly and shook his head. "You and everyone else." He pushed his knife into the block of wood with slow, practiced strokes.

Zo stayed against the wall clutching her stomach where her shirt had been cut away. Gryphon kept his eyes on his work, only sparing a glance when she slowly crept back to her bed.

She pulled the covers up to her chest again. "What do you want with me?"

Gryphon felt the color rise in his cheeks. Of course she would think he wanted her for his own devices. "To be honest, I want nothing to do with you. You've caused me a great deal of trouble."

"Then why keep me here?" she asked. "Why feed me?"

Gryphon stroked the wood, cutting deep into the middle of the block to form the neck of the animal. "I keep my promises," he mumbled.

Zo sat for a minute longer, watching him guardedly as he worked, until she finally reached for her plate and began picking at the food. A small part of him wanted to ease the sorrow on her face. To explain that the Wolf was alive. That he wasn't the monster she believed he was. Maybe if she knew she wouldn't hate him so. Maybe.

But then, why did he care?

They sat together with only the sound of Gryphon's humming to keep them company. It was fully dark before Gryphon heard the clinking bottles of Zo's kit.

"May I help you?" She gestured to his leg.

Zo opened her kit and began working on Gryphon's thigh. She reopened and cleaned the wound with graceful strokes that felt much more painful than they looked. Gryphon clamped down his jaw and tried to relax as she worked.

When she seemed satisfied that the wound was clean, she mixed a potent concoction of oils to make an ointment. After stitching him up, she wrapped a clean bandage around his leg. Her fingers were smooth and steady but freezing cold.

When she closed her eyes Gryphon stared openly at the subtle movement of her full lips as she muttered words of healing under her breath. She finished and rolled onto her side, wincing from pain, and fell asleep.

Gryphon forgot his carving and watched the rise and fall of her thin frame by the light of a lone candle.

Joshua found him there an hour later. "Hey, Gryph, how is she?" He settled onto the ground next to him.

Gryphon struggled to find his feet without tugging on his new stitches. "I'm sorry about this morning, Joshua. I shouldn't have yelled."

"You're stressed. I get it."

Gryphon ruffled his hair. "Go get her an extra blanket. Her fingers are freezing." He hobbled away imagining Joshua's stunned expression following him.

Chapter 22

The following day, Gryphon walked with only a minor limp down the road to Sara's family home for Eva's engagement ceremony. Each step away from home had him questioning the wisdom of leaving the Wolf unguarded. He carried the only key to the barn door on a string around his neck. The feel of the metal knocking against his chest gave him a small sense of security.

Soon all of his troubles would be behind him. His brothers would forgive him the inconsistent decisions of the past few weeks. Gryphon's triumphs on the battlefield would cloud the clan's memory of his dishonorable father. And Zo …

He cringed at his natural use of the girl's name.

The *healer* would melt into the background, living on his family land, away from harm and out of his notice forever. A tiny bit of hope buoyed up his mood. Everything would work out. It would.

The closer Gryphon came to Sara's family home, the more people joined him on the road. Though with all of the recent engagements inside the Gate, many of the Ram weren't headed for the same ceremony.

Gryphon spotted Ajax on the edge of his in-law's property line. They fell into step together and Ajax threw his arm around Gryphon.

"Where is your gift, brother?" He looked behind Gryphon for some invisible goat on a leash. "Tell me you didn't come without an offering for the bride!"

"It's taken care of." Gryphon, patted a pocket inside his fur vest.

Ajax didn't seem convinced. "Just don't make a fool of me. My father-in-law still wishes Sara hadn't accepted my claim a year ago."

"Funny. He likes me all right."

Ajax scowled but his nose wrinkled in the process, killing the effect. "Don't force me to end you, brother. Zander will be disappointed if I take out his famous Striker."

"I'll do my best."

Four long wooden tables sat in a square around a blazing fire. Next to the fire, two carved stones created the legs for an altar. Most of the guests clustered around the periphery, chatting in reverent tones while the would-be groom and a few of his mess brothers stood inside the ring of tables laughing and drinking.

"Taurus is an idiot." Ajax said, looking at Eva's soon-to-be husband. "I don't know why Eva accepted him."

Movement beside the family shed caught Gryphon's attention, though the smoke of the fire blurred his vision. He took a few steps away from the group to get a better look.

A burly man in Nameless rags stared at Taurus with unmasked hatred. Gryphon knew the expression well, had seen it countless times on the battlefield. The Nameless' concentrated stare moved from Taurus to Gryphon then to the dirt at his feet.

There was something about the man's look. His posture. His dark expression that didn't seem completely right— especially coming from a Nameless. A loud woman with wild russet hair moved into Gryphon's line of sight. He sidestepped the woman and went to confront the Nameless, but on second glance, the Nameless had disappeared.

"What's up?" Ajax moved to Gryphon's side and squinted into the forest.

Not wanting to cause a scene at Eva's ceremony, Gryphon said, "It's nothing."

A soft horn sounded and everyone took their seats around the outside of the square tables. Sara led Ajax away to sit with her family, leaving Gryphon to sit alone near the end of one of the four tables.

All talk ceased and all eyes stared at the backdoor of the house, awaiting the bride's entrance.

"May I sit with you?"

Gryphon looked up, surprised to see the white-haired Historian, Barnabas' grandmother. He fell over himself trying to stand, knocking the table with his knee in the process. "Of course."

The Historian's presence seemed to stop the whole ceremony. Sara and Eva's father stood from the center of the head table. "You do us a great honor, Wise One." He bowed to the Historian.

She nodded and gestured that the ceremony should continue before taking her seat next to Gryphon.

The backdoor to the home was painted red, representing the blood that accompanies new life. Eva stepped out of the house, and turned to shut the red door. The death of her old life. She stood before the engagement party dressed in fur boots and a long wool dress of simple design. Her hair fell down to the middle of her back. She was a plain girl with a small mouth and Ram nose, but the smoke of the fire and the whimsical mood of the evening made her breathtaking.

The Historian lifted a shaking hand to wipe a tear that escaped her lashless eyes. "Poor lamb," she mumbled to herself.

Gryphon wrinkled his brow. Wasn't this supposed to be a happy occasion?

And yet, Eva did seem somber, for some reason.

Eva stepped inside the square of tables where Taurus waited with a smile too large for his face. He handed Eva a wand of sage and placed his round shield at her feet. She stepped up to the altar, twisting the bundle of herbs in her hands.

Eva's whisper sent a wave of chills up Gryphon's back. "I claim your shield as my shield. May it protect our family and always bring you home." She dropped the sage into the fire. It hissed and cracked, causing fragrant clouds of smoke to rise from the flame and waft over the group.

Taurus drew his knife. He stepped closer to Eva and gathered her hair in his fist. "I claim your beauty and your womb. May our family bring honor to the Ram."

Gryphon flinched as Taurus pulled his knife through Eva's hair, leaving only a few inches from her scalp. Marking his territory.

The Historian seemed to exhale after holding her breath. "God protect that girl."

The couple turned to face each other. Taurus sheathed his blade and took his intended by the hands. Just as they bent to kiss—the last rite of the engagement ceremony—Gryphon again spotted the Nameless man in the forest. He looked wild and anguished. A bear caught in a deadly trap.

Gryphon unconsciously put hand to the hilt of his short sword, but the Historian touched his arm. She stared at the wounded-looking Nameless and subtly shook her head. Her lips formed the word, "No," though no sound escaped them.

The man in the forest bit into the back of his hand and stared one last time at the newly engaged couple, then darted away.

The couple kissed and the engagement was official. They would wait the standard month before the chief announced them man and wife, giving both bride and groom time to prepare for their new life together.

"Who was that man?"

The Historian studied Gryphon from the corner of her eye. "You have not earned the right to know that, Gryphon, son of Troy."

Gryphon blanched at the use of his father's name. "What does that mean?"

The Historian turned and took one of Gryphon's hands. She turned his palm to the sky and ran her finger along its creases. "You are a gifted warrior, Striker. But that tells me nothing of your character." Her knobby finger froze as the lines of his hand intersected. Her head whipped up, mouth open. Fast as an arrow, her hand reached up and took hold of

Gryphon's chin. She squinted, staring into the depths of his eyes for several seconds.

Just as quickly as it happened, the old woman dropped her hold. "How is the Nameless healer faring?"

"She is fine, I suppose." Gryphon didn't think it necessary to mention the fact that she'd been stabbed by a pitchfork within minutes of arriving at his family home.

The old woman snorted. She struggled to her feet as people around them took turns congratulating the newly engaged couple. She took hold of the key around Gryphon's neck. "Give the Wolf my greetings."

All of the blood rushed from Gryphon's face as the old woman, with cane in hand, hobbled over to Eva. The throng of well-wishers parted as the clan's matriarch approached the bride. She took Eva's face in her hands. The girl bent her head and accepted a light kiss on her brow. Gryphon couldn't hear the words the old woman whispered in the girl's ear, but Eva cracked her first genuine smile of the evening.

It was several minutes before Gryphon's shock wore off enough to approach the bride. He numbly pulled out a small dove-shaped carving and pressed it into Eva's hands before others would notice, still ashamed of his time-wasting talent.

"A dove for joy." He, like all the rest, bent to kiss her brow.

Eva looked up at him and a tear streaked down her cheek, chased immediately by a second. She shook her head. "You're wrong." A smile broke through the obvious, yet inexplicable agony in her face. "The dove is the symbol of hope, too, did you know?" She fingered the carving. "Thank you, Striker. For giving me hope."

Chapter 23

Gryphon's mother, Mrs. Drea, barged into the room carrying a bundle of clothing. "Well, I've finally found good use for you." She dropped a long, wool dress on the bed and urged Zo to change out of her worn Medica clothes.

"Our neighbor's best worker just broke his arm. They've promised me a barrel of apples if I send you to set it for him."

The stitches in Zo's stomach tugged as she pulled the threadbare shirt off over her head.

"Do you know how to set an arm?" Gryphon's mother put her hands on her hips. Clear definition cut into the woman's biceps and forearms.

"Yes, Mrs. Drea."

"Good. Joshua will take you."

Zo grabbed her kit and hurried after Mrs. Drea to meet Joshua on the road. "Do a good job," Mrs. Drea called after them.

After a short walk, Joshua led Zo down a narrow lane neighboring a flowering apple orchard. Several ragged-looking Nameless passed them, carrying buckets and shovels. The men kept their eyes trained on the ground until the last second, then stared accusingly at Zo. Like she'd done something wrong.

She pressed her hand to her stomach, as if to hide the clean clothes Mrs. Drea had given her. When they reached a farmhouse, Zo waited by the road while Joshua spoke with the Ram woman at the door. She tucked her short, strawberry hair behind one ear and laughed at something Joshua said while holding her ripe, pregnant belly. When the Ram woman spotted Zo, her whole demeanor darkened. With a sharp hand, she pointed around the house to a barn.

Zo nodded her understanding and walked along the curved cobblestone path to the barn. The wooden building looked similar to Gryphon's Nameless' quarters with one lone door hanging a little off square and a small window to let in light.

Zo knocked before entering. "Hello?" she called into the dark room.

"Over here." The male voice sounded strangely familiar. She followed the sound to a dim corner where the light didn't reach. The young man groaned as he sat up from a hay-lined cot. "Hello again, healer."

"Stone?" Of all the Nameless inside the Gate, she'd been called to help the rebel leader. The man, who not long ago, wanted to throw her off a cliff for information.

Zo took a step backward. Then another.

"There is no need to be afraid, healer. We are on the same team."

"It isn't safe to be with you." She looked at the door and

contemplated running out. "Is your arm even broken?"

In the dim light, the scar that ran along Stone's face caught a fraction of light. It was a gruesome blemish on an otherwise handsome face. He held his arm to his waist like a bird with a lame wing. "I promise I didn't even know you were coming." He looked down at her medical satchel and winced. "Can you at least give me something for the pain?"

Zo couldn't go back to Mrs. Drea and tell her she didn't perform her task.

She sighed. "I can treat you better in the light." Gesturing for him to sit down on the edge of a bed, she started mixing herbs and oils for pain. While she worked, Stone stared with eyes that seemed much older than his twenty-something years. She felt his intensity without needing to see the dark bags under his eyes that marked the nights spent working to overthrow the Ram.

"You know what you're doing is pointless," she whispered. "You're only going to get good people killed."

"No, healer. A bird in a cage is pointless. What we do might be insane, but it's *something*."

She stopped and looked up from her work. "How will you do it? Even the entire force of the Allies will struggle against the Ram. They are too strong. Too effective in battle."

"Yes. But they're dying."

Zo's hands froze. "How so?"

The corner of Stone's mouth hitched up into a crooked grin. "You aren't the only one who knows how to steal records, healer. Right now Nameless outnumber the Ram two to one."

The figure didn't surprise Zo in the least. For years, fugitives from all over the region came to the Gate as a last resort to starvation. And that number didn't include the Nameless born into slavery. "But you have no weapons. No training. Shovels and fists make little impact on the Ram shield. They will mow you over like dry wheat."

Zo measured his forearm for a splint and he slapped her hand away with his good arm. "We will find a way to escape our slavery." His shaking finger pointed down on her.

Zo saw something in him then. Something she understood more than he could possibly know.

Pain.

An awful brand that seeps into the heart and burns hot like smithy coals.

Head bent, she gently took hold of his broken arm. "May I?" When he offered no objection, she spread the healing poultice from wrist to elbow. The healing words flowed from her lips with the desperation of one who has struggled toward something for so long and still not found reprieve. She ached for this man and willed his strength to return.

Because he could not lead his revolution with a broken arm.

The blessing ended and Zo slumped over to catch herself. Her vision spun as she collected his pain. She closed her eyes and waited until her body felt right again.

"That was amazing." Stone looked at her in awe.

"You're not going to like this next part." Zo prepared some linen to make a sling then set the splint on the bed next to them.

Stone said, "So how does it feel knowing you're worth more to that Ram, Gryphon, than a new commission?"

"What do you mean?" Zo examined the break with a frown.

"Gryphon killed the Wolf prisoner. He could have asked

for anything, but he took you." Stone shook his head as he studied her. "I watch people, healer. I saw the way Gryphon looked at the Gate Master when he kicked you. I know what it feels like to want to protect someone you care for."

Zo snorted. "Gryphon cares nothing for me."

Stone shook his head, unconvinced.

"Is that why you fight, Stone? Who are you trying to protect?"

Stone sat silent for a moment then whispered, "If this Ram is willing to give up his commission to protect a lone Nameless, he might help others."

Zo walked her fingers up Stone's forearm until he let out a yelp of pain. The break was just below the elbow joint. "How did you do this?" she asked.

"I fell." Sweat beaded his brow. "You're changing the subject."

Zo didn't have time for this. "You fell," she said flatly.

"I was sleeping in a tree."

"Intelligent." Zo handed him a strip of leather. "I'm going to set the bone. Bite down on this."

"I need to ask you a favor, first."

She sighed. "What?"

"I am in love, healer. With a girl I shouldn't be. She is ... " he swallowed and looked away. "She is carrying my child and will be killed for it."

Zo inhaled. "Not a Ram?"

Stone nodded. The fire that ignited his talk of rebellion melted into agony. He rubbed his free palm into his forehead. "If I can't get her out of the Gate before they discover her condition they will send her and our child over the cliff."

Zo swallowed, feeling a heavy weight dumped upon her shoulders. "What is your favor?"

"If you and your sister find a way out of this hell, promise you'll take her with you."

Zo's face was damp. She wanted to pull her hair out and scream. To scratch and bite and kick and wail all at once. But instead she nodded. "I'll do my best."

Stone mumbled a somber "thank you" and put the leather in his mouth. He gripped the side of the bed, all the while keeping his gaze locked with hers.

Zo's mother could slip a bone back into place with so much speed the pain was over almost before it began. Too bad Zo hadn't inherited that gift.

"Ready?"

He nodded.

"One, two, … " Zo pushed with one hand and pulled with the other. The bone snapped into place and the young man passed out. Joshua and the strawberry-haired Ram woman walked into the barn just as Zo secured the splint to his arm.

"What did you do to him?" said Joshua.

"He's fine." Zo turned to the woman of the household and stared at her feet. "I've made him a sling that will hold his arm close to his body. The bone won't heal right if he takes it off. When he wakes he'll be in pain. He won't be able to work. After seven days have him come see me so I can make sure the bone hasn't shifted."

"How old are you, Nameless?" the Ram woman asked in a melodic, high-pitched voice.

Zo straightened to take advantage of her full height. "Seventeen, ma'am."

"A seventeen-year-old Nameless who has no problem giving a Ram instructions?" The woman shook her head.

Zo didn't have to look up to feel the weight of her stare. "I'm sorry, ma'am. In the Medica I became accustomed to speaking that way." She put her head lower to show submission.

The woman sighed and turned to Joshua. "Tie her to the post outside."

"Excuse me?" Joshua openly gawked.

"Do it."

The woman walked out and Zo nudged Joshua to follow. "I'll be fine, Joshua. Just do as she says."

Outside the sunlight glared through the thick pine trees surrounding the barn. Zo walked over to a tree trunk chopped at eye level with a rope secured around the middle. Joshua stood, arms hanging at his sides, while Zo put her hands in the straps. "Drea will not approve of this," said Joshua. "Not without her consent."

"Quiet, boy." The woman picked up a long, thin stick from the ground. Zo closed her eyes and tensed the muscles in her back, trusting that the extremely pregnant woman couldn't hit that hard.

The stick cut through the air making a whistle sound then connected with a *crack* on Zo's back. Skin ripped; fire spread down her spine and throughout every nerve ending in her body. Zo didn't even have time to cry out as another whistle cut through air and skin. The stick cracked again and again. Zo melted to her knees, too dizzy with pain to stand.

With every strike, Zo's hatred solidified. This was why she was here! The Ram would all pay for their cruelty. She would show them what it meant to bow their heads and submit like animals. She would show them …

"Enough!" Joshua took the whipping stick from the woman and launched it into the trees.

"I was done anyway." The woman laughed. She caressed her round belly as she stood over Zo. Her voice was pure honey. "My Nameless will visit you in seven days. Give my regards to Drea. Tell her the apples are on their way."

Joshua was careful not to touch Zo's back as he helped her home. He walked her to the bed but with the stitches from the pitchfork still fresh, she didn't want to lie on her stomach. "I'll just sit." The room spun in circles. She rested her hands on her knees and tried to get a handle on her breathing.

Joshua ran off and was back a moment later with both Mrs. Drea and a furious-looking Gryphon. "All she did was explain how to care for his arm and ask that he come back in a week to have it looked at. That's *it!*"

Mrs. Drea pushed both boys aside. Zo flinched under her hands as Mrs. Drea peeled away the remains of the ruined dress. "We've never had a Nameless healer. Ram women don't like being told what to do," said Mrs. Drea.

"This isn't her fault," Joshua protested. "She was only doing what you asked."

Mrs. Drea shook her head. "No. This is my fault. I should have warned the girl." It was the first time Zo had heard an admission of guilt from a Ram.

Gryphon picked up Zo's kit and started gathering oils. He motioned to Joshua. "Use your knife to cut the back out of the dress."

Mrs. Drea walked toward the door. "I'm going to pay a little visit. I'll come with another one of my old dresses later. I have a feeling the Nameless won't want anything touching her back any time soon."

She was giving Zo some of her own clothes. Something that she'd actually worn. The simple offering made Zo's eyes sting. She sniffled, confused by the kindness that contradicted what she knew to be true about the Ram. "You'll want to cut one inch strips out of the cloth," Zo said to Joshua as he gently cut a giant square into the fabric on her back. With every tiny movement a new wave of pain prickled throughout her body.

But all she could think about was Tess, the Ram woman Stone loved whose fate she now carried, and the red brand of hatred burning a hole in her chest.

Chapter 24

"Tell me what to do." Gryphon felt like they had just done this. Probably because they had.

"Soak the cloth in this, this, and this." She pointed to three different oddly shaped bottles. "Then lay them along the cuts."

Gryphon obeyed. She flinched every time he touched her. Every time.

And how could he blame her when nearly every experience she'd had with Ram ended violently? Beatings from Gate Master Leon, the pitchfork, and now this. Even he had handled her roughly in the forest and practically strangled her in the cave. He placed another strip. The oils ran down her back like tears.

"I'm so sorry, Zo." Joshua gave voice to the way Gryphon felt.

"It's not your fault, Ginger."

She shivered under Gryphon's touch as he placed another strip of cloth on her back. "I'll start a fire," he offered.

Zo nodded, but her eyes stayed frozen on the ground. Her dark hair fell in layers around her face.

"I'll do it!" Joshua rushed outside to gather wood, leaving Gryphon alone with Zo.

"I really am sorry, Zo." Gryphon soaked another strip of cloth before gently placing it on her back. It was becoming easier to say her name.

The girl blinked hard, as if awakening from a serious train of thought. "For what? My back? For murdering the Wolf? For taking me away from … " She wiped fresh tears and dropped her head. "You warned me about my tongue."

Gryphon wished he could explain. Wished he could make some of this—any of this—right. But how could he tell her about the Wolf in the barn without ruining all of his plans? The Wolves were making alliances with the other clans. This was bigger than his unfathomable desire to please Zo. His enemy.

It just was.

Fresh lyrics came to his mind. The melody carrying them was ragged and slow. Pathetic like he was. A song about midnight hair and hypnotizing blue eyes.

Ajax was right. He was weak.

[•]

Zo spent two long nights sitting on a bench with her head resting on a table for support. She fell in and out of sleep, usually waking to the sound of her own screams. Nightmares of Tess and the Gate Master filled her mind. Sometimes the

Seer, with her dark beady eyes, would stare down at her and say, "I can still see you, Wolf." At other times her dreams took her to a room without doors or windows. Just her and her guilt filling up every inch of space.

She knew it wasn't reasonable to take blame for what had happened to her parents, or Tess, or even Gabe. They had all made their decisions or been affected by the hatred of others. While her waking brain comprehended such logic, her subconscious disagreed. Then there was the added pressure of trying to escape. Plus the confusion that accompanied trying to help the mysterious Ram carrying a Nameless babe.

Zo closed her eyes to attempt sleep when the door to the Nameless quarters flew open and banged against the wall. "Zo, we need you!" Gryphon stood with his mess brother, Ajax, bouncing impatiently at his side.

"What is it?" she stammered, raising one hand to block out the blinding light of Gryphon's torch.

"Just bring your kit and come."

The fresh scabs on her back tugged and split as she obeyed the order. Once outside, Gryphon grabbed Zo's hand and raced after Ajax into the darkness. Every footstep sparked fire to her back, but Zo didn't bother complaining.

"Not much farther." Gryphon seemed to read her mind. She wanted to collapse from pain.

They approached a farm set back in the trees. The flicker of candlelight pulsed from the windows of the small house, making it seem alive from a distance. By the time they reached the porch, warm trails of blood rolled down Zo's back. She swayed and Gryphon had to catch her before she fell walking up the wooden steps.

Ajax turned on them both before they could enter the house. "No one can know what you're about to see, Gryph." He ran a shaking hand through his hair and paced. "Can you trust her not to talk?" He eyed Zo.

Gryphon didn't hesitate. "She's safe, Jax."

His expression made it clear that Ajax wouldn't have trusted Zo to sweep his tent, but he dropped his head and ushered them inside.

The metallic smell of blood, earth, and a hint of parsnips hung in the room. Zo turned to Ajax with wide eyes. "Where's the baby?" She had helped her mother deliver enough newborns to recognize the unique smell.

Ajax led her through a short hallway. "How did you—"

"Birth smells the same outside the Gate." She should have guarded her tongue, but the pain from her back muddled her resolve.

Ajax spared her a furrowed glance before pulling her into a dimly lit bedroom. In true Ram fashion, the walls and floors were bare with the exception of a lone log framed bed and a few baskets in the corner. On the bed, a pale young woman held an infant to her chest. Both mother and baby seemed to be asleep.

"She delivered so fast. I didn't have time to call for a healer," said Ajax.

The sleeping mother stirred and Ajax was instantly at her side, smoothing the hair from her face. "I've brought the Nameless healer, Sara."

The scowl Zo usually received from the women inside the Gate was notably absent from the young woman's hopeful face. "Please, tell me. Can you help my son?" She handed the swaddled bundle to Zo.

Zo accepted him with trembling hands. "May I sit?" She was still shaken from her run, and the sting in her back was almost blinding.

"Of course." The desperation in the woman's voice frightened her.

Zo peeled back the blankets to find a pink baby boy. Thick dark hair curled atop his head. There was a thin gap separating the upper lip on one side. It ran half the distance to the nose. In her training, Zo had seen two similar cases where the baby's nose was deformed in the process and the fissure extended all the way through the nose to the roof of the mouth. This didn't look so bad, but there was no way to tell without feeling inside the cavity.

"I need to wash my hands to examine him properly." She handed the warm, sleeping bundle back to his mother. Gryphon kept a firm grip above her elbow as he silently led her to the kitchen area to wash in a basin of cold water. When they came back, Sara hissed something under her breath, a vow of some sort. Ajax draped his arms around his wife and child and spoke soft words of comfort, almost too quiet for Zo to hear. He kissed her forehead and stepped back as Zo and Gryphon entered the room.

Zo accepted the baby again from his mother and instantly started humming a soothing lullaby as she used her finger to rub the infant's upper lip. The baby, still fast asleep, opened his mouth to suck. Zo slipped her finger in the child's mouth and felt for a break in the roof of the mouth.

She smiled relief when her fingers met a firm upper palate. The baby would be fine.

"Sometimes when babies are growing in the womb the lip doesn't come together and form properly. When that happens there is often a hole in the roof of the mouth that makes it difficult for the child to eat and drink."

Sara's eyes grew wide.

Zo put a reassuring hand out to the new mother but flinched at her own boldness. She cleared her throat. "Your son doesn't have that problem. I've seen a procedure to correct the lip. He's going to be just fine."

Sara gripped her arm. "Can you fix his lip?"

The baby stirred and Zo gently rocked him. "I can try. But the surgery is too dangerous for a newborn. You'll have to wait until he's at least a few months old."

"A few months?" Sara looked up to Ajax, wild fear making her eyes double in size. "Oh no, Ajax. No." She burst into tears. The strong warrior dropped to his knees and rested his head in his wife's lap. They wept together openly.

Zo looked up into Gryphon's stricken face. "I don't understand," she said. "The boy will be fine."

Gryphon walked over to Ajax and rested a hand on his shoulder. "You're sure no one knows she delivered?"

Ajax pushed the moisture from his face. "Positive. My Nameless were in the fields. When I saw his misshapen lip, I didn't dare send for a healer from the Medica."

"Then there is still hope for the child, as long as the Seer isn't suspicious and we make a good show of the burial."

"But what will happen when he's well? I can't present a two year old to the Horn and claim him as my legitimate son. Without passing the birth rituals he cannot be a part of our clan."

Zo handed the baby back to his mother. She stood but kept

one hand on the bed frame for support. She shouldn't draw attention to herself, but she had to make sense of the madness. "The child is healthy. Why would he not pass your rituals?"

"Because he is not perfect." Gryphon's clipped tone left no room for argument.

"What will they do to him?"

Gryphon took hold of her arm and led her from the room. He paused at the door and looked back to Sara and Ajax. "Don't let anyone know she's delivered, Jax. We'll find a way to make this work. Nothing will happen to your son."

"Thank you, brother." But Ajax didn't sound reassured.

"I'll think of something," said Gryphon.

Once they were outside, Zo yanked her arm from Gryphon's grasp. "What will the Ram do to that baby, Gryphon?" It sounded like a threat, even to her own ears.

Gryphon helped her down the trail, traveling at a slow pace for her sake. "There is a reason the Ram are known for their warriors, Zo."

She waved away his words. "Yeah, because you train your children like animals and have no regard for anything that doesn't involve bloodshed."

She covered her mouth with both hands. Gryphon had been tolerant, but she'd finally crossed the line. He raised his hand and Zo closed her eyes and flinched, ready for the beating she knew was coming.

Nothing happened.

She opened her eyes to find Gryphon holding back the branch of a tree she hadn't noticed before. His lips were screwed into a knot and heavy lines streaked his brow. She stepped away but her foot caught on something in the darkness and she fell with a near silent cry to the ground. Several scabs on her back ripped open in the process.

Gryphon bent to help her up. "I have no intention of hurting you, Zo. You should know that by now."

Zo's shirt was damp with blood from her back. Gryphon must have noticed because he wiped his hand on his pants. "I guess I can't blame you for being afraid of me."

"What will happen to the baby?" she persisted.

Gryphon sighed. "If a newborn doesn't pass inspection, it is taken outside the Gate. The Ram don't kill the child, but they also can't protect or care for it either. Only the healthy earn the right to citizenship in the Gate." His jaw flexed in the torchlight, his eyes pinched and he looked away from her.

"Who takes care of the infant outside of the Gate? Is it left to the Nameless?" Zo could sense his answer, but it was too horrible to be true. Not even the Ram would banish an infant. Would they?

His silence confirmed her fears. "Gryphon, we can't let that baby die!"

"I know!" he shouted, and she cowered away from him again out of humiliating instinct. "I'll think of something." His Adam's apple jumped up and down as he swallowed.

Zo didn't sleep the rest of the night. Up until now, she had felt the distance between her and Tess—though painfully difficult—was something of a protection to her sister.

After tonight that sense of safety was stripped from her. Zo couldn't handle another night wondering about Tess. Not after learning that her sister's innocence would not save her any more than it would that newborn. There was only one clear course of action ...

Zo had to smuggle Tess away from the Nameless' barracks and find some way to leave the Gate before anything happened to her, even if it meant forsaking the Cause.

Chapter 25

Before the sun rose in the morning, with almost no sleep, and his leg still healing from his wounds from the Wolf, Gryphon hurried to find the Historian. He didn't know exactly what he planned to say, he only hoped his instinct about her was right.

Would she help Sara and Ajax and their new baby? It was a big risk, but what other option did he have?

He rehearsed his excuse for visiting with Barnabas' grandmother over and over again. No doubt the guards would find his request even more baffling than when he came to meet with Barnabas himself. Just as he made the final turn down the road that led to the chief's home he stopped dead at the sight of the old woman sitting with her thin legs crossed on the ground. In her hands she held a small pouch of, what appeared to be, dark sand. She scooped up a handful of the interesting powder and let it fall back into the bag in thin streams between her knobby fingers.

"There you are." She didn't look at all surprised to see him, as if she'd been waiting there all night.

Gryphon pulled off his heavy cloak and flung it around the Historian's shoulders. "You must be freezing." She swatted away his concern as he helped her stand. The cloak dragged at least a foot on the ground.

"Well, it took you long enough." She looked over Gryphon's shoulder and smiled. "Come on out, young warrior. You are welcome to join us."

Gryphon whipped around to find a sheepish Joshua with bright cheeks step out from behind a nearby tree. The tip of his nose matched the flame of his red hair

"I'm sorry, Gryph. I just want to know what's going on."

The Historian hushed the boy and took his arm. "He doesn't mind," she answered for Gryphon.

"How did you know I was coming?" Gryphon still couldn't grasp the absurdity of the situation.

The old woman's eyes sparkled and she winked at Joshua, patting the top of his hand. "Call it a hunch."

The Historian led them silently through the town, past the platform in the square and through the maze of buildings until they reached a little, rundown shed at the edge of the forest.

"You leave for an excursion tomorrow." She unlocked the door with withered hands.

Gryphon didn't bother asking her how she knew about the secret excursion downstream to take out the Allied Camp. The old woman, with hair so white it almost glowed, seemed to know everything that happened inside the Gate. Not unlike the current Seer.

"Does your Nameless healer know you've uncovered her secret?"

Gryphon blanched. "How did you know about Zo and the bottles?" Gryphon's ears burned at his use of Zo's name. Joshua beamed.

"I've mastered harvesting information for most of my life, Striker." She looked down at the little bag in her hands. "Among other things." The lock of the door finally turned. "I might be old, but I still know what happens inside the Gate."

Gryphon felt completely naked with his treason exposed. "I know I should have reported her right away, but it didn't seem ... *right.*"

"You have no need to fear me, son of Troy. I have kept your secret, and will continue to do so." The Historian led him into the damp shed and lit a well-used candle on a worktable covered with odd glass instruments, scales, and bottles of strange liquids and powders. A sour smell burned the inside of Gryphon's nose.

"You have not sought me out to discuss the healer." She left her statement open to let Gryphon explain himself.

Gryphon paused to organize the mountain of questions rushing through his head. How did she know about the Wolf in his barn? Why hadn't she turned him in for treason? Who was that Nameless in the woods at Eva's engagement ceremony? And most of all, how could he help save Ajax's son?

For some reason, he never considered that she might turn his information about the new baby over to the Seer. He supposed he trusted her. But what if he was wrong?

"I know someone." He paused, unsure of how to proceed.

"Congratulations." The corner of her mouth rose as she measured out a small amount of liquid into a vial the size of

Gryphon's pinkie finger.

Joshua laughed, but one look from Gryphon silenced him.

"Well, you see. I need to help them with … The nature of the situation is … "

The Historian held up a hand. "May I tell you a story?"

Gryphon swallowed his angst and nodded.

"Generations ago, there was a mighty swordsman who loved a woman very much. When he approached her kingly father to ask for her hand in marriage, the wise king asked a simple question, 'How much do you love her?'

The man proceeded to express his feelings, comparing his love to mountains and great waters, treasures, and sky. The king listened intently and when the young man finished he was breathless from his oaths and speeches.

"The king had seen a great deal of the world. Had lived long enough to see past a man's infatuation to his heart. Atop his golden throne, the king nodded. 'Words are the trick of men. If you love her like you say, you will prove your words in a quest.'"

Gryphon cleared his throat. "I'm sorry, I think you might misunderstand my intentions, Historian. I am not in love."

The old woman stopped her stirring and gave him a look that made the great Striker blanch.

Gryphon bowed his head. "Sorry, please continue."

The Historian took a rattling breath and closed her eyes to continue. "The king first instructed the young man to sell everything he owned: his house, his land, his animals, everything but the clothes on his back and the boots on his feet. The young man, determined to win his love, obeyed. When he returned to the king, the king was pleased. 'Now,' the king replied, 'you must find a crucible and fill it to the brim with your tears. When that is done, you must travel until the land meets the sea and back without spilling a drop.'

The young man grew angry at the impossible request, but left, determined to have his bride at any cost."

Gryphon shifted the weight in his legs. How was this foolish story meant to help him with his own problems?

The Historian continued. "He filled his cup to the brim with his own tears of frustration and longing then set out on his journey over the difficult terrain and violent weather of the season, all without losing a single drop. When he returned to the king, his muscles ached and his hand shook as if the cup carried a great weight. The king examined the cup then drank the man's tears."

"Disgusting!" said Joshua.

"But the king wasn't quite satisfied. 'You have done well, but if you love my daughter you will perform one final task.'

The young swordsman's head hung low, but he raised it enough to meet the king's gaze. 'I have sold everything I own. I have taken an impossible journey. What more can you ask of me?'"

Gryphon found himself nodding his head in agreement. He couldn't imagine ever loving someone enough to go through so much trouble.

"The king motioned for one of his men to bring a heavy jeweled blade. 'Step forward.' The king set the tip of the blade on a wooden chopping block. 'Put out your right arm.'

The young man eyed the blade with fear, but only after a moment's hesitation, obeyed. His right arm was his best fighting arm, possibly his greatest physical possession. He closed his eyes, and tried to picture the woman he loved in his mind, repeating her name over and over again.

The king raised the sword, it sliced through the air and…" The Historian stopped and yawned. "The rest of the story doesn't matter."

"What happened?" Gryphon and Joshua spoke at the same time.

The woman shook her head and sighed. "I have information that can save your friend's baby, Striker. The question is, what are you willing to sacrifice to keep those around you safe?"

Gryphon immediately thought of the shield hanging in his family home. His desire to restore his family's honor. For so long it had been the most important thing in his life. The aspiration that eclipsed any other. Could he sacrifice that desire to save his friend?

The Historian patted him on the arm. "You've answered my question." She took a pinch of the powder she'd been mixing and set it on a metal dish.

"Tell me what I need to do," said Gryphon.

The Historian looked at him through the corner of her eye then poured a drop of liquid from the thin vial onto the small mound of powder. Light and heat exploded from the dish, causing Gryphon to yank the old woman away protectively. But the fire left as quickly as it came.

The Historian's face was black with ash in places and her wispy hair was singed, but she couldn't seem to stop the spread of a smile from lighting her face. "There are things happening inside the Gate, son of Troy. Great movements, or sparks, forming under your very nose, even in your very home. Imbalances will be restored. It will not be long before your own arm is set to the chopping block, Striker. When that time comes, you will have to decide if the people you love and the convictions of your heart are worthy of the sacrifice."

[•]

Zo's entire body ached as she slid out of bed the following night. A long, low creak sounded throughout the Nameless quarters as Zo opened the door. She didn't worry about waking Markus and the other Nameless who shared her room. After a hard day's work they dropped like stones into their straw beds.

She couldn't handle another night away from Tess, not after holding that helpless Ram baby in her arms. Zo used the thick forest for cover as she paralleled the path that connected with the main road. Her ears strained for the sound of footsteps on gravel, but she heard nothing other than the occasional twig breaking under her own foot. With only a sliver of moonlight for guidance, she made it to the Nameless' barracks in less than an hour.

As usual, no one watched the doors of the Nameless' barracks. And it was no wonder. Who would dare defy the Ram? And where would a Nameless go if he left?

Zo was the exception.

She stepped inside and was assaulted by the smell. Body odor and rotting teeth mixed with boiled egg. Surely it hadn't smelled so bad a few days ago. Zo covered her mouth and moved along the narrow aisle to find Tess' bed.

"Tess?" Zo sat on the edge of the bed and gently shook her sleeping sister. "Tess, it's me. Wake up."

Tess moaned then sat bolt upright. "Zo!"

Zo clasped her hand over Tess' mouth. "Outside," she

whispered, leading Tess to the door.

Away from the stench of the barracks, Zo pulled Tess into a hug and held her until the screaming cuts on her back couldn't handle anymore. "I'm so sorry, mouse."

Tess wept. Every little sob was a knife to Zo's heart. "Gabe … stabbed … and then they took you." She hiccupped into Zo's chest. "I … don't understand."

Zo pulled Tess to sit in her lap on the ground, ignoring the tugging pain in her back. She rocked them back and forth, stroking Tess' hair and humming a lullaby their mother used to sing. Tess wouldn't remember it, but for Zo it was an important piece of her shattered life. One of the few things she got to take with her after the raid.

After a while, Tess interrupted. "Who is the bald man we met at the gate?"

Any comfort Zo had found in that moment evaporated. "The Gate Master?"

"He visited me in the fields today. Said you and he were friends and that I could come and live with him if I wanted."

Zo swallowed her own tongue.

"I told him, 'No, thank you.'"

Zo cleared her throat, forcing her voice to sound casual. "And wh … what did he say?"

"He just smiled and went to talk to the man at the big house."

Zo shook her head. "You're never going to see that man again, Tess. I'm taking you with me tonight. Then we're going to find a way outside the Gate. I promise."

Instead of looking comforted, Tess' body went rigid in Zo's arms, her eyes wide, her finger trembling as it pointed behind Zo. Then she screamed.

Chapter 26

Gryphon sat on his porch, digesting the riddled words of
the Historian when the door to the Nameless quarters
squeaked and a slight figure emerged. Instead of calling out
to Zo, he pushed off from the porch and followed to see if she
planned to drop more bottles.

The thought of her betrayal affected him more than it
should have. She was only a spy doing what she'd been trained
to do. So why did he take her actions personally? He'd been
kind to her, hadn't he? If he was honest with himself, he'd
foolishly thought that she would resign herself to his home
and abandon her mission. But now, seeing her deft movements
through the brush, he realized just how naive he'd been.

When she turned from the path that led to the river, a flood
of relief cleansed his anger. If she wasn't dropping bottles
then where was she going? He continued to follow her at a

safe distance until she reached one of the Seer's Nameless' barracks for slaves not assigned to a Ram family.

Zo slipped inside the door and returned moments later with a young girl in tow. Even in the darkness, it only took one glance to realize the relation. Same pronounced cheekbones, same almond eyes. If their looks hadn't proved their relation, their actions and words did.

Zo mothered the girl with such attention, absorbed the child's pain with such emotion, that Gryphon's throat constricted and he had to look away. Why had the Wolves allowed this young girl to enter the Gate? Zo was one thing, but a child!

He needed to hit something.

The child spoke about Gate Master Leon. Gryphon moved closer to catch every word, to catch a better glimpse of Zo's silhouette in the moonlight. But, somehow, the child spotted him in the trees.

"Run! He'll kill you, just like Gabe. Please!"

Zo pulled her sister to the ground and covered her mouth. "Quiet. Someone will hear you!" she shouted a whisper. Zo stood in front of her sister and stepped into a sliver of light. Gryphon could just make out the pained expression on her face. "I wasn't running away. She's my sister. I had to see if she was all right."

Gryphon looked at the pair through heavy-lidded eyes. Just when he thought things couldn't get more complicated, life slapped him in the face with one more obstacle. One more test of loyalty that he would fail.

Zo stared at the ground in submission. "I know it's not my place to ask, but ... " Even in the semi-darkness he could see her lower lip tremble as she inhaled a long shaky breath. "I can't leave her here alone."

Gryphon's heart contracted at the pathetic scene before him. But he couldn't bring himself to say the words she wanted to hear. The Seer kept careful track of all the Nameless inside the Gate. His home would be the first place she would look once the girl came up missing. Besides, Gate Master Leon already loathed Gryphon for taking Zo. It would be foolish to provoke him further. The only thing worse than an enemy outside the Gate was an enemy inside the Gate. Especially one with so much influence.

The image of the Gate Master caressing Zo's face only to use those same slimy hands to strike her later made him waver. The man wasn't used to being denied. Gryphon had overheard enough of the sisters' conversation to know that this frightened little girl would pay for the Gate Master's disappointment.

He'd seen it before.

"No one can know."

Zo took two steps toward him, one hand outstretched as if she might touch his chest. Gryphon's breath sped to dangerous levels. Dangerous because he knew in that moment he was just as foolish as the Wolf had been back in that cave. He would do anything for this girl if it meant filling the vacancy in her lifeless eyes.

He turned away with balled fists and headed home. The Wolf sisters followed, quiet as shadows. It felt like they'd been gone a lifetime before the forest opened to Gryphon's pastures. At the door of the Nameless' quarters he pointed to Zo's sister. "Don't let anyone see her. Not even the other Nameless. Keep her hidden in the blankets until all of the workers leave. I'll find a better place for her in the morning."

"What about the barn?" Zo offered, pointing to the building only fifty paces away where the Wolf was kept, bound and gagged.

"Do as I say!" Gryphon chided. He wanted to hate this girl for what she'd done to him. Emasculating him from the day they met.

Zo nodded and pushed Tess inside the door. She followed but stopped halfway through and turned back. Gryphon could see the shimmer of a tear roll down the healer's cheek. "Thank you."

His fingers tingled. He ached to reach out and capture the tear. To cup her tempting cheek in his palm. The sensation lasted long after she left him standing alone outside the door.

What was he thinking? She was a Nameless spy working to destroy his people! He shook his head and slogged off toward the house. Gryphon, the fearless Striker, was losing a battle to his greatest enemy.

Himself.

Nothing was worse than an enemy inside the Gate.

[◊]

Zo eyed a little cellar that was only accessible through a narrow gap in the floorboards. She'd never noticed the hollow wood under her feet. Gryphon was right, this was better than the old abandoned barn. No one would find Tess here and she would be safe and free from hard labor.

Tess eyed the hole with less optimism. "It's dark. Spiders like the dark."

"I have some herbs we can burn to keep the spiders away," said Zo, pulling back a few strands of Tess' light hair.

Zo looked up to find Gryphon's golden brown eyes on her. The line of his broad jaw cast a shadow on his neck. His chin carried a slight dimple she hadn't noticed before. "This is only temporary," he said. "At least until the Seer is satisfied we don't have her."

"How long will that be?" Tess still couldn't look at Gryphon, even when she complained. In her eyes, Gryphon would only be the man who killed Gabe. Nothing more. She was too young to appreciate the complexity of the situation.

But then maybe Zo was too.

"Probably several days," said Gryphon. He turned to Zo. "I'm leaving in a few hours for a brief excursion, but I should be back before nightfall. Don't let anyone find her while I'm gone."

[◆]

Zo refused to feel guilty as she ran to the river when Gryphon left. It was her job to inform the Allies of any movement at the Gate. This was what she had risked everything to do. No matter how generous Gryphon had been to rescue Tess from the Nameless' barracks, he was still the enemy.

Right?

She watched a bottle get absorbed into the steady current and sighed. She didn't have much to offer Commander Laden and the Allies downriver. Gryphon and his mess would leave soon. She didn't know the nature of his mission, but the fact that there was some movement seemed worthy of mention.

She wrote briefly about the Nameless' rebellion, intentionally leaving out her reckless promise to help a pregnant Ram woman escape. She ended the missive by reemphasizing that the Ram planned to relocate south before winter this year.

Living with an actual Ram soldier on the outskirts of the city made things both better and worse for Zo. Better, because, like today, she noticed when Gryphon left on excursion, warning the Allies to have scouts follow them, worse because it made reaching the heart of the city, where all the tactical decisions were made, nearly impossible. Still, she had to confirm her suspicions about the Ram's relocation. She couldn't shake the feeling that the Valley of Wolves was the targeted destination.

Zo dropped her last bottle into the rushing river and settled to rest against a nearby mulberry tree. The sound of water always brought back memories of Gabe. Not many people found tromping through a freezing river invigorating. Gabe had. The only thing he liked better was throwing Zo over his shoulder and dunking her with him. Tess would laugh and Zo would hold his head under for as long as she could before marching out to find dry clothes and a fire.

At least he died fighting. Gryphon had given him that small gift. Zo ripped apart a piece of newly shed bark. The wood crumbled in a satisfying way in her hands while a hundred questions zigzagged across the streets of her mind.

Zo shook her head, blinking away tears of guilt.

If she had accepted Gabe from the beginning, she likely wouldn't have come on this suicide mission. Tess wouldn't have followed her into the Gate. Gabe wouldn't have brought his men so close to the wall to wait for her. He'd still be alive, resting his lean muscled arms around her on cold spring nights like this one. Promising there wouldn't be another raid. Vowing to protect her and Tess.

Zo wiped at tears with her forearm and laughed. It wasn't a healthy laugh—the kind that begins in your stomach and rolls out unaffected. It was dark delirium, without the slightest bit of mirth attached. Hollow.

It wasn't reasonable to think of such things. Zo's hatred of the Ram clouded every other emotion. She could never have been happy with Gabe. He wasn't broken like she was. He could have given a woman everything she could ever want or need from a man. His whole self.

Zo didn't have room enough to love him and hate the Ram. Hers was an all-consuming hatred. The kind held until reaching the grave. Zo had been broken so long, she didn't know how to fix herself. She didn't care to fix herself.

Run bottles. Run.

Chapter 27

It didn't take long for Gryphon and his mess to find remnants of the small enemy outpost the Wolf prisoner had mentioned. The grass lay flattened where tents once sat. A circle of hollow logs surrounded charred ground where a fire had been. Gryphon walked to the bank of the river where a small, man-made dam and rigging of nets had been hastily destroyed.

"Someone warned them," said Zander as he squatted near the fresh tracks.

"Scouts?" asked one of Gryphon's mess brothers.

Zander rested his thick forearms on his knees, still crouched on the ground. "S'possible." He turned to Gryphon and narrowed his gaze. "But my gut disagrees."

Gryphon's hands turned cold. Rushing water tugged on what remained of the wrecked nets. The stale air tasted wrong. He jogged over to the ashy circle where the campfire had been.

"Warm," he said, more to himself than anyone else.

"A scout couldn't have given them more than a half hour's notice. We're only five miles from the Gate," said Ajax.

Gryphon slowly rose to his feet, his golden eyes unfocused. He refused to believe Zo dropped bottles this morning before they left. She wouldn't. Not after he'd just taken her sister in.

But he had mentioned that he was leaving …

Gryphon looked around the small clearing and wrinkled his brow. "Something's wrong here." He marched to the edge of the abandoned camp and scanned the thick trees. The rest of the men followed his example, fanning out to form a standard search along the perimeter.

A deafening blast erupted from the camp as one of the hollow logs exploded. Lethal flying darts of debris soared in every direction. One of Gryphon's mess brothers cried out in pain.

Gryphon spotted the distant figure of a man through the thick forest.

"Jax!" he called, through the chaos. His voice sounded muffled in his ears.

Ajax was only a few feet away. "There." He motioned with a slight tilt of his head in the direction where he'd spotted the movement in the forest. Ajax nodded his understanding and the two brothers took off in opposite directions under the cover of the commotion to investigate.

Gryphon ran in a wide arc around the spot where he thought the scout was positioned. Wild rose thorns snagged his pant legs and tore his skin as he silently covered ground. The flower's deadly beauty made him think of Zo. He closed in on the point where he thought his enemy lay hidden and spotted a lone soldier with long black hair braided down the middle of his back. Two feathers hung from the leather band about his neck.

Raven. Low rank. Probably here to report the damage of the blast.

The young soldier carried an unstrung bow in one hand and a hatchet at his hip as he crouched behind the trunk of a tree.

Gryphon couldn't spot Ajax in the dense foliage. Of course, that was the whole point. The man was more panther than human.

Trusting Ajax to be in place, Gryphon picked up a dried stick from the ground and snapped it in two. The Raven whipped around and strung his bow with eerie speed.

Gryphon stepped out from behind his cover and caught the Raven's arrow with his shield. Ajax exploded from the brush and tackled the Raven to the ground. They bound his wrists behind his back and hauled him away without a word. The interrogators would get all the information they needed from this kid. If they were lucky, they might even learn the location of the Raven's grain stores.

As usual, everything boiled down to food. Survival.

Gryphon and Ajax arrived just in time to see Zander remove an inch-thick splinter from their mess brother's calf. He nodded approval when he saw the Raven prisoner. "Let's get back. This wound is going to need stitching."

One of the men mumbled something about Gryphon loaning out his Nameless healer, and everyone chuckled.

"That's enough," said Zander. He pulled his spear from the ground and led the group out of the clearing with a scowl on his face.

The sun was at its highest point in the sky when they reached the Gate. "Hasn't your wife had that baby yet?" One of the mess brothers asked Ajax as Nameless turned the massive wheel and chains to open the gate.

Ajax gave an unsteady laugh. "The healers think she is still several weeks away." He looked at Gryphon and forced a smile.

[♦]

Two days, and the Seer still hadn't come looking for Tess. Meanwhile, Zo's reputation as the Nameless healer spread like wildfire throughout the neighboring homes. Gryphon's mother arranged for slaves to come to Zo in the Nameless' quarters on Gryphon's property. If they couldn't travel, Zo went to them.

Sitting on the edge of her bed, Zo soaked strong-smelling tobacco leaves in boiling water then placed the soggy plants on the swollen ankle of a neighbor's field worker. "It's just a sprain." She wrapped the ankle in linen. "Keep it elevated as often as possible."

"I'll do my best, ma'am." The man must have been in his late forties, but with Nameless it was always hard to tell. The man straightened his tattered shirt and nodded gratefully as he rose to leave. Just as he reached the door, it flung open, banging against the wall. The Nameless field worker fell to the ground, unable to balance himself at the surprise of seeing Gryphon seething in the doorway. The slave covered his head with his arms and whimpered for mercy like he expected a fatal beating.

"Get out." Gryphon barely offered the Nameless a glance.

The man crawled like a frightened spider out the door without looking back.

Zo didn't remember gathering her feet to stand, but her body reacted to Gryphon's scowl. Dark hair fell forward to cover one side of his face. In that moment, she felt she caught a glimpse of what Gryphon's enemies saw in battle. This was not the merciful Gryphon who'd risked his own standing with the Ram to save Tess. This was Gryphon the warrior.

She craned her neck to meet his gaze, refusing to be intimidated. She should have cowered in the corner, but anger was her first language, and she wouldn't back down.

"I could have died today." He pushed air out of his nose, like a bull ready to charge. "Two of my brothers were injured. One seriously."

Zo didn't understand why his anger would be directed at her … unless he knew about the bottles. Again, she should have faked submission, said the right things. But she couldn't.

"My people die every day, Striker. Get over it."

Gryphon growled and grabbed the chair by Zo's bed. He flung it across the room. It connected with the wall and shattered to pieces.

Tess began to cry from her little hole in the floor.

Gryphon looked down at her place in the ground and frowned. The wind of his storm completely vanished. He grabbed the hair above his ears and groaned. "What am I doing?"

He left without another word.

Did he know about the bottles? If so, why had he shown her so much compassion? Why hadn't he stopped her?

No. It was impossible.

Chapter 28

G ryphon took a moment to look around the splintered barn where the Wolf was kept to make sure he was alone. Long grass swayed around him in the morning breeze. He could hear a hundred different rhythms in that sound. A hundred melodies to match them. Most were conflicted, melancholy bits, while others were sweet and docile. Like a soft caress.

The barn reeked of stale urine. Gryphon closed the creaking door behind him and walked across the dilapidated floor carrying a satchel of supplies. The Wolf slept, his bare chest rising and falling in even time. His hair was a nest of muddy blond knots. The beginnings of a beard covered half of his face. After several days of healing, the bandage on his shoulder was finally dry. Thanks to Zo, Gryphon had managed to clean the wound and sew him up the morning after the stabbing.

When Gryphon cut the ropes the Wolf groaned awake.

"Ahhh … finally."

"You stink," said Gryphon tossing him a pair of fresh clothes.

Joshua's knock came right on cue. "I have the bucket." He spilled half of its contents before setting it next to the prisoner. "There's a brick of soap in the bottom. Should be nice and soggy by now."

"How is she?" said the Wolf.

Joshua looked from the Wolf to Gryphon for explanation. "Who … Zo?"

Gryphon rolled his eyes. "They know each other. We practically have our own little Wolf pack staying here on the farm."

Joshua paled. He knew the consequences of harboring one Wolf. "Three Wolves." He let the thought simmer for a while then pointed to their prisoner. "Does Zo know he's alive?"

Gryphon shook his head. "I can't risk her telling anyone."

Joshua swallowed.

The Wolf pushed up to his hands and knees. He worked up a good lather on the bar of soap. "Three?"

"Zo's little sister," Joshua blurted. Gryphon glared his rebuke.

The Wolf washed in something of a daze, seeming barely to notice his two enemies. "You know I could solve all of your problems, right?" He stared past them at the wall. "I could take them with me. Get them back home."

"Where is their family?" Gryphon asked. He knew there was some logic in the Wolf's words, but he needed more time to think things through before making any rash decisions.

"Their mother and father were killed in a raid several years ago." The Wolf stopped scrubbing and looked Gryphon directly in the eyes. "Your people, of course."

Gryphon nodded, his mouth dry. "I see."

The Wolf dressed in fresh clothes and settled back down into a small mound of hay. "I feel human again. Thank you."

Gryphon waved his hand. He didn't want this man's gratitude. Soon this whole ordeal would be over, and he could get back to serving his people with a guilt-free conscience.

The Wolf offered his hands for Joshua to bind him. While the boy worked, the Wolf gave him a few pointers on the proper way to secure the knot. Gryphon shook his head and cast his eyes to the rafters of the barn. The world was backward and upside-down. Every black and white was now a muddy gray.

"You're right, that is better," said Joshua, nodding his head. He tightened the gag covering the Wolf's mouth. "See you tomorrow." The boy waved before shutting the door.

Gryphon locked the door behind them and crossed his arms in front of his chest.

"What?" said Joshua, his hands outstretched in innocence.

"He's not our friend, kid. You know that, right?"

"I'm not an idiot, Gryph. I know what he is."

"Good."

Joshua ran off toward the main road leading into town. "Why the hurry?" Gryphon called after him.

"I want to get home early. Zo's healing a Nameless family this evening. She might need my help," he hollered over his shoulder.

Gryphon's stomach twisted. All he could see was gray.

(•)

On her way back from washing her and Tess' clothes in the nearby stream, Zo spotted Stone in the forest. He held possessively to a girl's hand as they navigated the trees ahead of her. If she didn't know better, she would have thought they were headed right for Gryphon's family land. They stopped just before the forest thinned to fields. The Ram girl knotted her fists into the front of Stone's shirt while he stroked her butchered hair. There was something about this girl that seemed familiar, even though Zo knew she'd never seen her before.

The couple exchanged soft words, indecipherable to Zo. Stone interrupted the girl several times with a kiss on her cheek, her forehead, the tip of her nose. The girl began to cry and Stone dropped to his knees, burying his face into her stomach with his arms locked around her.

The impact of what she saw made Zo forget, just for a minute, the anger and fear that she'd carried around every moment since entering the Gate. Seeing these two completely different people so much in love was like seeing the impossible in action. She found herself aching for them—not just Stone, but the Ram girl as well.

Strange.

Zo took a step closer and Stone, with some crazy extra sense, turned his head and pushed the girl behind him in the same instant. His feral features transformed to relief at the sight of Zo.

He led the young woman to Zo's side.

"Eva, this is the healer I was telling you about. She has Striker Gryphon's protection. The Historian says she is the key to getting you out of the Gate."

Zo blanched. She had promised to help, but didn't want them to think she had any influence over Gryphon that wasn't true. "Who is the Historian?"

Eva came forward. Zo didn't remember offering her hand, but before she knew it, Eva had taken it in both of hers. "The Historian is a friend to the resistance. She also happens to be Chief Barnabas' grandmother."

Zo gently pulled her hand away. She flexed her fingers open and shut. "And you trust her?"

Eva shrugged. "We have to. She's been our only hope until you've come along." Eva took a step closer. "People of the rebellion say you are working with others outside the Gate. People who want to help the Nameless."

It wasn't exactly true. The Allies had never focused much on the Nameless slaves of the Ram. But the enemy of the enemy is your friend. Why not enlist the Nameless to help with the Allies? If they somehow managed to escape, they could be a great help to the Cause, maybe the difference between victory and defeat.

"I've been sending them messages, but I don't know how much good has come from it." Zo looked from Stone to Eva and sighed. "I'll do whatever I can to help you. Only don't expect a miracle. I'm stuck inside the Gate, just like you are."

"But the Historian said—"

"She's wrong. I am a slave in Gryphon's household. He has shown me some mercy, but he is not my friend or ally."

Eva's expression faltered, and Zo found herself desperate to say something, anything to give the Ram girl some comfort. "I'll do what I can, but I just can't make you any promises."

The girl rubbed her stomach as she bit into her bottom lip.

"Thank you."

Stone stepped behind the woman he loved and kissed the top of her head. "I'll find a way for us, Eva." He laid his hand over Eva's, still resting on her stomach. "For all of us."

"Let me have a look at that broken arm," said Zo.

Eva slipped out of Stone's embrace. "I have to go check on my sister Sara. She's due to have her baby any moment, and she still won't let anyone near the house."

Eva ran off and Zo stared after her with mouth gaping.

Eva and Sara were sisters! Neither knew of the other's plight.

It took Zo several minutes to digest this new information. She wanted to run to Gryphon and explain the situation, but she still didn't know if he could be trusted. Trying to help a newborn survive the Ram's cruel expectations was one thing. Condoning a relationship between a Nameless and a Ram was quite another.

Chapter 29

Three little girls and two boys, all under the age of ten, huddled around their mother as Zo felt their foreheads. All were hot with sticky sweat. They wheezed through half-open lips, like little birds waiting to be fed. Their large round eyes looked to her with caution, piercing the dimly lit room. Zo wiped her hands on her apron. The youngest boy coughed into his threadbare sleeve. He sounded more goose than child.

"How long have they been breathing like this?" asked Zo.

"Maybe two weeks." The Nameless mother had red, sullen eyes that had clearly not seen sleep for too many nights. The baby in her arms was Zo's biggest concern. She could barely hear its shallow breath; the babe's throat passage was all but closed. Slowly suffocating.

Zo went right to work, enlisting Joshua and the oldest girl to help grind ingredients while Zo took the baby from her mother.

Breathe. She hummed another of her mother's lullabies while rubbing healing oils on the little chest. *Breathe, my sweet.* She bounced the child in her arms and applied more oil to the baby's neck. *Release and breathe.*

If only every healing came so naturally. How could Zo not love this little angel? She rocked and loved the child until it passed into an easy slumber. Already its airway had opened considerably.

"Thank you! Oh bless you and thank you!" The mother cried without shame. Her sobs were interrupted by her own heavy wheezing.

"I think you're next, ma'am." Zo took the woman's arm and led her to a straw-stuffed mattress.

"No. My children. I'm fine."

Zo held up a hand. "You need to sleep. How will you care for them if you're not well? I doubt I'll be allowed to come another night."

The woman didn't fight her further. Zo administered to the worn woman who fell asleep halfway through the treatments. She, like the others, would recover with rest and medicine.

After several hours of working, Joshua slumped forward in a chair. "Go home, Ginger," said Zo.

"No." He yawned. "I'm not leaving you alone."

"You have training in the morning and you need your rest. I'm almost done here. I know the way back."

"You sure?"

Zo nodded while humming the simple healing melody her mother had taught her. In truth it would be hours before she finished. There were still two children she needed to work on. "Just tell Tess not to wait up for me."

"I will." Joshua came over and kissed Zo's cheek like a good boy kissing his mother goodnight. "Hurry home, Zo."

When the door shut behind Joshua, Zo touched her cheek where he had kissed her. "Good night," she whispered to no one.

[●]

Walking home that night, Zo's hands burned. Some of the oils tended to irritate if used in excess. A cool wind rolled over her body as she walked under the bright stars. She found herself singing lightly, swinging her medical kit as if it were a basket of flowers in summer.

She'd done some good tonight. Made a real difference in someone's life. Those children would survive and have a mother to watch them grow up. All because of her knowledge. A gift from her own mother.

Maybe this was what she was meant to do: help the Nameless inside the Gate! A sense of power surged throughout her body, lifting a fraction of the darkness of her past. Maybe she did have a purpose beyond this suicide mission. She could help people.

Zo turned left onto the main road and practically ran into a tall figure with a terrifyingly familiar bald head and popping eyes.

"I must be doing something right." The Gate Master grabbed the collar of her shirt before she could escape. "I was just on my way to visit you, and here you come to me instead. How fortuitous."

An explosion of panic expanded from Zo's heart throughout her whole body. She dropped her kit in the dirt. The Gate Master at night. Alone on an empty road. No one to hear her screams.

"The Seer wanted to come in the morning, but I thought it would be better to surprise you. Wouldn't want to give you time to hide your little sister." He pulled Zo to him, whipping her like a length of rope, and placed his hands on her lower back. He licked his lips. "Surprise." His rotten breath made a stream of bile jump up her throat.

"My sister lives in the Nameless' barracks, sir." She turned her head and grimaced as his lips grazed her neck, just below the ear.

He laughed, his hot breath a poisonous vapor of warning. "Fine. Lie, if you think it will buy you time. If I don't find her tonight, the Seer will in the morning. Nothing happens inside the Gate that she or her spies don't see." His hands moved to Zo's rib cage. "Nothing." He kissed the corner of her lips.

Stop! She screamed inside. In her mind she raked her long nails across his face, gouged out his protuberant eyes, spit down his throat. In her mind she took the knife from his belt and thrust it into his cold heart. Once. Twice. A thousand times.

Outside she was a perfect statue. It was the only way to survive. For Tess. For the Nameless. For the Cause.

The Gate Master pulled her closer still, pressing her body to his. He kissed her again, this time finding her full lips. "You. Are. Mine." He grabbed her by the waist and threw her several feet into the thick trunk of a tree. Her head cracked against a branch. Blood ran from the corner of her mouth after she bit off a piece of her own tongue.

He charged with all his Ram speed to tackle her to the ground.

"Stop!" called a wild, deep voice.

The Gate Master turned his rage on a dark figure in the road. She didn't even see him reach for the daggers in his hands. It was as if they just appeared. Zo heard fists connect with flesh as the two men engaged, but didn't bother to watch the fray. She crawled away as fast as her throbbing head allowed. Several stitches on her stomach were torn open. Blood soaked into Mrs. Drea's old dress.

Men shouted over the pounding in her head. Zo was too frazzled to understand what they were saying. She found a good tree fifteen yards from the road and climbed until the branches were barely thick enough to support her weight.

[•]

"Yield!" said Gryphon, forcing his knee deeper into the Gate Master's spine while stretching back the man's arms.

The Gate Master growled something incoherent. That was good enough for Gryphon. He released his superior officer and climbed to his feet.

"I could have your hands chopped off at the wrists," Master Leon raged.

Gryphon was still too heated to say what he should. "Not for self-defense, *Sir*. You attacked me." Gryphon couldn't stop seeing Zo's body connect with the tree. The fear in her face as Master Leon charged.

The Gate Master stepped closer, his boot inches from Gryphon's, and thrust a fat finger into his chest. "You were in my business."

Gryphon leaned into his superior's finger. His voice could barely be heard over the wind. "The girl *is* my business, Sir.

She belongs to me."

A slow smile spread across the Gate Master's face. Gryphon felt the hair on his neck raise. "The healer is yours, but the little sister is mine. I've come to collect her."

"I don't know what you're talking about."

The Gate Master raised his hand to silence Gryphon. "You're losing your edge, soldier. When the Seer comes tomorrow, produce the child." He took several steps away then turned. The same dangerous smile plastered to his face was made worse by the harsh shadows of night. "The healer might live in your household, but she belongs to the Ram." Gryphon could translate that easy enough. *"She might be yours, but I'll still have my portion."*

Gryphon shuddered and stepped off the trail in search of Zo. He found her clinging to a high branch in a tree. Her almond eyes were closed. Her breath caught as she tried to calm her nerves. Even though the wind had died down, the leaves on her branch shook as she trembled.

"You can come down now."

She opened her eyes slowly, like the sun takes its time cresting a horizon. When she recognized Gryphon she didn't speak, but started to climb down with sticky, choppy movements.

"Slowly," he said when she almost stumbled. She winced from pain as she moved. The poor creature had endured so much. When she came within reach, he offered his hand. To his surprise, she practically fell into his arms.

He set her on the ground and without thinking, pulled her into an embrace. She hesitated then leaned into his chest. He rested his chin on her head and rubbed warmth back into her arms. She was fragile. Like brittle glass that might break into a hundred pieces and slice him open if he wasn't careful. What could he say to fix what had just happened? Nothing sounded quite right in his mind. So he held her.

Until she shoved him away. "Why did you do that?" she hissed.

Gryphon felt like he'd swallowed his tongue.

"Why did you stop him?" She covered her face with her hands. "At least it would have been over."

Gryphon shook his head. Surely he'd misheard her.

"Men like that are in it for the hunt. Every time you get in his way he'll only try that much harder. It will be worse next time."

"He hasn't ever … " for some reason Gryphon couldn't finish the question. "Has he?"

Zo stared down the road, holding one hand to her stomach. "Does it really matter?"

A lion roared in Gryphon's chest. For some reason beyond his understanding it mattered very much. Too much. But there was something in the way she avoided his eyes, something about the shy set of her jaw that made him think she'd escaped Gate Master Leon's clutches so far.

"That's why you always caked mud on your face, isn't it?"

Zo bit her bottom lip and gave a quick nod.

The fabric to cover her silk hair, the oversized clothing that made a mystery of her pleasant figure. It all made sense to Gryphon now. He was blind not to see it sooner. She wouldn't have lasted long without those simple defenses.

"He can't touch you now, Zo. I won't let him."

Zo stopped walking. She peered at him from the corner of

her eyes. Untrusting. "Why, because I belong to you?"

Gryphon winced. The suggestion made his cheeks warm. He looked away, grateful for the cover of night. "Despite what you think, I am not a monster."

"No." She picked up her kit from the ground and wiped blood from the corner of her mouth. "You are a Ram."

Chapter 30

Zo had said the hateful words aloud because in her heart she couldn't quite form them. Gryphon was an unfathomable being. A creature of his own mold. The Ram uniform didn't fit a man who preferred using his blade to whittle designs into pieces of wood. He'd done so much for her and Tess. His mere presence tonight meant that he had been on his way to check on her.

Zo shook the fog from her thoughts. A wolf dressed in sheep's clothing was still a wolf.

The irony of the comparison just angered her further. Wasn't she the Wolf wearing the wool of the Ram? The world didn't make sense.

"When do you leave again?" she asked, partly because she could pass along that information to Commander Laden, partly because she didn't want him to go.

Gryphon scowled. "Why do you want to know?"

"Just thinking about Tess. When you leave, what will keep the Gate Master from finding her?"

Gryphon kicked a rock off the dark road. "I have a plan."

They turned off the road and up a dirt trail. Zo's head throbbed as she shivered from the night chill. They reached the Nameless' quarters on Gryphon's property. The crooked door did little to block the sounds of whispering coming from inside.

Someone's in the room with Tess! She tugged on Gryphon's arm. Both of her hands could hardly fit around the circumference of his bicep.

Gryphon pushed Zo behind him and opened the door.

The floorboards that covered Tess' underground hiding place sat in a disorderly pile. Joshua and Tess were hunched over an oil lamp while the rest of the room slept. They seemed to be in the middle of a great, whispered debate because Tess had on her "argument" face.

"What's going on here?" Gryphon and Zo spoke at the exact same time. Zo almost laughed. Almost.

"I came to tell Tess not to wait up for Zo," Joshua said, looking mostly at Gryphon.

"You left me hours ago," said Zo.

Joshua shrugged his shoulders.

"It wasn't his fault! *I* had questions," said Tess.

"Lots of questions." Joshua rubbed his eyes.

Tess smacked his arm with the back of her hand. "I wasn't the only one."

"Enough." Gryphon pinched the bridge of his nose. "I have to get you two out of here. The Seer is coming in the morning. She knows when people lie."

Joshua jumped to his feet. "The Seer? Coming here?

Gryph, what about the other W—"

"I know." Gryphon spoke over him. "Trust me. I know." Gryphon turned away, as if it were easier to think without them in his line of vision. Something about his posture changed. Perhaps the set of his shoulders or the stiffness in his stance. Zo couldn't decide. When he turned to face them again he was no longer Gryphon, he was a leader of men. Someone to follow.

"Here's the plan." He looked directly at Zo as he spoke. "Joshua will take Tess into the woods for the night. They can hide there until I come looking for them. You need to leave as well, Zo."

"Why?"

"Because you're too easy to read. It's your eyes." Gryphon swallowed in chagrin. Joshua wore a curious smile.

Zo took Gryphon by the sleeve and led him a few feet away from Tess and Joshua. "I don't think it's a good idea to leave them alone in the woods." She whispered so only he could hear. She looked back to see Joshua wearing the same foolish grin. "Why can't they leave at first light?"

"That's no good. They could be seen without the cover of night. Besides, we don't know when the Seer's coming." Gryphon rested his heavy hand on the side of her arm and gently squeezed. "Joshua will take care of your sister. Trust me. This is our only option."

Zo couldn't remember the key points to her argument. She watched Gryphon's hand fall away from her arm then looked up into the warmth of his earthy eyes. "I ... I trust you." Suddenly she felt like she'd fallen off a cliff. There was nothing to hold on to. Nothing to break her fall. Just wind and a rapidly approaching bed of rocks below. She couldn't seem to catch her breath.

The corner of Gryphon's lip raised in a subtle smile. "I'll tell my mother you went to check on the family you helped last night. It shouldn't raise suspicion. Thankfully, she knows nothing of Tess."

Zo barely heard him, but nodded anyway.

"Joshua, two bedrolls, rations, water, knife, bow. Take her to my spot. Not too fast, she's young. If I haven't come for you by sundown, find Ajax. Tell him I'll explain later."

"Got it." Joshua bounced on his toes like this was all just some grand adventure.

"Go!" Gryphon ordered.

"Oh yeah." The boy shot out of the building.

"What can I do?" Zo asked.

"Hug your sister and get some rest. I have a feeling tomorrow is going to be a big day."

She'd said she trusted Gryphon, even as the words came out, she knew it was true. "There's something else you need to know."

Gryphon crossed his arms and frowned. She had the impression that he thought he knew what she was about to tell him.

"You are good friends with Sara, right?"

Gryphon obviously hadn't planned for that response. "She's like a sister."

Zo dug her toe into the ground.

"What do you know?" He urged her on.

"It's about her sister, Eva. She's in trouble."

[•]

Gryphon sat awake for most of the night whittling down a piece of pine into the shape of a Ram. His attention divided between Joshua and Tess hiding in the forest, Ajax's small family, the Gate Master, Eva and the unborn Nameless' child she carried, the Wolf hidden in the barn, and then, of course, Zo.

How did he find himself responsible for so many people? What would happen if he just closed his eyes, and let everything happen? Why did he care so much that Tess be spared from the Gate Master? Or that the Wolf be allowed to live? And Ajax really couldn't expect him to risk everything he'd worked for to help his child, could he?

Gryphon's knife slipped, and he accidently cut off one of the Ram horns on the wooden figure. He let the knife and wood block tumble to the bed and dropped his head into his hands. "I've lost control."

For as long as he remembered, Gryphon had only longed for one thing—to make up for the shield hanging on his wall. He'd done everything ever asked of him, trained harder and longer than anyone else in his mess.

It wasn't long ago that he would have done anything for the Ram without question. But times had changed, just like the unhealthy soil of the Ram over the years. His priorities had become diluted. The certainty of his situation dissolved.

All that remained was the core conviction that he wanted to make the right decision. Not the right decision for the Ram. Not even the right decision for himself.

Just the *right* decision.

And protecting the people around him seemed to be the only acceptable course of action. As hard as it was.

Chapter 31

Zo watched Gryphon from the corner of her eye as Sara and Ajax swaddled their small baby. "Give the medicine to him twice a day until the lip has healed," said Zo.

The couple nodded. Ajax draped his arm around his wife and squeezed both mother and child. Zo walked them to the door to bid farewell, the whole time listening to Gryphon's approaching footsteps behind her. He put his hands on her waist and spun her around. She melted into him, wrapping her arms completely around his waist.

"I'm exhausted." She sighed, content in his embrace.

Gryphon led her to their usual spot in the hayloft. He lowered her into the hay with his hand supporting her lower back while she clung to his neck. His lips were fire. She pulled him closer and let the hay envelop them.

In the corner of the barn, Zo's mother and father cried out as men with short swords slaughtered them.

Gryphon bent down to kiss Zo's cheek. "You trust me, don't you?"

Tess' scream filled her head. Growing louder and louder as the walls of the barn collapsed on top of them.

Zo sat up with a start. Markus, the Nameless who slept in the corner, hovered over her with his bushy gray eyebrows raised to his hairline. "You all right?"

Zo's chest pumped in and out, sweat trickled down the side of her face. "I can't do this anymore." She raked a hand through her long dark hair. Somewhere in the woods Joshua and Tess were camped like fugitives. That was, unless they had been discovered already.

Markus frowned, adding six new wrinkles to his already rippled face. "I know."

But he didn't know. No one really *knew* what it was like to carry this impossible weight. No one *knew* anything!

Gryphon burst through the door like a tornado. "You need to leave. Now."

Markus took a few steps away from Zo then quickly left the room as if Gryphon's words were intended for him.

"Is the Seer here?" Zo whispered. She couldn't quite look him in the eyes after that dream.

"Not yet, but we can't take any chances."

"Your mother—"

"Thinks you're headed to the Jordan home to follow up with the Nameless family you helped last night."

"Tess and Joshua—"

"Are safe in the forest." Gryphon's demeanor softened. He

reached out, almost taking her by the hand, then hesitated. Zo couldn't pull her gaze from his extended hand, even though yearning for his touch was a complete betrayal of everything she stood for.

When had it happened? The start of this inexplicable longing. Gryphon was everything Zo grew up hating. How could something feel so wrong and so right at the exact same time?

She thought of the kindness he'd shown her sister. Of the mercy he'd shown others. To her. Zo shook her head and tried to repress the contradictions of her thoughts to listen to Gryphon's instructions.

"You need to find Sara and Eva. Tell them to bring the baby and meet at my home this afternoon. I'll speak with Ajax at mess training."

"What are you planning?" Zo gathered her things, purposefully avoiding Tess' little hole in the floor. Her stomach dropped whenever she looked at it.

"There's no time for this." He guided her out the door and into the frosty morning air, his hand a whisper on her lower back. Gryphon's breath clouded as he spoke. "Stay off the main road until you reach the turnoff. You don't want to chance running into the Seer or Gate Master on your way."

Zo shivered. "What about you?" She blew into her cupped hands to warm them. "You said the Seer can tell when someone's lying."

"I've had interrogation training. Let's hope the system doesn't fail me." He smiled weakly.

A trained liar. She was putting her sister's life in the hands of a trained liar. Perfect.

[◦]

The most important part of deception happened inside the mind. Gryphon really needed to believe his own story, and if possible, avoid telling lies altogether, to convince the Seer. When he tweaked the timeline of events, everything he said was true.

Zo— no that wasn't right—*My Nameless healer never even mentioned she had a sister. The little girl is not here.*

Unfortunately Tess wasn't Gryphon's only problem.

Gryphon closed the old barn door behind him. He cut the ropes around the ankles of the Wolf and removed his gag. "What's going on?" the prisoner asked at once.

"I need to move you."

"And I was so comfortable here."

Gryphon didn't have time for the Wolf's sarcasm. "Tess is in danger. People are looking for her. They could be here any moment."

"Where is she?" All humor fell from the Wolf's face.

"Safe in the mountain forest with Joshua."

The Wolf nodded his understanding. "Are you being watched?"

Gryphon helped him up to his feet. "Maybe."

"Where is Zo? If they question her—"

"I know. She's a dead giveaway. I sent her away."

Again the Wolf nodded. "And you need me to hide, so they don't discover you spared my life."

Gryphon cracked open the door to the barn. "I'm going to walk back to the house and close the door behind me. I want you to crawl through this field until you reach the tree line east of the house. Watch and wait. I won't be able to meet you until later this afternoon. If you get caught, it's your own neck."

The Wolf regarded him from the side. "And you're not worried at all about me scaling that wall and running?"

"You won't leave without Zo and Tess."

"And when they return?" The Wolf's whole demeanor tensed in anticipation.

Gryphon had made the decision long ago, but it didn't make the words any easier to say. "You're all leaving Ram's Gate with my friend and his family."

"You're not coming?"

Gryphon thought of his mother. Of the shield hanging on his wall. Of his dreams to restore his family's honor. Of his own hopes for success. Of his love for the Ram in spite of the clan's many shortcomings.

"I can't."

[◆]

Gryphon pushed his knife into the block of wood that no longer resembled the Ram. Now it was nothing more than a sharpened stake. Curled shavings fell to the floor. The scent of pine tickled his nose as always. The familiar smell and the steady strokes of his blade helped calm his nerves as the Seer and two guards climbed the hill to his humble family home.

When they were twenty yards away he stood to give her the respect she was entitled as the chief's trusted counsel. Her black hair was pulled back into a severe bun at the nape of her neck. Her bird eyes examined the knife in his hand before scanning up to meet his face. Gryphon set the knife on the small deck table and walked down the steps to greet the Seer.

"Good morning, ma'am." He offered a slight bow of the head to show submission. He thought the guards would begin their search right away, but they just stood there with arms clasped in front of them.

"Soldier." She returned the gesture. "You've been expecting me." It wasn't a question. "Why are you not training with your mess?" she asked, her black Seer eyes unblinking.

"Zander was called in to meet with Chief Barnabas this morning. We aren't scheduled to meet for training until third horn." She likely knew the answer to her own question. She knew everyone's business inside the Gate.

She studied him, pulling her brows together just a fraction. "Your mess needs you at your best for a pending mission. Someone of your particular skill is too valuable to lose. Especially now."

Gryphon bowed his head again, wondering about the nature of his next excursion. "Thank you, ma'am."

The Seer's smile spread in a thin line across her face. "Which is why I sent Gate Master Leon last night."

"You sent him?" Fear rose from his toes to his forehead, fogging his mind with icy doubt.

"With the proper amount of pressure, the guilty incriminate themselves."

Gryphon couldn't breathe, but worked to keep his face neutral. "Excuse me?"

"We followed your little red-headed apprentice last night. He was caught smuggling one of my Nameless, the sister of your healer, into the forest. He admitted to stealing her from the Nameless' barracks and hiding her on your property for the last few nights to help your healer. I'm sorry he let you and his people down. "

The muscles in Gryphon's jaw tightened to the point where he couldn't speak. Joshua had taken the blame for all of it.

"We can only assume he was poisoned by your Nameless girl. I trust you will see her properly punished."

Gryphon could only nod.

The Seer smiled again. "I don't think I need to tell you how disappointed the Ram Council is with young Joshua. It reflects poorly on you. We can only assume he spoke the truth when he said you had nothing to do with this."

Gryphon held perfectly still. He thought of a hundred different scenarios, but the surest way to help Joshua and Tess was also the most disgusting. "Of course not."

The Seer nodded approvingly. "Good. I told them you had more sense than that. We'd hate to see our famous Striker tangled in such a mess."

"Where is the boy? He needs to be punished," said Gryphon, the words were acid to his tongue.

The Seer laughed without humor. "Oh, don't worry about that."

"He's my responsibility." Gryphon couldn't hide the tremor in his voice.

The Seer's smile melted like a wax candle. "We will take care of his punishment and assign him a new mentor. Trust me, this type of violation will never happen again. Ever."

Gryphon tried to swallow, but his dry throat made the effort impossible. "And the little Nameless girl?"

"She is where she belongs."

Chapter 32

The last time Zo went to Sara and Ajax's home had been in the middle of the night. Even then, she hadn't paid a great deal of attention to where it was because of her recent whipping. She wandered through fields and forest in the general direction she remembered traveling. But the area inside the Gate was extremely vast. She could spend the entire day searching, and still not find the right Ram farmhouse.

Joshua and Tess would be somewhere along the western edge of the forest, close to the mountainous cliffs that dropped off into freezing ocean. She hoped Tess had been warm enough the previous night, and that Joshua didn't feel over-burdened by the heavy responsibility entrusted him. The boy had become something of a little brother to Zo. She couldn't imagine losing either of them in this dangerous game they played against the Seer.

After an hour of wandering without hope of finding Sara's home, Zo collapsed on a log and buried her head in her hands. Why hadn't she thought to ask Gryphon for directions?

Deciding that sitting wouldn't help her sister or Joshua, Zo followed the familiar road she'd been avoiding through a blossoming apple orchard. Zo skirted the house, careful to avoid being seen by the violent pregnant woman she'd had the unfortunate opportunity to meet already. She hurriedly turned the corner to walk behind the house and ran directly into Stone.

Zo bounced off the Nameless revolutionary's chest and landed ungracefully on her backside.

Stone reacted without pause, lifting her by the arm and hauling her back behind the Nameless' shed near the border of forest. "What's wrong? Why are you here?" He looked in every direction to make certain they weren't followed. "You can't *be* here. It isn't safe for anyone."

"I need to find Eva and Sara. Can you take me to them?"

"What's going on?" His grip on her arm tightened with worry.

"It's a long story. Gryphon has agreed to help Eva. We're meeting this afternoon at his family home." She didn't bother mentioning her sister or the Seer. She couldn't stomach saying the words out loud. As if that would make the situation less dire.

Stone blanched. "Does the Striker know anything about the rebellion? About me?"

Zo shook her head. "He only knows that Eva is carrying a Nameless' child." She touched Stone's hand to remind him that he was still squeezing her arm. "Gryphon will help her."

Tears sprang to Stone's eyes and he quickly wiped them

away. "I don't know what sort of power you hold over this Ram, but ... " he cleared his throat, "this is a miracle. Thank you."

"Nameless!" a shrill, familiar voice called from the front of the main house.

The muscles in Zo's back flexed at the sound. She cast a sideways glance at the whipping post and felt her knees buckle.

"You can't be seen here," said Stone. He quickly went about explaining how to find Eva's family home. "Thank you. Thank you." He took Zo by the shoulders and kissed her full on the lips. "Thank you!"

He left her standing alone on the fringe of the wood, stunned.

Zo immediately set out to find Eva's family home while Stone's directions were still fresh in her mind. Thankfully, it wasn't far. She wouldn't be able to relax until she held Tess in her arms.

The house, like most other Ram homes, was likely constructed from the very pine trees chopped down to clear the land on which it sat. Goats roamed free on either side of the cobbled path leading to the house. They bleated a welcome as Zo passed, then returned to their loud grass chomping. The stone path led to a small porch where an elderly man and woman sat on a bench staring at her.

Zo stopped at the sight of them. Why hadn't she thought this through? A Nameless couldn't just walk up to the door and ask for a Ram. She needed a solid story to explain her presence.

The old man pulled himself to his feet, leaning heavily on a wooden walking stick. He didn't question Zo, just stared expectantly.

"I've … I'm … I've come to deliver a message to Eva." Zo stared at the man's boots and inwardly prayed she didn't look suspicious.

The old woman walked into the house, leaving the unnerving man on the porch. "Who sent you?" His voice cracked, but carried a baritone warning.

"Striker Gryphon." Zo hoped it wasn't a mistake to use Gryphon's name, but she had to say something, and didn't dare use Mrs. Drea's name.

The old man squinted. "You are the Nameless healer. Gryphon's newest pet." His deep laugh barely carried to Zo's ears but sent a shiver up her arms.

The door to the house opened. Eva bounded down the steps and took long, purposeful steps to Zo's side. Her hopeful expression contradicted the disdain in her voice. "How dare you summon me, Nameless."

The old man on the porch settled back into his chair, as if satisfied by Eva's ability to handle a sub-human.

Desperation laced Zo's whispered plea as they put some distance between them and the house. "You need to come with me to Gryphon's family home. He wants to help you and your sister."

Eva's eyes became round. "Really? And he knows … " she touched her flat stomach, "everything?"

Zo nodded.

"What is wrong with Sara?" Eva's brows knit in concern.

"What does it want?" The old man called from the porch.

Eva didn't even hesitate. She called over her shoulder, "Gryphon and his mother want to discuss a trade for goat's milk. I'll take care of it, grandfather."

Eva walked down the path, and Zo followed an appropriate distance behind. Once they were a safe distance from the house Eva whipped around. "Does Stone know?"

"Yes. He's very happy." Zo blushed at the thought of Stone's lips pressed against hers in celebration.

Eva stared off, her gaze unfocused. If Zo didn't know better, she'd think Eva looked disappointed.

"Is everything all right?" Zo asked. "I thought this was what you wanted."

Eva sighed. "It is. I just ... " she pushed her short-chopped hair out of her face. "If I leave the Gate, I won't be with Stone."

"But if you stay, you'll have to marry that Ram. Both you and the baby will die when they discover you're pregnant. I'm sure Gryphon would help Stone leave with you. I know people outside the Gate who can help. You could start your life together in another clan."

Eva shook her head. "You don't understand. Stone won't leave his cause here. Not yet. And what if he needs my help?"

Zo could only imagine what had brought this Nameless and Ram together in the first place. A love impossible to understand. "There is someone else who needs your help right now."

Zo told Eva all about Sara and Ajax's deformed child. "Gryphon asked me to find you and Sara and have you meet at his family home after mess training. He'll speak to Ajax."

"I still can't believe she didn't say anything to me." She touched her stomach again. "I guess we were both afraid."

Zo was relieved when Eva agreed to retrieve her sister Sara, alone. The sun was already at its highest point in the sky and Zo thought she might die if she didn't get back to Tess and Joshua soon. The Seer would have left hours ago, and it wouldn't be too much longer before Gryphon came back from training.

[♦]

At mess training, Zander didn't bother disclosing the details of his meeting with the chief and his advisors that morning at training. He pushed Gryphon and his brothers harder than normal. Sprints, weighted weapon drills, circuit training, sparring, phalanx formations, it didn't matter the task, Zander stood with arms folded, appraising his men with hooded eyes, impossible to please.

"Again!" he ordered.

Gryphon and his brothers put their hands to the massive tree trunk that had been stripped of its limbs and rested at the side of the open field. They drove their feet into the ground and pushed, grunting and sweating as they rolled the giant log the entire length of the field. Gryphon's shoulders burned, his legs felt ready to give out, but all he could think about was Joshua.

The boy had gone through so much. Losing his mother at birth and his father only a few years later, on the battlefield. And yet he was always so happy and desperate to please Gryphon, his mentor.

Gryphon pushed harder, growling and pumping his legs.

Joshua was his responsibility. And he'd let him down.

He'd let him down …

The log crashed into a heavy pine at the other end of the field. All of the men of his mess stood and placed their hands on knees to gather breath, but Gryphon just kept pushing. Kept working his legs, digging trenches into the soft spring ground like a mad man. He had to do something to help Joshua. He had to save that poor little girl from the Gate Master.

Even if it meant placing his own arm on the chopping block.

After training, Zander called everyone around. "Good work, today." His gaze rested on Gryphon. "As you know, I met with the chief at the Horn this morning. The Raven soldier that Gryphon and Ajax captured finally broke. I don't have many details yet, but plan on meeting at barracks tonight at dusk for a bonfire. We should have our orders by then."

As everyone gathered shields and weapons to leave, Gryphon pulled Ajax aside. "You're coming with me."

"I have to get home to Sara."

Gryphon kept hold of Ajax's arm. "Sara and the baby are at my family home."

Ajax outpaced Gryphon as they headed down the path that led to Gryphon's home. "What's going on?"

Gryphon didn't mince words. "Would you leave the Gate to save your child?"

Ajax's eyes doubled in size. "You can't be serious. My family can't survive alone outside the Gate."

"What if I found someone to help you? Someone who could take you to another clan? Would you go?" Gryphon didn't dare mention that Ajax's family would be traveling with three Wolves and most likely, Joshua. Better to ease him into the idea.

Ajax's eyes grew clouded. His grip tightened around his spear. "I ... Is there no other option that you can think of?"

Gryphon put his hand on his friend's shoulder. "I can't see another course, brother."

Ajax still couldn't seem to answer.

"Joshua's in trouble, Jax. I don't have time to explain, but if you want to leave the Gate, I will help get your family outside the walls."

"When?"

Gryphon didn't have an answer. It seemed like his whole life was swirling faster and faster into a dangerous vortex. "Soon. Maybe tomorrow. ."

Ajax looked like Gryphon had just punched him in the face. "Would you come with us?" he gasped.

Gryphon grabbed a fistful of his own hair. "I don't know."

He couldn't imagine not having Joshua in his life, but knew Zo would kill for the boy. Her face instantly came to mind: her full lips and defined cheekbones, her perfect blue eyes and defiant stare. The idea of losing both her and Joshua forever was almost as terrifying as losing his home. His honor. Everything he'd worked for.

I'm going insane.

Zo didn't even care about Gryphon. Likely hated him. But for some ill-conceived reason, that didn't matter. Gryphon wanted to be near her, wherever that was.

But then he thought of the Wolf. Zo would never prefer Gryphon, her enemy, to one of her own kind. And did he really want to leave everything to watch Zo commit to another man?

For the first time ever, he suddenly regretted sparing Gabe's life.

Chapter 33

Zo ran through the thick foliage at a reckless pace. Branches and briars tugged and tore her dress as she moved. But she didn't care. Nothing mattered until she held her little sister in her arms.

When she reached the farmland surrounding Gryphon's home she was completely out of breath. Mrs. Drea had her back to Zo, beating out the wool rugs. Zo didn't want to explain her frazzled state to Gryphon's mother, so she made a large arc around the field near the edge of the woods, and approached the log house from the rear.

Gryphon must be inside, she thought.

Suddenly, a large man stepped out of the trees. His clothes were tattered rags, his messy light blond hair matched a patchy beard and mustache. Zo tensed and took a step backward.

Gabe?

He couldn't be real. She'd seen him die with her own eyes. Gryphon had strangled him the same way he'd almost killed her in the cave.

Not strangled. Just rendered unconscious.

The trees around her began to spin. Zo dropped to her knees and gasped.

Gryphon stepped out of the trees to join Gabe. The two men walked toward her like giant sentinels. Gryphon, dark as midnight. Gabe, light in both features and aura.

Gabe rushed forward and scooped her into a spinning embrace with his good arm. His left shoulder was bandaged over the stab wound Gryphon had inflicted on the platform.

It was too much to believe possible. Zo couldn't find her voice.

"I never thought I'd see you again!" said Gabe. His grip on her was painfully tight.

"Gabe," she gasped. "You're such an idiot. You should have stayed away." Zo didn't remember giving herself permission to cry. She wiped tears on her sleeve and searched his face to make sure it was really him. "You died. I watched you."

But he hadn't died. And that could mean only one thing. She turned to Gryphon. "You spared him?" Her tone was laced with accusation and awe. "Why didn't you tell me?"

Who was this Ram? Why would he risk everything to save Gabe? She shouldn't have been angry, but all she could think about was punching Gryphon in the face.

Gryphon glanced away. Harsh shadows cast heavy lines around the strong line of his jaw and beneath the heavy hood of his brow.

"What's wrong?" She looked at Gabe. His smile faltered

then died. He rested his forehead on Zo's, cupping the back of her head with one hand.

Zo took him by the wrists. "What happened?"

Gabe shook his head.

Zo pushed him away. "Tess. Where are Tess and Joshua?"

Gryphon kept his voice even, but the muscles in his neck jumped and contracted as he spoke. "Tess is with the Gate Master."

Zo melted to the ground. "How ... ."

"The Seer sent the Gate Master as a decoy. She guessed we'd move Tess if he warned us of her visit. Spies followed Joshua last night. I'm sure he and Tess didn't make it more than a mile from the house before they were captured."

"And Joshua?" Zo whispered.

Gryphon cleared his throat. "Told the Seer I knew nothing of Tess. That he acted alone."

Zo's head whipped up. Gabe's arms fell away as she took a step closer to Gryphon. "They'll punish him. They'll hurt him!"

Gryphon walked over to rest his forehead on the trunk of a tall pine tree. He covered his face in his hands.

"No!" Zo ran up to him in anger. "You don't get to be weak! I trusted you, Ram! I *trusted* you!" Zo yelled. Gabe held back her arms, but Zo wasn't through with Gryphon. "You should have known the Seer would do that." She kicked and struggled until her whole body went limp in Gabe's arms. "You should have stopped them!"

It was so much easier to be angry at Gryphon than herself. Zo had been so oblivious back home. Not seeing that her little sister needed her there. Not getting to know Tess well enough to predict her following. This was her fault. After her parents died she'd been too blinded by her own pain to recognize Tess'. The poor girl didn't just lose her parents; Tess had lost her only sister as well.

Selfish.

Through the trees Gryphon's mutinous-looking friend Ajax stood like a stone statue in the forest. A livid rock with arms crossed in front of his chest, ready to kill someone. Zo was too distraught to care about him or his heavy glare.

Gabe rested a hand on Gryphon's shoulder. "How do we get them back?"

"We have to break Joshua and Tess out at the same time. It's the only way," said Gryphon.

That much was obvious. "But they'll know it was you," said Gabe.

"Joshua will not take my punishment. This was not his fault. I let things get out of control." He swept his hand in Zo and Gabe's direction, as if they didn't realize he meant them.

Zo's anger flared again. "That's right. You should have slaughtered me the moment you discovered I was a Wolf!" Zo had no right to goad him in his pain. But her own anguish was a venom she couldn't contain.

"Zo, be reasonable," said Gabe. "He's just trying to do the right thing."

But Gabe didn't understand. Zo had had everything perfectly worked out in her mind. For as long as she could remember, she'd hated the Ram. By admitting Gryphon was a decent person, she was admitting that other soldiers inside the Gate might be somewhat decent as well. It was all or nothing, and she'd staked her life's mission on the ideal that every Ram soldier needed to die for the world to be a better place. Every

Ram. Without that foundation, what did she have? Where could her hate go?

Zo bent her head and buried her wet face in Gabe's side, too confused to even meet Gryphon's devastated expression.

A rustling in the trees sent Ajax running to discover the source. Moments later Eva, Sara, and a baby-carrying Ajax came to stand next to Gryphon. They all looked at Gabe like he had horns sprouting from his forehead. Ajax's face was red with anger.

Gabe's voice rumbled in his chest as he spoke. "What is your plan, Gryphon?"

【◆】

Gryphon and the others sat in a circle on the ground, with the exception of Ajax, who stood guard behind his wife and sister-in-law. Ajax had remained silent throughout the whole discussion, leaving Gryphon, Gabe, and the others to sort out a great deal of the particulars.

Gryphon had suggested that he and Gabe retrieve Tess that night at the Gate Master's home. Then, before sunup, they would go for Joshua. Ajax would stay with the women and help Sara prepare the baby for the journey. Gryphon would contact the Historian for help. If they didn't find a way to open the gate without alerting the clan, all of their efforts of freeing Joshua and Tess would be for naught. For some reason, he felt he could trust the old woman to help them escape.

Timing would be vital to the plan, because once the Gate Master discovered Tess was missing from his household he would come immediately for Gryphon. And the last thing any of them wanted was the whole of the Ram forces on their tail.

Gryphon tried not to think about their chances if Barnabas sent a mess to recover them outside the Gate.

Eva spent most of the meeting scanning the forest, for what, Gryphon did not know. Sara rocked her already sleeping babe and kept glancing up at Ajax, as if making sure he was still there.

Zo hugged her knees to her chest and stared at her feet. She nodded her consent, and spoke up when her opinion was called for, but otherwise remained silent in her desperation. Every now and then she would catch Gryphon's eye. Without words or gestures, she seemed to apologize.

Gryphon resisted the urge to comfort her. To pull her under the wing of his arm and hold her. If he was honest with himself, he needed the physical contact likely as much as she did.

But Zo had Gabe for that.

[♦]

Gryphon met Ajax that evening on his way to their barracks to conference with Zander and the rest of the mess. He'd worn his long, dark cape made of fine-spun wool that wisped around his ankles as he walked. His father's cape. It seemed fitting since the rest of Gryphon's world was cast in harsh shadow.

The two mess brothers fell in line without a word. The rhythm of their swords hitting against the giant round shields at their backs mingled with the soft footfalls of their heavy, fur-lined boots.

After a while, Gryphon couldn't stand the silence. "You're angry."

Ajax stopped on the road. "I can't believe you didn't tell me you spared the Wolf," he hissed. "You, my shield brother and friend, deceived me and every other Ram inside the Gate." He ground his teeth together and sneered. "Why did you do it, Gryph? How can you sleep knowing you're a traitor?"

Gryphon felt like the ground beneath him gave way. "I'm just trying to do what I feel is right, brother."

"Don't call me 'brother,'" Ajax spat. "And don't expect me or my family to join you in your treason."

"But the baby ... and Eva."

"I will take care of my family, just like you should have been man enough to take care of Joshua. Instead, you let these Wolves invade our home. You've betrayed the clan." The fire went out of Ajax's eyes and his head sunk so low his chin touched his chest. "You've betrayed me."

He turned and walked ahead of Gryphon, even though they were headed to the same bonfire.

Chapter 34

S harp laughter carried on the breeze as they approached the fire.

"Poor Joshua," said a hushed voice. "Must have seen how much fun Gryph was having with his Nameless girl, and thought he'd get his own."

Gryphon stepped into the light of the fire and the men of his mess quieted. Ajax frowned and found a seat not far from Gryphon at the back of the group.

As the last of the mess brothers arrived, no one else commented on Joshua's alleged transgression. It was a stain on all of them. A foe best handled by looking forward to the next victory.

Gryphon settled in as Zander spoke, careful not to meet Ajax's reproachful gaze. "Now that we're all here, let's begin. Our orders come from the chief himself. The information gathered from the Raven we captured during our last mission has led us to the Raven clan's stronghold. A hidden location less than fifty miles north of here."

"So close?" Ajax interjected. "Why haven't we discovered it sooner?"

Gryphon wondered the very same thing. Countless mess units had scouted the lands surrounding the Gate for Raven settlements. On his excursions the most they ever found were empty campsites abandoned by enemy soldiers. Never any sign of women or children.

"The settlement is protected by a natural canyon on all sides. Its only access is a hidden bridge of some sort. They'll have a defensive advantage, but we should have surprise on our side."

"How many mess units are joining?" asked one of Gryphon's brothers.

"Ten."

Ajax gave Gryphon a significant look. Ten of the fifty mess units in the Gate were commissioned. One mess of fifteen to twenty Ram could easily wipe out a hundred trained soldiers under decent circumstances. Gryphon shuddered to think what a force of two hundred would do.

This wasn't your everyday excursion. It was a full-scale attack on the Raven population. A genocide, if women and children were involved.

"Why not just take their food?" asked Gryphon, in spite of himself. "They aren't strong enough to be considered a military threat."

Zander narrowed his eyes at Gryphon. "The Great Move is happening. Last year our dead soils barely produced enough food to keep us alive. Wild game in this region has dwindled as well. After harvest, the Ram will move south to confront the Wolves. But first we have to destroy those who would get in our way. For the sake of our children."

"When do we leave?" Gryphon said, clearing his gravelly throat.

"We will report at the platform tomorrow morning for a briefing with the chief then leave the Gate by afternoon. We'll attack under the cover of night. We can't risk alerting them. This might be our only chance."

Gryphon looked around at his brothers. They seemed resigned to the chief's decision to attack not the just the soldiers of the Raven but their families as well. Their elderly, their women, their children.

What is happening to my people?

All his life Gryphon had been taught to hate the other clans. That they were less than human. Enemies who didn't have the right to harvest food in this region. But what he never thought to ask his own mentor was the simple question: why? Why couldn't the people of the Kodiak, Raven, Wolves and other lesser clans come to a compromise? Couldn't they work together to find food? Couldn't they build relationships of trade?

Hate didn't speak the language of compromise. Looking around at his brothers he saw nothing but a desire for power. Power for which the innocent would pay the ultimate price.

"This is wrong," whispered Gryphon to Ajax. "Will you kill children?"

Ajax paled but didn't respond. When Zander excused them for the night, Ajax pulled Gryphon aside. In the faint light of the fire Ajax looked older, with harsh shadows resting beneath his weary cheekbones. "I'm sorry I can't stand with you on this, Gryph. But a man has to draw the line somewhere."

Gryphon felt like bricks had been gradually piled on his back, pinning him down, making it harder and harder to breathe.

"Help the Wolf escape, if you must. We'll find another way to save Joshua and Jaxson."

"Jaxson?"

Ajax rubbed the back of his head and looked away. "We haven't had an official naming ceremony, but that is the name Sara and I chose for the baby. You always call me Jax ... " Ajax swallowed hard, and looked away.

"How does Sara feel about your decision to stay?" Gryphon whispered.

Ajax didn't answer. Both men walked back up the road that led to their family homes. "I'm hoping we can convince an official to help us after your healer does the surgery. That is, if you will agree to keep her here until then."

Gryphon shook his head. "What if the officials aren't lenient, Jax? What if the Seer discovers your son beforehand?"

The muscles in Ajax's neck leapt with tension. "I'll find a way. I will *not* lose my son."

The road came to a fork and Gryphon and Ajax stood before the divide.

"Abandon this plan. Stay and help me work things out. You say you are my brother. Prove it. Choose me and my family over these Wolves."

Gryphon's hands and feet felt cold and a chill crawled up his spine. "Do you know what will happen to that girl if she stays with the Gate Master? Do you know what kind of torture the Seer has in store for Joshua?" Gryphon fought to keep his voice down. "Joshua *is* family. I'll do whatever it takes to protect him." He tried not to think about what the boy was going through at this very moment. "I can't help you both unless you agree to leave with them tomorrow morning."

All hope drained from Ajax's face. "So, you will follow in your father's footsteps."

Gryphon grabbed Ajax by the shirt and growled. "I'm am sorry that you feel betrayed, Jax. But you are wrong about this."

(•)

Gabe didn't flinch as Zo examined his shoulder. He also didn't let his hands fall from her waist. Zo understood how he felt. Like they'd found something lost and cheated death to have it back.

"I'm not going to disappear, you know." Her lips hitched into a half smile that, given the circumstances, felt strange on her face. She peeled away the bandage to reveal Gryphon's neat stitches. He really was good at stitches. What surprised her even more was the healthy coloring around the wound. Gryphon had a natural healer's touch.

Zo had trained for several years to find her own abilities. Her mother used to lecture her on finding compassion for those she healed.

"The more you open your heart to the patient the faster they will recover. Love can heal even the deepest wounds if you let it."

Some thought healing was witchcraft or magic, and in a

way, it was. Healing required giving a portion of one's self. A small sacrifice to bring about a greater good. Wasn't loving someone more than yourself—when survival dominated the human mind—a form of sacrifice?

But even in healing you could love too much—try too hard to override the ailments of the human body. Zo had seen it happen.

Zo wondered if her mother's last thoughts were compassionate when the Ram entered their home five years ago. She wished she could remember everything that had happened that day, but no matter how hard she tried to fight through the veil protecting her from her own memories, she just couldn't remember.

Zo wondered if love could have saved her and her three-year-old sister had the Ram soldiers found them hiding in wicker baskets only a room's length away.

Zo snorted. *Unlikely.*

"What are you thinking?" Gabe used his rough fingers to brush away a tear on her face. Zo hadn't realized it was there. She'd been doing that a lot lately.

A hard spring rain beat upon the ill-constructed barn roof. A chill rolled up her arms.

"We'll get Tess back," Gabe said, guessing her thoughts.

But would they be too late? And even if, by some miracle, they did succeed, where would they go? The Ram would track them and kill them like dogs before they had a moment to enjoy their freedom.

Gabe must have sensed her despair. He cupped her chin and forced her to look into his light-blue eyes. "I promise."

She pushed his hand away, but the conviction in his fierce

gaze didn't waver. "This Ram, Gryphon. I've seen what he is capable of. If he fights to help us tomorrow we will be successful. I know it," he said.

Zo turned toward the corner of the dusty barn. The flickering light of their meager candle danced along the splintered walls to the subtle rhythm of the rain outside. "You've been living in a barn, Gabe. Your wrists and ankles are worn raw from ropes. Look at your hands!" She held up his hands for him to see. As if the loss of his pinkie fingers wasn't apparent enough. "How can you trust Gryphon or any Ram? How?" she demanded.

Zo had been counting on Gabe's cynicism to break the spell Gryphon had cast over her, but he only made it worse. A frown sagged on Gabe's face as he studied Zo. "How can you not trust him?" He bent down to kiss her forehead. She leaned into the kiss, needing any comfort she could get. Gabe was alive! That pillar of hope was all that kept her from crumbling.

Gryphon yanked open the door just as Gabe pulled away. He carried his sword and shield under a damp cloak. Rainwater drizzled from his dark hair, banking as it rolled off his square jaw. "I've got some news." He pulled a dusty three-legged stool from the corner of the room and set it down heavily in front of Zo. "Sit," he said.

Zo eyed the stool like it had teeth but eventually inclined her head. Perhaps sitting wasn't a bad idea after all. Gabe stood behind her and placed his hands on her shoulders. For some reason, Zo was more self-conscious of Gabe's touch in front of Gryphon. "What's going on?" she asked.

When Gryphon finished explaining the Ram's plan, she was glad to be sitting. "You're certain they know the Raven settlement's location?" Lightning rattled the shabby walls of the barn as she thought about little children playing freely in front of their humble homes.

Gryphon shifted his feet and looked at his hands. "My people captured a Raven a few days ago. He must have broken under interrogations."

Gabe's hands became heavy on Zo's shoulders. "No," he murmured.

"Wait!" said Zo. "Didn't you and your men leave only a few days ago?"

Gryphon looked up with a scowl, like he dared her to condemn him. "Yes, Zo. It was my mess."

"It was *you*?" She felt suddenly dizzy.

Gryphon growled. "And it was *you* and your bottles that let them know when I left. My brothers and I could have died!" Gryphon turned and slammed his palm on the rickety door. One of the wood panels flew out into the treacherous night.

"You knew about the bottles?" Zo looked up at Gabe who nodded confirmation. "You knew and you didn't stop me?"

Gryphon pulled at his hair, like he always seemed to do when he was upset. He closed his eyes. "After Tess ... I just didn't think you'd do it."

The color drained from her cheeks, like a spiderweb of ice shrouding her face. He'd trusted her and she'd let him down.

Yet he still came to check on her last night when the Gate Master had almost ...

Gabe stepped between them. "That is history. We need to focus on the future. Specifically the two hundred Ram leaving to massacre the Raven tomorrow." He turned to Gryphon. "You need to get us out. I've been to their settlement. I have to warn them."

"But what about Tess and Joshua? We can't leave them behind!" said Zo.

Gryphon raised his hands to calm Zo. "Gabe and I will get them tonight. The three of you will only have a few hours' head start. Ram soldiers travel fast."

"What about you? Will you and Joshua and the others not come with us?"

Gryphon sighed. "Ajax and his family are not leaving the Gate."

Zo grabbed Gryphon's arm with both hands. Red panic fringed her sight. "What about Sara and the baby? And Eva? The Ram will kill her when they discover she's pregnant." How could Ajax choose the Ram over his own child? He'd seemed so attentive and concerned for his family. And Eva. Stone had been so relieved that his lover would be safe. Zo looked into Gryphon's golden-brown eyes and pleaded. "You have to convince them to come, Gryphon." Her lower lip trembled of its own volition. "Please."

Gryphon searched Zo's face. His lips parted, like he was about to speak, but closed again. He focused on her with acute attention, like she was a critical target in an important mission.

Gabe coughed into his fist and Gryphon shook his head. "I'll try." His voice was dry and scratchy.

Gabe said, "What if you can't convince them? Will you and Joshua travel with us to warn the Raven? We could use your help with the evacuation."

Gryphon studied his hands. "I don't think I can leave."

Zo suddenly realized how difficult this must have been for Gryphon. He was proud. A fallen patriot of a clan that he loved. The clan of his parents and friends. She wished there was something, anything she could do to compensate him for the sacrifices he had made for her and those she loved.

"If you don't leave, what will happen to Joshua? The boy can't live his whole life in hiding. Ram's Gate is vast, but the Seer will find him eventually," said Zo. "Come with us. I can keep you safe. Take you away from this life."

Gryphon bristled. "The Ram aren't perfect, Zo. Our society is flawed in more ways than I'd like to consider. However, these are my people and I will not desert them. Someone has to help them understand that there is value in life outside of our own blood. If we can't learn that, there can never be peace between the clans."

Gryphon closed his eyes and pinched the bridge of his nose. "I will send Joshua with you."

"But—" For some reason, she couldn't imagine leaving the Gate without Gryphon. Why had she always assumed he'd come with her? Moreover, why did she feel rejected?

Gryphon pushed open the creaky door to leave. "Get some rest, Gabe. We leave in three hours."

"What about me?" Zo found herself desperate not to have him close the door. "Let me come with you tonight. I could be your lookout."

"No," both Gabe and Gryphon said at the same time.

Gryphon sighed. "We'll come for you as soon as we have Tess and Joshua." He held open the door for Zo to follow him out. When she didn't move he hesitated on shifting feet and studied the splintered doorframe. Gryphon cleared his throat. "There is no bed here, Zo. Gabe can't be seen, but you can sleep on your bed in the Nameless' quarters if you like."

Gabe's hands tightened on Zo's shoulders.

"Or I could move your bed in here." Gryphon spared her a quick glance. His eyes were liquid brown in the low light.

"I'll just sleep here in the hay," she said. For some reason, it sounded like an apology.

Gryphon pursed his lips, nodded, and left.

Chapter 35

Gryphon and Gabe traveled through the dark brush with weapons in hand. The devil in Gryphon resisted the urge to turn around and disfigure the Wolf's face. He had no good reason to feel that way.

But he did.

"Why don't you just say it?" whispered Gabe.

Gryphon ignored him. They still had another half mile before they reached the Gate Master's property where Tess was being held.

"You're in love with her."

Gryphon snorted and pushed on.

"Don't be ashamed. I don't think I could respect you if you didn't care for her. She is as mysterious as she is beautiful."

Gryphon almost laughed at the understatement. She was unearthly and dangerous. She made him lose touch with all rational thinking. She was both wonderful and terrible in one delicate package. More intimidating than any man could ever be on a battlefield.

"It gets worse," the Wolf continued to whisper. "Just wait until she's gone. Wait until you have to go to sleep and wonder if she's still alive. If she ever, even for a moment, felt for you the way you feel for her."

Shut up, Wolf!

"I don't envy you that," Gabe said.

Gryphon sheathed his sword, whipped around, and with both hands shoved Gabe in the chest. The Wolf stumbled but didn't fall.

"Be quiet or go back. I'm good with either."

The Wolf showed his hands in surrender. "Sorry."

Gryphon had the impression that Gabe was apologizing for more than his words. He didn't want or need the Wolf's pity. Zo was just a silly girl, and in a few hours she wouldn't be his problem any longer.

All was quiet as they crept through the forest. Only the lonely song of a nightingale accompanied them. The bird trilled into a great crescendo then carried its song into a deeper, more somber tone. Melancholy prose flitted into Gryphon's mind. A song of things that would never be.

They reached the road that led to the Gate Master's land. Gryphon met Gabe's stare as he pulled out his sword. In that moment both men lost themselves to the soldier within. Only their objective mattered now. Find and retrieve Tess without being seen.

Gryphon and Gabe kept to the shadows of the path until the large house came into view. The building was twice the size of Gryphon's home. It divided into two distinct sections in the shape of an arrow with a large wooden door at the point. A small stable stood fifty yards away from the house attached to another building that he assumed was the Nameless' quarters.

Gryphon pointed to the mud-walled stable. Gabe nodded and crept through the field to skirt the building from one direction while Gryphon approached from another. Under the cover of night, he could barely see the Wolf's form as he moved.

There was only one door to the building. The Wolf nodded to Gryphon then slipped inside while Gryphon crouched at the corner outside, studying the property for any signs of life. But by this hour, even the crickets had abandoned their songs to sleep.

A minute later the door to the Nameless quarters clicked open as the Wolf slipped out. He shook his head. "She's not in there."

That meant only one thing. Tess was inside the main house.

[●]

When she was sure Gabe and Gryphon were gone, Zo slipped out of the door to the barn to warn Stone about Eva. The night was as still as it was dark. She silently crept through the fields of sprouting wheat to the edge of the forest. The walk took a lifetime. When she finally found the path leading to her destination, a man stepped out from behind a night-black apple tree.

His giant hand covered her mouth before she could scream. "It's me," said Stone. His massive Kodiak frame cut a terrifying figure in the dark. Zo sighed, grateful to know this cunning man was a friend and not an enemy.

"What is on your face?" Zo gestured to the black and brown smudges covering his face and hands.

"Extra cover. Tonight is an important night."

Zo didn't have time to get involved with Stone's Nameless rebellion. "Listen. I've come to warn you about Eva."

"What's happened? You're still planning to escape the Gate in the morning, right?"

The anxiety in his voice made it hard for Zo to continue. "Ajax has forbidden her to leave with us."

Stone literally growled like the bear his likely-ancestors were named for. "The hell she isn't." He took both of Zo's shoulders and shook her so hard her teeth rattled. "You listen to me. I will make sure Eva is near the gate in the morning. I'm going to try and help you all escape. Give the stinking Ram something else to worry about besides a few innocents leaving the Gate." He shook her again, the whites of his eyes glistening wild in the blackness of his complexion. "You will take her with you. Do you understand me?"

Zo nodded, wincing under the pressure of his hands as his fingers dug into her skin.

"Take her and whichever Nameless leave with you to your friends, the Allies. I will find you both there."

"But—"

"I'll find you!" he nearly shouted then shook his head and sighed. "She is carrying my child, healer. My flesh and blood. Nothing can keep us apart. Nothing."

Zo pulled away, her face flushed.

"Now go back to where you came from. You don't want to

be involved with my lot tonight." He ran off in the direction of Eva's family home without a backward glance. Zo didn't have a chance to mention the Raven before he disappeared into the darkness. It was no wonder he'd been so successful with leading the Nameless. He never gave anyone a chance to speak against him.

What did he mean "whichever Nameless leave with you?" Were there more people planning to leave the Gate in the morning? When had she agreed to take responsibility for the fate of the Nameless' rebellion?

It took most of the walk back to Gryphon's home to regain her breath. She couldn't stop thinking about Stone and the ferocity of his love for Eva. Love that the Ram girl reciprocated without question. She found herself desperate to help them even though Stone hadn't given her the option. The desire was irrational. As if by preserving their love she was preserving any hope of goodness still left in this wretched region. Preserving the hope that two people, so obviously different, could look beyond their differences and find happiness.

If only there was some way to convince Ajax to let Sara and the baby leave as well.

Zo took her time walking back to Gryphon's family home, knowing she wouldn't be able to sleep when she got there. The barn door whined as she pulled it open. She sank into the hay and stared up at the black rafters trying not to think of Tess and Joshua. Of the danger Gryphon and Gabe had entered to save them. It was strange to think that she could be outside the wall in only a few hours.

The barn door whined again, and Zo sat up.

"Gryphon?" she called into the darkness.

Four black figures entered the room. A man she didn't know grabbed her wrist and cupped her mouth before she could scream. Something struck the back of her head. As her vision faded, the familiar voice of the Seer carried over the haze. "That was easier than we could have hoped."

Chapter 36

Gryphon and Gabe sat hunched in the cover of the brush alongside the trail that led up to the Gate Master's house. Their whispers seemed like shouts in the too-quiet night.

"How many entrances?" said the Wolf. His chest rose and fell with anger.

"Not sure. I see one door and two front windows. There are likely more in the back."

Gryphon had heard rumors about the Gate Master and his unusual household. After his wife passed, he'd never remarried. The men from Gryphon's mess used to joke around that no respectable Ram woman would share her husband with that many Nameless.

The thought made him ill.

"You go right. I'll go left," Gryphon ordered.

As he approached the house, Gryphon couldn't stop thinking

about Tess. Her wild blond hair and eyes that doubled in size whenever she was the least bit nervous. She was a bold little thing, but always looked to Zo with unwavering confidence.

He shuddered.

Gryphon saw nothing through the first window except the vague outline of a hearth and a few chairs. He crept along the side of the house, grateful for the rain that made the ground damp and quiet. He paused at the muffled sound of heavy snoring. Gryphon peeked through the window but a thick covering blocked his view.

He hurried around the back of the house where Gabe waited by a window on his side.

"I count five cots. One is empty," said Gabe.

A giant wave of adrenaline pumped through Gryphon's veins. He wanted to tear apart the log house with his bare hands. "Tess?"

The Wolf shook his head. "Too dark to tell."

"Give me a leg up," said Gryphon.

"No. I should go. If they see you—"

"Fine," Gryphon snarled. He hoisted the Wolf up through the window then circled back to the side of the house where the Gate Master slept. To Gryphon's relief, the Gate Master's snoring continued. Gryphon matched his breathing to the awful sound. As long as he heard it, they were safe.

A shrill scream came from the other room followed by a great commotion. The Gate Master snorted awake. Gryphon ran around the other side of the house just as Tess' head popped out of the window. When she saw Gryphon she reached for him but was pulled back in at the last second.

Gryphon didn't hesitate. He jumped in after with sword

in hand. Chaos reigned inside the house. Women screamed, pressing themselves to the outer walls, while Gabe and the Gate Master moved through a series of attacks. Tess cried, her big eyes wide with fear as the Gate Master clung to a section of her shirt to keep her from running.

"Release her!" ordered Gryphon. The room fell silent as Gryphon held the point of his sword an arm's length from the Gate Master. Even the Wolf stopped fighting.

"Fool!" The Gate Master seethed. "Traitor!" His whole body shook with rage. He yanked Tess in front of him as a shield. "You're no better than your pathetic father."

"Drop your sword and step away. You can't defeat us both," said Gryphon.

The Gate Master curled his lips into a smile. "You've lost, boy." He looked outside and laughed. There was maybe an hour until dawn. "The Seer loved my idea. The healer gets her justice and you learn your lesson. Everybody wins."

Master Leon wasn't making sense. "The girl!" Gryphon demanded. "Hand her over!"

The Gate Master held Tess by the neck. His eyes shifted back and forth between Gryphon and Gabe. It would only take one swift movement to snap her neck.

Time slowed. Gryphon could see the slight bulge in his leader's arm, how his hand braced the girl's shoulder for leverage.

Under his cloak, Gryphon inched the knife out of the sheath at his side.

There would be no turning back after this.

The dagger whipped through the air and sank to the hilt in the Gate Master's arm, only inches from Tess' head. The

Gate Master released the girl and dropped to his knees before wrenching the dagger out of his arm. "You missed," he said, breathing hard through the pain.

"I never miss," said Gryphon. He dropped his sword and shield on the ground and charged the Gate Master, throwing him into the wall behind them. Gryphon punched him in the nose and felt a satisfying crunch beneath his fist. He struck him again and again, every hit stronger than the next. He would make the Gate Master pay for every time he'd beaten Zo. For the fear in Tess' innocent face.

"Not as fun when someone hits back, is it!" Gryphon roared like a feral animal and delivered another blow to the man's head. The Gate Master's body slumped. But Gryphon wasn't through with him yet. He grabbed him by the shirt and threw him across the room. The women screamed.

Gabe put a hand on Gryphon's shoulder. "Enough."

Gryphon's chest heaved for want of breath. The Gate Master didn't move. Gabe went to check his pulse and Tess ran for Gryphon. He pulled her into his arms, concealing her under a portion of his cloak.

"He's dead. Let's get out of here," said the Wolf as he climbed out the window.

Gryphon handed Tess to Gabe then joined them behind the house. They ran most of the way to Gryphon's home. The Wolf carried Tess on his back.

The sky was gray in anticipation of dawn. The men slowed to a brisk walk. Tess climbed down to carry herself. She had tears in her eyes. "I thought you were a ghost when you came into the house," she explained to Gabe. "I watched you die on the platform!"

She turned to Gryphon. "Why didn't you tell me?"

Gabe spared him from answering. "Gryphon was trying to protect you, bug."

"Well, that doesn't make any sense." She clung to Gabe's side. "Please don't die again."

Gabe laughed. "I'll do my best."

She looked over to Gryphon and frowned. "I don't want you to die either."

A knot locked up Gryphon's throat. He nodded and looked forward to watch the wooded trail leading to his family home. He'd just killed a high-ranking Ram officer. When the Seer discovered Tess and Zo missing, she would immediately suspect him. It would not take much to get the Nameless women in the Gate Master's home to talk.

They had maybe another hour before the next shift change at the Gate. It would be their only chance to get out alive. "You grab Zo. I'll gather my packs."

"Your packs?" Gabe's brow rose.

"Just go! Meet me out front in five minutes. We need to get Joshua before sunup."

Gryphon bounded into the house. "Mother!" he called, as he ran around his room collecting his things. "Mother, get dressed!"

His mother rushed into the room in panic. "What is it?"

"We're leaving." He stuffed a bag with supplies.

"I thought your mess didn't leave until this afternoon?"

"No, mother. We're *leaving*. You and I."

Gryphon would have said more, but his mother's distant expression confirmed that she understood his full meaning. "I want you to come with me."

She took a step back and shook her head.

"Please, mother. Pack a light bag. We have to leave at once."

Her face twisted into rage. She took another step back. "Not. You. Too."

She turned around to show him her back. "If you step out that door, you're dead to me." Gryphon put his arms around her but she would not turn to face him.

"Please, Mother!"

"Leave if you must, son. But I will not follow you." She pushed his arms away. "Just like I would not follow your father."

She went into her room and slammed the door behind her.

Gryphon couldn't seem to command his body. He stared at the closed door and found his face wet with tears.

Gabe charged into the house just as deep Ram horns sounded in the distance.

"Gryphon!" he panted. Tess stood behind him, misery etched into her forehead. "I can't find Zo."

[◊]

Zo couldn't keep her body from shaking. She sat on her knees, folded into a tight ball on the floor of the cave. Her arms hung from the ice cold chains bolted into the rock wall above her. The metal dug into her wrists as she let it support her weight. The darkness was alive, filled with breath and movement. It was an evil shadow ready to envelop her forever. A tangible fiend meant to erase everything worth living for while exposing every reason why giving up was almost certainly the best option.

A light pierced the darkness. She'd only been in the cave for a few hours, but the brightness blinded her. "S'time to get you ready," said a gravelly voice. "I just have one question." The man walked closer. The contrast of light and shadow made his nose appear twice its size. "How are you with a sword?"

The man unleashed her wrists and led her to a vacant room filled with weapons. *A torture chamber?* Zo thought. But the old soldier didn't bother tying her down. Instead he selected a sword from the wall and offered Zo the hilt.

"How's that? Too heavy?"

When Zo didn't say anything he handed her another. "What about that? Better?"

Zo nodded. "What's going on?" she finally asked.

The old man smiled, revealing a mouth more gums than teeth. "The chief wants the Nameless to at least give the people a show. S'no fun if they only last five seconds."

Understanding hit Zo like a wave to the chest. "A prizefight."

The man lifted his bushy eyebrows and tilted his head forward. An expression that said, *Naturally.* As if this was something she should have assumed from the beginning.

"Now," he picked up a sword and held it relaxed in his hands, "I want you to attack. Let's see what you know."

Zo just stood there, arms and sword hanging at her side. "What's the point? I don't have a chance of winning."

The man smiled and lunged at her with the sword. Instinct won out, and she deflected the attack with both hands desperately gripping the hilt.

"Good. Now what if I do this?" He attacked again, only this time at an angle that forced her to change direction. He advanced again and again, and Zo was barely able to keep his blade away from her body.

The man looked impressed. "You've had some training."

"Only a little," said Zo, panting. Usually Wolf women didn't fight, but when she joined the Allies, Commander Laden had insisted she receive training in basic combat. It seemed silly at the time. A healer with a sword.

The old man set down his weapon and took Zo's from her. "Just be sure you protect your back. The faster you are, the longer you'll last." He led her out to a group of women who'd obviously been waiting for her. "Good luck!" He winked and walked away whistling.

The women were less cordial. They forced her to undress in the middle of an open room. Cold air swept over her bare skin. With buckets of water and pumice soap they scrubbed the dirt from her naked body. The women smacked her arms every time she attempted to cover up. By the time they finished, Zo's skin burned raw, and her dark hair dripped down her back. They used wool blankets to dry her skin and sat her in front of a blazing hearth to help dry her hair.

Two women brushed and braided Zo's hair while another sat before her with a tray of paints. The woman grabbed a thin brush and dipped it in a smoky, charcoal mixture before painting her eyelids. She added rose-colored chalk to her cheeks and finished with a burnt-red paste for her lips.

Last, they dressed her in a simple white tunic that barely reached her knees with a feather woven belt around her waist. Her arms and legs were bare. Zo didn't bother asking these women questions. She'd figured it out on her own well enough. This prizefight was a production of sorts. A theatrical performance that would end the way every sort of Ram entertainment ended.

In bloodshed.

She only hoped that Gryphon and Gabe had been able to free Tess and Joshua. That Gabe had the good sense to leave her behind and get Tess and Joshua to safety.

Please keep them safe.

She thought of Gryphon and blinked hard against the memory of him. "Keep him safe, too."

Chapter 37

They had less than an hour before the sun would crest the great wall and their hopes of recovering Zo and Joshua and fleeing the Gate would be lost. Gryphon hid Tess behind a neatly stacked woodpile near the Medica. Already, Ram and Nameless were gathering in the square, for what purpose Gryphon could only guess. Gryphon handed the shaking child his packs, keeping his shield secured to his back, his spear in hand, and his short sword at his hip.

Gabe crouched down and whispered. "We will be back for you soon, bug. No matter what happens, don't leave this spot until we come for you."

"Will you find Zo?" The desperation in the little girl's voice kindled Gryphon's resolve. He *would* find her. And kill the man holding her, and anyone else who stood in his way. He felt like he could even lift up the wall if that is what it took to protect Zo.

They arranged the logs to cover Tess' hiding place and set off at a run. "They must be holding Joshua in the prison," Gryphon called over his shoulder.

They ran through the woods, skirting the village packed with Ram and Nameless. The prison wasn't even a half-mile away, leaving little time to plot a way to free Joshua and Zo. *If they are even there.*

They crossed the wild stretch of ground like bloodthirsty demons. Every moment wasted brought them closer to failure. Gabe dropped behind as Gryphon calmly approached the entrance to the mountain prison. One boy, barely older than Joshua, guarded the tall doors to the cave. His breastplate hung cockeyed and his teeth seemed too large for his mouth, but he stood at full attention as Gryphon drew near.

"Where is everyone?" Gryphon asked.

The boy brightened. "You're Striker Gryphon, aren't you, Sir?"

Gryphon grimaced, then nodded. "I'm looking for one of my Nameless. She was—"

"The healer? She's here, sir! Or was, before they took her to the prizefight." The boy scrunched his eyebrows together. "Why aren't you there, Sir?"

"Where?"

"The prizefight. As Joshua's mentor, I thought you'd be his greatest supporter."

Gryphon iced over. "I was just heading there. Thank you, soldier."

Gryphon trotted down toward the town center cursing under his breath. Joshua was too young for his prizefight! The Seer was known for finding the most effective punishments.

This was her way of making Gryphon pay the price indirectly. Hurting him at his weakest point. He'd admire the strategy if it wasn't his life being destroyed.

Gabe joined Gryphon on the vacant trail. When Gryphon didn't slow his pace, Gabe asked, "What's happened?"

Gryphon told him about Joshua and the prizefight with a bitter tone. "He's just a boy! He shouldn't be fighting in a life-or-death situation."

"And from what you've told me, almost every Ram soldier will be there to watch. How will we get him out before the alarm is raised?"

The noise of the looming crowd pushed the men off the trail and back into the thick forest. They crept up to the tree line but couldn't see anything over the heads of the boisterous congregation.

Gabe looked at him like a soldier awaiting a command. The simple gesture pressed heavily on Gryphon—the knowledge that if anyone could save them from almost certain death, it was he.

"Pull your hood lower, you're about to enter a crowd of soldiers thirsty for a Wolf killing," said Gryphon.

To the Wolf's credit, he didn't even look disturbed.

"Look for Zo in the crowd while I get a better view of the platform." Gryphon would have his spear in case Joshua needed him in the fight. This was one attack as Striker in which he would not falter.

"Zo will be guarded." The Wolf grimaced. "If I make a scene we'll find twenty spears in our backs before we have time to run ten steps.

They needed some sort of diversion.

A crazy idea came to Gryphon, something he never would have even considered a year ago. But then, the image of Zo with a spear in her back inspired irrational thinking. "I'll think of something. Wait for my signal. I'm going to see if I can get the gate open for us. Once you've got Zo, retrieve Tess and get outside the wall. If Joshua and I don't make it out, go on to warn the Raven."

"How will I know your signal?" said the Wolf, eyeing him skeptically.

"Trust me. You'll know."

[•]

The deep sound of a single horn called in the distance. The old man from the armory returned bearing Zo's weapon. When he looked at her his eyes widened. "You might not last very long, Nameless. But at least the men will get a nice show." He led her out of the rocky tunnel into the reluctant light of morning. A family of birds chirped from their lofty nest. The sound didn't belong in Zo's world. Not as she walked down the dirt road to her death.

Zo's hands flexed into fists then released. Flexed then released. She used her forefinger to pick at the skin on the side of her thumb. Her face revealed nothing but the mask of calm she intended. She heard the gathering crowd of both Nameless and Ram long before they turned the final bend in the trail that led to the center of town. The deep horn sounded again, only this time the vibration rattled Zo's chest.

Eva, with her chopped hair and wrinkled brow, was one of the first faces she recognized among the throng who'd gathered to witness her death. She was a year or two older than Zo, but she clutched a traveling pack to her chest like it was a comfort blanket. Nameless men stood in conspicuous groups, whispering to each other and casting shifty glances in Zo's direction.

She had a distinct feeling like something was happening inside the Gate. Something bigger than the prizefight. Some Nameless faces carried the burden of fear while others stood with arms folded across their chests, with chins set high in defiance.

What is going on? Only one man could be responsible for the tension in the clan. One revolutionary so blinded by love that he'd lead men to their deaths to protect his mate. *Stone, what have you done?*

A wave of nausea crossed over her, painful and threatening. She walked on, one foot in front of the other. Had Gryphon and Gabe been successful? Was Tess safe? And what of Joshua? She *needed* to know that they would live. She *needed* to know that Gabe would alert the Raven before the Ram invaded. That candlelight of hope would give her strength beyond measure. Perhaps even strength enough to defeat whatever budding young man she was put up against and walk away from the Gate a free woman.

The trail opened up to the main square. A mass of bodies clamored around the platform. As Zo passed, excited voices diminished to whispers. Zo didn't have her mud and wrap to hide behind. Her ebony hair was braided along the crown of her head to frame all of her damning features.

"Wolf," a soldier exclaimed. Others joined; speculation of what she was dawned like a sporadic wave across the stunned crowd. The horn sounded a third time, silencing all but Zo's pounding heart.

A Ram wearing a string of ancient metal coins climbed the wooden stairs of the waist-high platform and held up his hands to address the crowd. The old man escorting Zo nudged her up the steps.

The old man's instructions along with the white noise of the crowd were lost to Zo—the sound choked to death by fear and utter shock.

For on the other side of the platform stood a young boy with a short sword in his limp hand. He was all red hair and freckles, looking at her with large eyes rimmed with tears.

Her opponent. Joshua.

Chapter 38

Gryphon raced to the Chief's home before reason could catch up to him. He skirted the square by weaving between the main buildings of the town. At every opportunity, he glanced into the growing crowd, hoping to be rewarded with a glimpse of Joshua or Zo, but only managed to stumble over an old man pushing a cart of wool.

When he finally made it to the other side of the square Gryphon ran down the cobbled road to Barnabas' home. The guards at the massive oak doors aimed their spears at his chest. "Stop," they ordered.

Gryphon ran so hard he almost fell over trying to stop in time to avoid the guards' spears. It took him a moment to catch his breath. "I need to speak with the Historian."

"What do you want with my grandmother?"

Gryphon whipped around to find the chief looking like he

wanted to filet Gryphon's innards in the belly of his shield. The Historian rested a withered hand on her grandson's arm. Gryphon had hoped to convince the old woman to use her authority to open the Gate. But now …

He stammered an apology, but the Historian cut him off. "Gryphon, I'm so glad you made it. Look for my Nameless man back in the square. He'll assist you in your goals."

"My goals," Gryphon repeated flatly.

"Yes, a big fellow with a red tie wrapped around his arm. I require him to wear it. All those cattle look alike to me."

Barnabas patted his grandmother's hand. The old woman sighed. "I imagine he's helping Eva as we speak."

"Eva?" Gryphon knew he sounded ridiculous, but he had absolutely no idea what the crazy woman meant.

Chief Barnabas' lips formed a tight line. "What are you up to, Gryphon?" he asked. "And why does it involve my grandmother?" He placed a protective arm around the woman's frail back.

"I'm sorry, Sir. It's just—"

"I'll fill you in on everything on our way to the prizefight, dear. They can't begin without you." The Historian pulled the reluctant chief away from the house. She turned back and winked at Gryphon when Barnabas wasn't looking.

Gryphon didn't waste time contemplating the Historian's words. He ducked off the path and into the woods again, jumping over logs and pushing away branches until he broke through the tree line at a sprint and entered the throng of Ram and Nameless gathered in the center of town for the prizefight.

A sea of Ram surrounded the platform. The tips of spears stood out in the crowd like porcupine quills, swords reflected the early morning light, blinding Gryphon as he looked up to find Joshua huddled in one corner of the platform. He kept his arms folded and his head down. His eyes were trained on the floor in the center of the platform, as if trying to avoid the hundreds of eyes trained on him. Mostly he just looked small. Too young for what lay ahead.

Joshua's challenger was yet to arrive, but Gryphon knew it wouldn't be long. He searched the crowd for Eva and the mysterious Nameless with the red strip of cloth tied to his arm. He had no idea how this man was supposed to help him, but he knew the Historian mentioned the Nameless for a reason. After several minutes of searching, Gryphon couldn't help but feel like he was wasting time.

Joshua wasn't ready for a prizefight. What if the kid lost?

A horn sounded and most of the crowd quieted as Joshua's opponent walked through a tall aisle of Ram toward the platform. Gryphon stood on his toes to get a look at the Nameless, but was too far away to see anything. Ram soldiers gasped, the hum of their reaction to the challenger filling the square.

Gryphon was out of time. Barnabas would be here any moment and the fight would commence.

"Gryphon!" Eva rushed over to meet him, carrying a light pack and bedroll. She stood with the Nameless along the outer rim of the crowd. "You have to stop them!"

Another horn sounded announcing the entrance of the chief, but Gryphon didn't bother looking at the platform. Instead he approached the tall Nameless at Eva's side. His arm was cast in a sling, but Gryphon would have recognized the man even without the red fabric tied to his bicep. It was the same Nameless he'd seen at Eva's wedding. "The Historian told me to find you."

The man nodded. "She asked me to give you this." He handed Gryphon a small linen bag. Its contents clinked together and a strong-smelling powder puffed through the unseen holes of the fabric, smelling very much like the Historian's shed.

"Careful, Striker." The Nameless explained the volatile nature of bag and its purpose. "Attach it to the front of your spear. A ladder is set up behind the Building of Records. You'll only have one chance at this. The Historian and I will help you open the gate, but you must hurry!"

"I can't just—"

The giant Nameless took Gryphon's arm and squeezed. "I'm told many of your men will leave today to slaughter the Raven."

Gryphon couldn't believe this man, this *Nameless*, knew of the Ram's plans.

"The Historian said to tell you that if you want to save those you love, you must be willing to cut off your arm."

Eva couldn't stop staring at the platform. "Just go, Gryph," she shrieked. "They need you!"

Gryphon saw the flame of Joshua's hair out of the corner of his eye as he pushed his way out of the square. He hoped Gabe had found Zo and was ready to free her once Gryphon created the diversion. He found the wooden ladder propped up against the records building, right where the Nameless said it would be.

A pearl of sweat rolled into his eyes as he tied one final knot securing the dangerous bundle onto the end of his spear. He worked in a daze, not knowing if he could do what was required to save Joshua and Zo. He placed one heavy boot on the ladder, pulled a deep breath through his nose then started the climb with one hand holding the deadly spear. Every rung of the ladder brought him closer to his doom, but as if propelled by strength that wasn't his own, he kept reaching for the next rung. Then the next.

The booming voice of the Master of Arms carried across the square. "On this day, Joshua, son of Kote, and former apprentice to Striker Gryphon, challenges this Nameless in a prizefight for his shield."

The sound of Joshua's name sent a ripple of gooseflesh over his arms. He shimmied up the slick rooftop on his stomach—an awkward feat considering the sword at his hip and the deadly spear in his hand. When he finally reached the peak of the roof and looked down on the fighting platform, he nearly fell from shock.

He first saw Joshua's brilliant red hair, but standing on the opposite side of the platform, wearing nothing but a tiny tunic revealing her slight frame, was Zo. She held a sword in her hand like it was a snake that might bite her.

"Fight!" the Master of Arms called.

(•)

A guard slapped Zo's backside, inspiring raucous laughter from the crowd. Joshua's ghostly face haunted her when she looked up to meet his eyes. *The poor boy!* Zo dropped her sword and turned around to run off the platform but hit the chest of a brawny guard instead. He whipped her around and shoved her back into the center of the ring.

Joshua peered down at the ground, refusing to even look at Zo. Her mind raced for a solution, a way to save this boy's life without causing Tess pain. There were just too many Ram surrounding them for an escape. They couldn't surrender—a prizefight ended only when one of the fighters expired on the platform.

There was really only one course of action.

Zo charged Joshua. His eyes doubled in size at her attack. Out of instinct, his hands met her shoulders to block.

"Fight me, Joshua." She pushed against him, their arms locked together like the horns of two butting ram. "This needs to look convincing."

Joshua dug in his feet and pushed against her with surprising force for a thirteen-year-old boy.

Thank you! Zo could have cried in relief.

With a quick move, Joshua whipped Zo's legs out from under her. She hit the ground hard and lost her breath. The crowd cheered. Joshua jumped on Zo's chest, pinning her arms with his knees.

"It will be all right, Ginger," she encouraged him. "Please," she panted, "please, just do it." Tess would be devastated, but Gabe would look after her.

Joshua yanked a knife from its sheath and held it above his head. Moisture formed in his eyes. "I love you, Zo." His lower lip trembled. "My sister." His warm tears splattered on Zo's cheek as he hovered above her.

Zo wished she could at least hug him one last time. To pull him to her chest and rock him back and forth until his tears dried up and he could smile again. It was bad enough to have to watch those you loved die. She couldn't imagine his pain at having to be the one who killed her.

"I love you, too." Zo's voice shook. "Escape this place, Joshua. Tell Tess I'm sorry and that I love her. Tell Gryphon—"

The knife came down. Zo winced but opened her eyes in time to see Joshua plunge it into his own stomach.

"NO!" Zo wailed. The world turned white streaked with red. All noise vanished.

Joshua's body collapsed onto hers like a limp fish. She tasted his hot blood in her mouth. It soaked her braids and pooled in the hollow of her neck. Her heart echoed in her ears for two beats then everything around her turned to absolute chaos.

Chapter 39

G ryphon threw the spear.

He didn't think, only reacted to the sight of Joshua stabbing himself. The slender shaft of his spear wobbled in the air from the force of the throw as it sailed over the heads of the crowd gathered in the square. It struck the bed of a wooden vegetable cart and exploded, sending the whole cart and its contents flying into the air. The Historian's chemicals erupted into a ball of flame that licked the two-story rooftops. Gryphon felt the heat of the blast on his face as he leapt off his lofty perch into the riot below.

He landed hard. The hilt of his sword jammed into his ribs as he rolled out of the fall. Everywhere he looked Ram scattered in all directions, some looking for relatives and friends, others looking for a fight. Clumsy arrows poured down from Nameless archers positioned on rooftops. Nameless men carried weapons they didn't know how to wield while women and children ran from the square, their wails ringing like demon bells in Gryphon's ears, as their men were quickly chopped down.

In the back of his mind, Gryphon thought of Ajax and his mess brothers. He hoped they were all right. He thought the spear was only supposed to be a diversion to save Joshua and Zo, not the signal for a planned rebellion!

What was the Historian thinking?

Gryphon sprinted toward the platform, jumping over bodies and dodging Nameless and Ram locked in battle. He noticed Stone from the corner of his eye, shoving a pack into Eva's arms and pointing emphatically toward the direction of the gate.

Gabe reached the center of the square at the same time as Gryphon. They cleared the steps of the platform in a single bound and raced to Joshua and Zo, anonymous in the madness surrounding them.

Joshua's blood formed a giant puddle. Zo had managed to roll him onto his back. She covered his stomach with two dripping red hands. Her hair fell around her bare shoulders like a veil of black despair. "Gryphon!" She sobbed his name. "I couldn't stop him in time. The wound … it's deep … " She ran at him like she might charge, she reached for his knife and sliced his shirt enough to tear it.

Zo sobbed as she tied the cloth around Joshua's waist. It soaked through even before she finished. The pitch of her cry made Gryphon want to stop and pull her and Joshua both to him. To wrap his arms around them and expel their fear by sheer force. But there wasn't time.

Gryphon's legs nearly gave out as he took the final steps to Joshua's side. In one motion, he scooped the boy up into his arms. Gabe helped Zo to her feet and together they scrambled off the platform and ran toward the gate, cloaked by the mayhem of the bloody square.

"Where is my sister?" Zo shouted over the noise of clanking swords and swooshing arrows.

"I sent Tess ahead to wait for us at the gate," said Gabe. Zo tripped and Gabe turned back to help her.

Gryphon tried not to look at Joshua, tried not to interpret his dead weight or his unfocused eyes. *He'll be all right.* He repeated the mantra over and over again. Willing it to be true. Needing it to be true.

They ran out of the square and passed the string of buildings and mess barracks.

No one followed them. When they reached the perimeter of the great wall they heard the gears and chains of the massive gate opening.

[●]

Zo's vision tunneled as they ran, blurring in and out. She fell and hands snatched her up. It took several moments for her to recognize Gabe helping her forward.

"Joshua," she croaked, her legs unsteady. "He tried to kill himself so I could escape."

Gabe's grip was as firm as the look on his face. "You can save him, Zo. We're all going to make it."

Running. Running. Running. Looking over at Joshua's limp form in Gryphon's arms. Smelling the slick layer of blood on her skin. Feeling it dry and cake on her chest. Too much blood.

It's happening again. Her parents' lifeless bodies. Too much blood. Not being able to save them.

Knowing it was her fault.

[●]

The Historian stood near the gate entrance with Eva as hundreds of Nameless fled the walls. It was only a small percentage of the thousands of Nameless inside Ram's Gate, but still the sight of them made Gryphon stop short. They carried packs filled with provisions on their backs. Four guards lay dead, their lifeless bodies trampled under the feet of the Nameless as they made their frantic exodus. The lookouts were missing from the high walls. Likely sharing the other guards' fate.

Gryphon set Joshua on his feet but still supported most of the boy's weight. Shouts and cries of pain wafted over from the square only a few hundred yards away. The distraction wouldn't last long.

"You must hurry!" The Historian ushered them to the narrow opening behind the last of the escapees. She nodded to the forty Nameless manning the wheel that opened the gate. "My men will close it behind you."

Your men? Gryphon's cheeks grew hot. If this woman hadn't been helping them escape he'd be furious. How many of his friends had died today because of her scheming? Gryphon understood now that he'd only been a pawn in her little game. Manipulated by a foolish bedtime story. Yes, Barnabas was evil, and the Ram had many flaws, but to organize a rebellion inside the Gate?

It put his own treason to shame.

Tess ran to Zo's side, her face white at the sight of Joshua covered in his own blood.

"Zo and I know of a good place to hide. It's not far," said Gabe.

Shouts called out from behind them. Barnabas' voice boomed unintelligible orders that carried over the dying noise of the square.

The Ram were coming.

Gryphon and Gabe immediately locked eyes. They both knew their chances of survival if something wasn't done to stop the Ram from leaving the gate. In one glance, everything important passed between them. Strategy, oaths, respect. Gabe ripped off his pack and handed it to Zo.

"What are you doing?" she said.

Gabe wordlessly reached out to free Gryphon of the task of supporting Joshua. "Gryphon will be right behind us. He just needs to make sure no one follows."

Zo had been in a state of shock since the prizefight, but snapped her head to Gryphon and reached out to grasp his arm. "No." The word came out hoarse and trembling. Tears instantly sprang to her eyes.

Gryphon, who'd always been so careful not to touch her, didn't think twice about resting his hands on either side of her cheeks and letting his fingertips weave into the dark tangles of her hair. The moment was fleeting but if Gryphon survived the next five minutes of his life, he knew he'd never forget the feel of her soft cheeks against his palms, the look of affection in her blue eyes that—until today—had always been so guarded.

"Save Joshua. I'll be with you soon."

Zo was still shaking her head when Gabe pulled her under

the gate with Tess right behind. She looked back, pleading for him to follow.

Eva stared back in the direction of the square, uncertain and unmoving.

"Go, Eva. Now!" said Gryphon.

"But, Stone."

Gryphon took her by the upper arm and forced her out the gate. "If you love him like you say, show him by leaving."

Gryphon turned back to the Historian. She held her arms folded over her chest, appraising him with hooded eyes.

"Close the gate!" Gryphon called to the Nameless at the giant wheel. Each link of chain connected to the wheel was a foot in diameter. The heavy chain connected to a massive boulder held aloft by a pulley system. The counterweight of the boulder was all that kept the gate open.

The sound of the Ram army grew louder. Gryphon had only minutes before they reached the gate and discovered the dead guards and the missing Nameless.

Gryphon retrieved a spear from one of the lifeless guards on the ground. Holding the spear gave him courage and balance, but it wouldn't be enough to stop the strongest army in the region.

The Historian pulled out a bundle from inside her cloak, greatly resembling the one he'd tied to his spear only a few minutes earlier.

The Ram army sounded like approaching thunder.

Gryphon snatched the bundle from the Historian's hands and sprinted to the wheel where all of the Nameless still stood. "Get out of here!" Gryphon ordered. He wedged the bundle of chemicals inside the one of the links in the chain then raced up the five flights of stairs that hugged the great wall.

The army turned the final corner and marched to the gate. The Historian had vanished.

From high on the wall Gryphon took a moment to catch his breath while he did his best to judge the distance.

"There, up on the wall!" a voice cried from below.

Gryphon held his spear aloft. The target of explosives seemed tiny from this great height.

"Striker!" Barnabas growled in fury. Men began to climb the walls. Spears flew up to meet Gryphon.

It would be not only his death if he failed, but Joshua and Zo's, Tess and Eva's, not to mention countless Nameless. All of their faces passed before his eyes as he reached back then threw his weight forward, his arm arching past his ear last, propelled by all the momentum he possessed.

He knew his aim had been sure even before the spear connected with the explosive pouch. On impact, light, heat, and a deafening boom brought Gryphon to one knee. Chains rattled as the gargantuan boulder acting as the gate's counterweight dropped from the air and cracked in two as it hit the ground. The wall shook, knocking several of the men pursuing Gryphon off the stairs and plummeting to their deaths.

"I will kill you for this!" Barnabas yelled.

The wood beneath his feet swayed and groaned. With no other options before him, Gryphon pulled both of his daggers from their sheaths. He climbed over the pointed shafts of the fifty-foot wall just as the platform toppled beneath him.

Chapter 40

The first blast was immediately followed by a loud cracking sound that made the earth shake.

Gryphon.

Zo didn't dare stop to look back at the distant wall. No matter how desperate she was to know if Gryphon survived the impossible task of blocking the Gate, she only allowed herself to think about saving Joshua.

Ahead, Gabe ran with Joshua in tow. The boy's limbs flopped up and down and side to side as Gabe navigated the rocks and trees of the downward slope. Even with Joshua's weight, Gabe traveled faster than Tess was able.

Zo turned to Eva, who'd been silently running at their side. "Can you help Tess? I need to get to Joshua."

Eva nodded and took Tess' hand before Zo took off after Gabe. She did her best to block out the scenes from so many of her nightmares of her past, but the macabre images flashed before her eyes without volition.

Mom forces the lid over the basket to hide us just before the Ram enter our hut. She doesn't realize the basket has holes big enough to peek through.

It all happens fast. The whites of Dad's eyes catch the light of the low fire. They change like a cloud passing before the sun when the blade of the Ram's sword slides through his chest to the hilt. Another Ram slices the backs of his knees. Dad crumbles to the ground like a sack of potatoes falling off a cart.

A man covered in fur carries a large round shield in one hand. He holds the tip of his spear to Mom's neck. He wants to know where the food is, but all Mom can do is stare at Dad and try not to look at the large wicker basket in the corner where I am hiding with my baby sister.

Tess is asleep in my arms and I know any moment she will wake and wonder why Dad can't get up and blow raspberries into her round tummy. It's their favorite game.

And that's all I can think of. Who will blow raspberries in Tess' belly if Dad doesn't get up?

Zo tripped, but gathered herself. She needed to get to Joshua before he bled out. They approached the large tree tucked into a corner of rock. The same tree they'd hidden beneath the night before Zo entered the Gate.

Other memories surfaced. Things Zo had somehow forgotten.

Mom shakes her head over and over. She's crying. Pleading. But the fur-covered man won't listen. Mom has her hands raised as she steps backward until she is out of our hut. She steps to the side, out of my line of sight, but what I can't see I can hear. Her screams shatter something fragile within me. Something important that can't ever be fixed.

I sit with Tess in my lap, my hands blocking her ears as I rock her. And rock her. And rock her. I don't want her to hear our mother's screams. Especially the last one that ends so abruptly.

Zo lifted the low-sweeping evergreen boughs from the ground while Gabe crawled under the tree. He set Joshua between two large branching roots near the trunk. "His breath is so shallow," he said. "Is he going to make it?" Gabe sounded like he knew the answer to his question. He put a hand on Zo's shoulder as she used the pack to prop up his legs. "Just do your best, Zo. No one can ask more of you than that." He crawled back out from under the tree, likely off to see if Gryphon survived.

The morning light filtering through the branches didn't seem to belong to the gory sight of Joshua covered in blood. Zo knelt down and stared as the horrible memories of her past crept over her skin. She tried to think of what she was supposed to do first, but couldn't seem to remember anything but the nightmares.

I wait until I'm sure the soldiers have left before setting my sleeping sister down. I leave the basket and run for my Mom's medical kit. I am her apprentice and I can save my parents!

I go to Dad first. I feel for a pulse. His hand is already cold and I know he is gone. The kit knocks against my shins as I

*hurry outside to help Mom. She's on her back, lying perfectly
still except for the slight rise and fall of her chest. Her body is
covered in weeping red gashes and a thick line of blood runs
from her neck where her artery is severed.*

*She doesn't have much time. And I can heal her. The words
of the blessing always come easily to me.*

*But all I can do is stare at Mom covered in gore. I feel
myself melt to my knees. And I stare. Willing myself into action,
but my body won't obey. I forget how to breathe. I think I hear
Tess crying in the hut, but I'm not sure.*

Mom dies before my eyes and all I do is watch …

"No!" Zo's crippling fear would not control her. Not
ever again. She instinctively reached for her medical kit, and
realized too late that it was still back in Gryphon's barn.

Frustrated, she ripped the fabric from Joshua's stomach to
expose a long gash that reminded her too much of her mother's
so many years ago.

Her mind wanted to retreat into a safe place burrowed deep
within her own oblivion. This time she fought the safety. She
pumped her hands to bring them warmth and forced herself to
act.

"Joshua, can you hear me?"

Of course he couldn't. The flow of blood had slowed, but
that wasn't surprising considering how much he had already
lost in the last fifteen minutes.

She stripped another piece of cloth from Joshua's shirt and
held it over the fatal wound. The words of the blessing seemed
just outside her mental reach.

Please remember!

Then, like a splash of water to her face, her mother's bell-like voice entered her head.

"Love, Zo. Just love."

Could she give Joshua everything she'd worked so hard to bury? With hands pressed to his stomach, Zo stopped struggling to find the words of the blessing. She stopped worrying about what would happen if she failed. Instead, she only thought about Joshua. Always so loyal, defending her against Gryphon in the woods, joining her to visit sick Nameless families, his insistence on calling her Zo when he was raised to think of Nameless as animals, his freckled smile and clumsy feet, the puppy dog eyes that worshipped Gryphon's every move.

Loving Joshua wasn't hard.

A small hand touched her back. "I can help."

Zo shrugged Tess away. But it was too late. Her concentration slipped and the darkness slipped back through her defenses.

"Tess, go back outside with Eva. I need to do this."

But Tess wouldn't move. "I can *help*." She bit down on her bottom lip like she might cry. "I need to, Zo. Please let me."

With hands still pressed to the wound on Joshua's abdomen, Zo saw something in her sister that she didn't dare refuse. She'd never realized just how much Tess looked like their mother. Zo's mouth was dry as she nodded her answer.

Tess dropped to her knees beside Joshua and placed her hands over Zo's.

A vein throbbed in Zo's forehead as she battled past her parents' death and focused on her feelings for Joshua. Her hands shook against the boy's neck. She didn't feel a pulse, but refused to acknowledge what that meant.

This isn't happening again. He will live!

Zo's lips set in a thin line, her head bent, her mind centered. She repeated the promise over and over again until every cobweb of doubt was cleared to reveal pure determination. Her hands warmed. It was a while before she realized her lips were moving. She gave the words breath and spoke foreign strings of ancient words that carried power. There were several phrases she didn't even remember learning, but they rolled off her tongue seamlessly.

Tess picked up on the words of the blessing and chanted with her sister. A current of energy emanated from the little girl's hands. It was a familiar, stubborn energy that wouldn't be ignored. Much like Tess.

[●]

Gryphon drove his knives into the wood like pickaxes as he descended along the massive wall. His arms shook with exertion. Sweat rolled into his eyes. One stab at a time, he moved lower and lower along the wall until he was nearly fifteen feet off the ground. Freedom.

He dropped and winced as a spear thumped into the earth next to his boot. Gryphon leapt into a roll to dodge a second one. He took off at a run into the thickest section of the outlying trees for cover. Shouts followed after him, but he knew it would be some time before anyone followed.

A whistle sounded from somewhere to the left. Gryphon followed the sound until he found Gabe. "Joshua?"

Gabe put a finger to his lips and shook his head. He signaled for him to follow. They zigzagged through the woods, often jumping from rock to log to make it harder for a tracker to find their trail.

They weren't more than a few minutes run from the Gate when Gryphon spotted Eva. She held her arms crossed over her chest, a pained look on her face as she paced back and forth in front of a thick fir tree.

"How is he?" Gryphon asked.

Eva's brows knit together and she pinched her lips. Gabe held up one of the sweeping boughs of the fir tree for Gryphon to climb under.

Gryphon shed his weapons and pack as fast as he could, then dove under the prickly branches.

[♦]

What began as gentle warmth around Joshua's wound turned into electric heat. Zo lost all sense of gravity and space. Her body swayed into something solid. *The tree?* It didn't matter.

"Are you all right?" said a clouded, masculine voice that sounded like a dream.

Zo continued the blessing. The words consumed her every thought. She hardly heard the men arguing about something in the background. Her skin was numb to the large hands on her shoulders, even though she was pretty sure they supported a good portion of her weight.

Heat rose up from Joshua's wound into Zo's forearms and gathered in her elbows.

Someone shouted something Zo couldn't comprehend. Tess cried out and her hands fells away.

The heat reached Zo's shoulders.

Someone tried to pull her away. But Zo would not be moved. Joshua needed her. And she would not fail him like she'd failed her parents.

Just as the heat filled her chest a large force knocked her to the ground. She raked her arms and chest as a searing pain boiled throughout her body.

Chapter 41

A single drop of rain rolled down Zo's forehead and into her eye. She blinked awake from a deep sleep she wasn't quite ready to part from and yawned. Rolling onto her other side, she nuzzled into the warmth beside her. A heavy arm draped around her shoulder in welcome.

Zo froze as memory caught up with consciousness. "Joshua!" She pushed off from the ground beside Gryphon, wondering vaguely how she'd gotten there.

Gryphon pulled her back to him and clamped his hand over her mouth. Outside, the sky was overcast and the sun seemed prepared to relinquish its hold on the day.

She looked around, surprised to find everyone but Gabe sleeping near the trunk of the enormous spruce. The lowest branches brushed the ground, making it impossible to see outside of their little haven. Thunder rolled in the late afternoon sky. Crunching feet and calls of men's voices carried in the distance.

The Ram. Searching for them.

Zo nodded her understanding and peeled Gryphon's warm fingers away from her mouth. Joshua rested peacefully along Gryphon's other side. Zo ran her fingers over the cut along his exposed stomach. By some miracle, the wound had sealed into a pink, branded line of flesh.

Impossible.

She went to take Joshua's pulse but froze at the sight of her hands.

Heavy black mounds callused her fingertips and knuckles. Angry red boils dotted the pads of her palms and the backs of her hands. The slightest movement tugged uncomfortably at the traumatized skin.

Gryphon frowned and with two careful fingers, took her by the wrist and kissed her open hands one by one. "I don't know how you saved him, but I can never thank you enough."

A warm blush crept into Zo's cheeks, which was completely ridiculous considering the imminent danger surrounding them. "I love him, too." She looked up into Gryphon's eyes, but was too self-conscious to hold his gaze. There was absolutely nothing casual about the way he studied her. She couldn't decide if it was terrifying or wonderful. Perhaps it was both.

"Where is Gabe?"

Gryphon cleared his throat and carefully set her hand back into her lap. "He's scouting the area for the group of Nameless who escaped the wall. We need to know where they are and whether or not the Ram will pursue them or keep to their plans to attack the Raven."

Zo squirmed under the idea of Gabe running through a Ram-infested forest, but if anyone could do it … "What is our plan?"

"We need to warn the Raven."

Zo nodded. "What about the Nameless? Do you think the Ram will go after them?" Stone had given her responsibility for them, somehow.

Gryphon shrugged then picked up a pinecone. "Even if they don't, the Nameless won't survive outside the Gate without the protection of a clan. We can't take them to the Raven, and many of the Kodiak have migrated south."

Zo nodded. "What about the Allies? They would take the Nameless under their protection without question."

Gryphon crumpled the pinecone in his hand and let the wood litter the earth. Lines of worry etched his brow, his lips turned down in firm concentration.

"You don't want to travel to the Allies, do you?" Zo leaned forward. She reached out to touch him, persuade him, but even the slightest brush of her hand sent a shock of pain up her wrist and into her arm.

Gryphon rubbed his hands together to remove the debris from the pinecone. "I would not be welcome." He raised a hand to silence Zo's rebuttal. "And I don't think I could live with myself if I joined the Allies—my people's greatest enemy."

"How can you still think of the Ram that way? After everything they've done." Zo gestured to Joshua, like Gryphon needed the reminder. "*We're* your family now, Gryphon. You can't just wander the wilderness alone."

Gryphon opened his mouth to speak, his eyes round. But no words came.

As if out of nowhere, Gabe slipped under the bough. He looked between Gryphon and Zo and frowned.

"What did you find?" Gryphon managed. He seemed grateful for the chance to focus on someone else.

"The Ram still haven't managed to open the gate." He slapped Gryphon's shoulder and let go a silent laugh. Zo didn't know what Gryphon had done to earn the look of esteem on Gabe's face, but it must have been incredible. "Their scouts climb a rope ladder to get in and out of the wall. It's a slow process."

"What about the Nameless?" said Gryphon.

"They've left an obvious trail heading south from the Gate. Impossible to miss, but the Ram don't seem interested in the Nameless. They only sent one scout after them. Probably to gather information. They've dedicated most of their manpower to tracking us. Our initial tracks have brought them close, but I don't think they'll find us if they haven't already."

Gryphon's head hung a little as he sighed, but his weariness didn't last long. "Barnabas will not rest until he has his revenge. He sees me as the rebel leader of the Nameless. I've insulted him."

"But what will he do to the Nameless?" asked Gabe.

"A few hundred Nameless aren't important to him. He's been searching for the Raven for too long not to strike. The Ram need the bird-people's resources."

Gabe nodded. "So we get a head start. I've been to the Raven stronghold on assignment from Commander Laden. I can get us there."

"Laden?" Gryphon raised a brow.

"The Allied commander."

Zo rolled onto her knees. "We can't just let those Nameless wander aimlessly. Someone needs to take them to the Allies. Besides, Joshua isn't going to be fit to travel yet. Not at the pace needed to help the Raven. Tess will struggle, too."

It seemed everyone had a reason to look away. No one wanted to consider the risk of separating. Gabe was the only one who knew how to find the Raven. With help, Zo might make it to the Allies, but with her charred hands, she'd have no way of defending herself from wild animals and nomadic clans.

"We're not splitting up," said Gryphon.

"He's right," said Gabe. "It might be several days before the Ram can open the gate."

"What about the Nameless?" said Zo.

"They're a large group. There's a chance they will survive."

Eva sat up from where she lay on the ground. Her hair was matted with pine needles, but she seemed so alert that there was no question she'd heard the whole conversation. "Stone will find the Nameless. He'll make sure they are taken care of."

Gabe and Gryphon exchanged looks that said, *If he's still alive.*

"You said the Nameless moved south. I'm going to follow them."

Gryphon said, "Eva, be reasonable. I can't let you wander off into the wilderness to find those people. There are wild animals and dangerous Clanless who wander the hills."

"I'm going." She set her chin, daring anyone to contradict her.

Gryphon took her by the arm. "Ajax is my brother, Eva. I

will not let you risk your life on the gamble that your Nameless lover survived the rebellion."

Eva whipped her hand back and slapped Gryphon across the face. "Don't you *dare* talk to me like that. Stone is alive."

She turned onto her side and showed the whole group her back. Her body shook with silent tears as she wrapped her arms around her frame. Zo wanted to go to the poor girl, to offer some token of comfort. But what could she possibly say to make things better?

Gryphon turned wearily to Gabe. "I'll help you evacuate the Raven, but Joshua and I will make our own way from there."

"But—"

"Those are my terms, Wolf. Take them or leave them."

Gabe considered for a moment then put out his hand. Gryphon closed the handshake, effectively settling the matter.

They would leave before first light to save the Raven from massacre. All of them.

That night, Zo rested with Tess curled against her side. Joshua put off a pleasant amount of heat at her back. She couldn't help but think of all of the escaped Nameless and their doomed fate if they didn't reach the Allies. She thought of Eva's desperation to be with the father of her unborn child, wishing there was something she could do to help. Stone was counting on her to get them all to the Allies safely. Could she really abandon them?

[•]

Gryphon spent most of his watch that night watching Zo as she slept with one arm around Tess and the other around Joshua, as if they were her baby chicks. He wondered what it would be like to have someone care for him with the passion that Eva cared for Stone. In the last few years, whenever he imagined belonging to a woman he never managed to picture the girl's face.

Now, even when he fought the tendency, he always saw Zo. It was part of the reason he could never travel to the Allies. He'd rather rip out his eyes than watch Zo and Gabe share their lives together.

Gryphon wasn't quite sure when it happened, but somewhere in the trauma of the last two days he'd realized that he'd never really be happy without her. It was an awful feeling that gnawed at his gut and threatened all reason. Like discovering you'd lost your arm in battle. Living with the memory of what it was like to have that arm, and reminded every day of the loss.

Gryphon the deserter, son of Troy the deserter, was in love with a Wolf. A fitting end to the tragedy that was his life.

Chapter 42

Zo awoke with a start to a large, calloused hand cupping her mouth. The sky outside was too dark to be considered morning. When her eyes adjusted, Gryphon's face came into focus. His breath kissed her ear, their bodies sandwiched together, as he whispered, "Ram scouts." He put a finger to his lips and removed his hand. His words barely travelled over the breeze of the night. "They must have stumbled upon some of our tracks. Gabe went scouting. He said not to expect him back until dawn. I'm going to try to lure them away from the tree."

Zo grabbed the front of his shirt and pulled him close to whisper in his ear. "We can't all outrun them."

Gryphon nodded, his jaw flexed. "But I can."

Zo shook her head over and over. But what option did they have? "When it's safe to leave, I'll take Eva, Joshua, and Tess to the Allies. We'll find the Nameless on our way. You and

Gabe can go help the Raven."

The footsteps outside moved closer. Rock ground against rock in a chorus of danger. Gryphon cupped his hand around her ear to block his words. "The mountain isn't safe for you to travel without protection."

She sighed. "Gabe can't go alone. Too many people will die if he doesn't make it. Please promise me you'll help the Raven, Gryphon."

Gryphon pulled away, shaking his head. A shiver of steel rang in the early morning—a blade being drawn from its sheath not far away.

"Please." Zo mouthed the word.

The footsteps stopped just outside of the tree. Zo made out the fur-lined boots of three Ram. She worried her pounding heart might give them away if nothing else did. Tess ... Joshua ... How could she protect them when these men attacked?

Gryphon pushed Zo behind his back. More boots came. More crunching gravel—a sound that, if Zo survived, would forever haunt her nightmares.

Zo looked back to Joshua, Eva, and Tess sleeping around the trunk of the tree. Helpless.

Gryphon turned back to her, pain etched into his face. He must have realized that Zo's plan was the only option they had. He drew Zo close to him. This time Zo met and held his eyes. He pressed his cheek to hers and Zo felt her stomach drop to the ground. "Track the Nameless. Be careful with fires. Don't try to be a hero. Just do what you have to do to stay alive. I'll meet you at the Allied Camp."

Zo nodded. Tears sprang to her eyes. A rigid fear seized her, making her limbs stiff and breathing a chore.

Gryphon silently picked up his shield and turned to leave, but Zo caught his hand. She couldn't let him go.

He looked down at their connection in disbelief, like he didn't trust it.

Zo placed her charred hands on either side of his face and suddenly Gryphon's hand was at her back, a firm support. It belonged there, somehow. The Ram outside the tree walked the perimeter like starving wild dogs sniffing out a kill. At any moment someone would bend down to look under the heavy skirt of the tree and they would all be dead.

"Come back to me," Zo whispered. She leaned into him and hesitated for a thin moment before touching his lips with hers. His hand traveled up her side until he cupped her neck. The kiss turned urgent. His lips demanding and yielding all at once. In that short blink of time, something within Zo changed, an earthquake that shifted everything she believed. They rested their foreheads together and Gryphon brushed away one of her tears.

"They're here, Zander. I can feel it," someone whispered near the tree.

Gryphon stiffened at the mention of his mess captain's name.

His hands fell to her shoulders. "No matter what you hear in the next few minutes, promise me that you'll stay under this tree with the others." He didn't wait for a reply. On hands and knees he crawled to the opposite side of the tree, away from the guards and crept out into the darkness.

[•]

Gryphon carried his spear in one hand and his shield in his

other, but still his arms felt empty. He doubted they would ever feel full again without Zo.

Outside the tree, Gryphon slowly gathered his feet, careful not to make any noise. He would alert Zander and the others to his location eventually to draw them away from the tree, but it wouldn't be wise to do it yet. Apart from his mother, everyone he cared for was under that tree. Suddenly the Historian's story made complete sense. He would do anything to protect the people he loved.

Gryphon scanned the area for Gabe but he wasn't supposed to be back for hours. He knew the Wolf was out here hiding somewhere. If they could somehow work together they might make it out of this situation alive. Though the odds of two lone men against a Ram mess unit weren't ideal, Gryphon felt like he could do almost anything at that moment if it meant protecting his "family."

He held his breath then darted behind another tree to give him the angle he needed to view the enemies he'd once called "brother." It was too difficult to know for certain, but it looked like his entire mess unit, including Ajax, stood scattered about, studying prints in the ground and discussing strategy. He wasn't surprised that Barnabas had given his brothers the task of finding him. The chief would see it as a way for his mess to prove their loyalty.

Gryphon turned to put a little more distance between him and the tree, choosing each step with careful precision. He searched the woods for Gabe, but he could have been hiding anywhere in the almost darkness.

Just when he reached the next tree, four strong hands grabbed him as if out of nowhere. Gryphon elbowed and fought his way out of two of his mess brothers' grasp. He threw one man over his shoulder, and landed a wild punch to another brother's throat to free himself.

"Don't let him go!" Gryphon vaguely heard Zander's orders in the background.

Gryphon left three men on the ground, but before he staggered away, another Ram tackled him. Then another. They bound his wrists behind his back and pulled him to his feet.

Gryphon was glad Gabe hadn't come to his aid. The Wolf was the only one with the power to warn the Raven. No swords were drawn. His mess brothers would keep him alive long enough for Barnabas to make his death public.

Blood ran down Gryphon's nose and into his mouth. A ringing in his left ear made Zander's words foggy. "I accepted you into this mess." Zander cocked his arm back and threw his fist into Gryphon's stomach, causing him to double over and wheeze for breath. "I made you my second. Taught you everything I know." Again, Zander reared back, only this time his punch landed squarely on the jaw. Gryphon's vision faded. His legs forgot how to support his body.

"You've made me look like a fool." Zander reached back to deliver another blow to the head.

Gryphon's vision tilted as Zander turned to Ajax. His commander's words clouded in Gryphon's ear. "The healer can't be far. Find them and kill them,"

Zander looked back to Gryphon. "We have what we came for."

Gryphon bucked and kicked as his brothers dragged him back up the hill.

Back to the Gate.

Chapter 43

Z o dug her fingers into the ground to keep her rooted in place as Gryphon fought off his brothers. They couldn't have been more than twenty feet away. Eva crawled next to her and took her by the hand. She shook her head, pleading for Zo to stay still, like she knew that every muscle in Zo's body was tensed and ready to run to Gryphon's side.

Zo rocked back and sat on her heels, burying her face in the pine needles with arms reaching in Gryphon's direction. Silent sobs rocked her frame as she pinched her eyes together so hard they hurt.

When the sound of fighting ended, Zander's orders to find and kill her snapped Zo back to reality. She and Eva scampered back against the trunk of the tree, resting on either side of Tess and Joshua who still slept. Zo reached out to take the Ram girl's hand, ignoring the pain from the blisters.

Gryphon was gone. Gone. And no matter how hard she fought, she couldn't protect Tess and Joshua. It was over. The Ram had won.

Time passed, the sounds of Gryphon's struggle were lost in the distance separating them. A set of boots approached with little attempt made to silence the sound. Whoever this Ram was, he knew he had nothing to fear from the prey he hunted. The boots froze before the tree. Zo held tighter to Eva and kissed the top of Tess' sleeping head. The bough of the branch lifted to reveal Ajax. He stared at Zo for a long moment, his face twisted in agony. Then the bough of the tree branch dropped back to the ground and Ajax's boots carried him away.

He let us go.

Zo's breathing sped until she thought she might hyperventilate. They would survive. But even as the thought became reality, a black syrup of despair stretched its sinewy fingers around her heart.

She might not be able to help Gryphon, but she could get Tess, Joshua, Eva, and the rest of the Nameless to the Allies. Gryphon would want her to finish what they'd started.

Zo lifted a shaky hand to her lips, as if some remnant of Gryphon's touch still lingered there, and let her head fall back against the tree trunk to grieve for someone she never believed she was capable of loving: A Ram.

Epilogue

Gryphon couldn't stand to look at Ajax when he came back from fulfilling Zander's order. He'd been gone only minutes, but Zander didn't insult him by asking if he'd done the job. He wouldn't be there if he hadn't.

Iron manacles secured Gryphon's wrists behind his back as he stumbled along the rocky slope back to the Gate. He searched the trees for Gabe but his vision swam in tears that rolled down his cheeks into the beginnings of his dark beard.

He'd failed everyone. Joshua, Tess, Eva, the Raven, and Zo. He swallowed hard.

Especially Zo.

Ajax fell in line beside him, his expression neutral, as if this was just another assignment.

Gryphon shot spears at Ajax with his gaze. He didn't know what he wanted to see in his old friend. Regret? Sorrow?

Perhaps some confirmation to extinguish his denial that Zo was actually gone.

Ajax looked straight ahead. Lines wrinkled his brow. Sweat beaded down the side of his face. His Adam's apple bobbed up and down. He released a long breath and uncurled his clenched fist at his side to reveal the key to Gryphon's restraints.

The key to freedom.

ACKNOWLEDGEMENTS

I'm staring at a blinking cursor, completely at a loss of how to untangle the hundreds of "thank you threads" jumbled in my mind. While these few words will only shine a dim light on the support I've received with this book, I'll endeavor to try…

First and foremost, I have to thank the five talented writers who have traveled down this long road of publication with me. To Tahsha Wilson, Lois D. Brown, Margie Jordan, Jo Schaffer, and James Lewis: I love you and know that without your unfailing creative and emotional support, this book would never have happened. You've made the journey exciting, educational, and hilarious. With you, anything is possible. Watch out world, here they come.

My family is my secret weapon. Not once have I ever been told that this lofty dream was ridiculous or intangible. So thank you for the cheerleading, the babysitting, the edits, the story advice, and mostly your love. Casey, Liberty, and Boston: you'll always be my number one. Haley Woods, your battles fought and victories won inspired Zo's character. I'm stronger because I know you. Julie and Glayd, thanks for keeping me on the list. Special thanks to my parents, Lloyd and Haze Eldredge, who've always taught me that I can do anything with hard work and faith.

To the Game Night crew, my writing is officially not an "off-limits" subject any longer. I also need to send love to my fabulous beta readers: Brad Walker!, Stacy Jenkins, Kristen Whitely, Becca Gunyan, Jonathan Ryan, Micah Reese, Katie Jarvis, Whitney Rasmussen, and Haley Woods.

Special thanks to Georgia McBride and the Month9Books team for recognizing something special in Zo and Gryphon. You've been a joy to work with and have made me, as an author, feel so important and appreciated. NAMELESS is in wonderful hands!

In this tough industry it has become extremely difficult for a first time author to break through that illustrious glass ceiling of publishing. Thank you to my agent and friend, Amy Jameson, for taking a chance on a no-name girl with the curse of needing to tell stories. I consider myself deeply blessed to have you by my side in this journey. You are so sweet and kind and good, but as fierce as a lion when you need to be. I hope this is only the beginning in our happy partnership.

Clint, I dedicate this one to you. You believed in me when I struggled to believe in myself. You are the very definition of support. Thank you for being the foundation that I needed. For working so hard for us. I love you.

Jennifer Jenkins

With her degree in History and Secondary Education, Jennifer had every intention of teaching teens to love George Washington and appreciate the finer points of ancient battle stratagem. (Seriously, she's obsessed with ancient warfare.) However, life had different plans in store when the writing began. As a proud member of Writers Cubed, and a co-founder of the Teen Author Boot Camp, she feels blessed to be able to fulfill both her ambition to work with teens as well as write Young Adult fiction.

Jennifer has three children who are experts at naming her characters, one loving, supportive husband, a dog with little-man syndrome, and three chickens (of whom she is secretly afraid).

Visit her online at www.jajenkins.com.

OTHER MONTH9BOOKS TITLES YOU MIGHT LIKE

NOBODY'S GODDESS
THE ARTISANS
BRANDED
FIRE IN THE WOODS
THE EMISSARY

Find more awesome Teen books at Month9Books. com

Facebook: www.Facebook.com/Month9Books
Twitter: https://twitter.com/Month9Books
You Tube: www.youtube.com/user/Month9Books
Blog: www.month9booksblog.com
Instagram: https://instagram.com/month9books
Request review copies via publicity@month9books.com

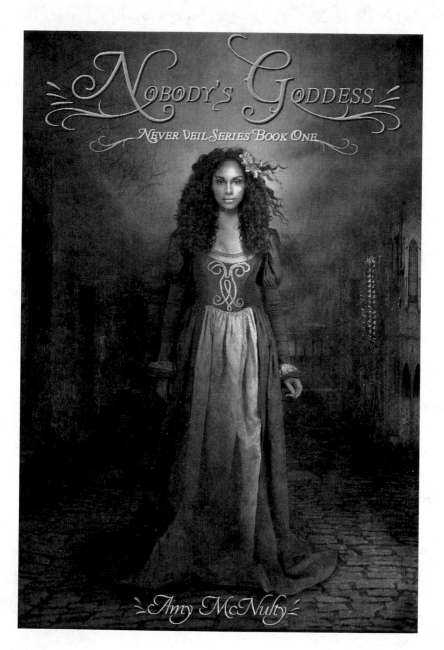

Nobody's Goddess

Never Veil Series Book One

Amy McNulty